TARRIS MARIE

BLAQUE PEARLE

BLACK
ODYSSEY
MEDIA

WWW.BLACKODYSSEY.NET

Published by
BLACK ODYSSEY MEDIA

www.blackodyssey.net
Email: info@blackodyssey.net

Library of Congress Control Number: 2023900478

First Trade Paperback Printing: October 2023
ISBN: 979-8-9855941-7-1
ISBN: 979-8-9855941-8-8 (e-book)

Cover Design by Ashlee Nassar of Designs With Sass
To the extent that the image or images on the cover of this book depict a person or persons, such person or persons are merely models and are not intended to portray any character in the book.

10 9 8 7 6 5 4 3 2 1

Manufactured in the United States of America

Distributed by Kensington Publishing Corp.

Dear Reader,

I want to thank you immensely for supporting Black Odyssey Media authors, and our ongoing efforts to spotlight more minority storytellers. The scariest and most challenging task for many writers is getting the story, or characters, out of our heads and onto the page. Having admitted that, with every manuscript that Kreceda and I acquire, we believe that it took talent, discipline, and remarkable courage to construct that story, flesh out those characters, and prepare it for the world. Debut or seasoned, our authors are the real heroes and heroines in *OUR* story. And for them, we are eternally grateful.

Whether you are new to Tarris Marie or Black Odyssey Media, we hope that you are here to stay. We also welcome your feedback and kindly ask that you leave a review. For upcoming releases, announcements, submission guidelines, etc., please be sure to visit our website at www.blackodyssey.net or scan the QR code below. We can also be found on social media using @iamblackodyssey. Until next time, take care and enjoy the journey!

Joyfully,

Shawanda Williams

Shawanda "N'Tyse" Williams
Founder/Publisher

AUTHOR'S NOTE

Writing *Blaque Pearle* was a spiritual journey for me. Its inception started with the character Pearle. Smart, sexy, talented, devoted, and flawed, her essence is a cumulation of different women from my past and present. She places the needs of her family ahead of her own and is not afraid to go dark for what she believes is her only means of survival.

Pearle's name is considered "old-school," but I knew she would carry it with confidence. Although she is a criminal, I wanted her name to symbolize characteristics all women could relate to—pearls, the universal gems of wisdom created in layers while trying to escape parasites in darkness. While trapped inside an oyster's shell, pearls develop beauty and don't shine until the oyster is done with them. Like women, pearls possess a value that appreciates as it ages, so I chose the name Pearle to represent the soul of a woman.

Christian "Blaque" Savage spoke to me immediately after Pearle. Blaque, like Pearle, is unlawful, but it is not my job to justify or judge them. His spirit was inspired by black men with whom I had come in contact throughout my life. He is intelligent, charming, protective, and, unfortunately, scarred. Loyal, loving, and respectful to the women in his life, Blaque is a powerful outlaw with a vulnerability I had never experienced in black male characters depicted in books or television.

Blaque's birth name, Christian Savage, represents the humanistic struggle between good and bad. Like other black men I've known, he wrestles with his chameleon ability to adapt to his legacy and environment, both of which he feels have been affected by societal factors outside his control.

Blaque Pearle is a soulful love story, and the title—like the gem, black pearl—is dark in color and symbolizes eternal love. I don't believe it is coincidental that black pearls are also legendary for healing wounded hearts because *Blaque Pearle* did more than heal me during my spiritual journey. It transformed me into a published author, and typing every word has been my pleasure. So please, kick back and find your inner Blaque Pearle.

PART ONE

CHAPTER 1
CALIFORNIA LOVE

PEARLE MONALISE BROWN
LOS ANGELES 1999

I KNEW THE ACADEMY Awards would never grant me the coveted Oscar for any of my performances, but the Hollywood sign would always be my inspiration. Summertime 1999 required me to use acting techniques that would forever change my life. It was a quiet summer night, and Mother Nature blew an unseasonably cool breeze over me. Standing on the balcony, I admired the Hollywood sign and gazed at the dazzling stars amidst the full moon and black sky.

Maxwell, a handsome, six-foot-five, newly-retired NBA point guard, stepped outside and wrapped his arms around my waist. My velvety chocolate mountain had recently moved to L.A. to escape the cold winters in Minnesota.

"Hey, Robyn, are you ready to come inside?" he asked, gently kissing my neck. "It's getting chilly."

Turning around, I gently grabbed his face, and we kissed softly. Maxwell was the best kisser; his warm lips gave me chills.

"Are you ready to warm me up?"

He effortlessly swept me into his power-forward arms and smiled beautifully as he carried me to his bedroom.

"I was born ready."

I loved the strength of his hands. He lifted my red dress with

3

one hand and spread my bare lips with the other. As the fullness of his tongue moved deep between my thighs, I closed my eyes and reminded myself this was the longest relationship I'd been involved in. He was unlike the others. Being a guard on the court for twenty years must have also taught him to be an expert in guarding his heart.

I slowly unbuttoned his dress shirt while he removed his pants. He was always so gentle with me because, as he pointed out, I was the most petite woman he had ever dated. When he entered me, I gasped softly from his Magnum size, but he muffled my sounds with his full lips. I never had to fake the pleasure Maxwell provided.

My arms and legs grabbed him tightly, and he released passionately inside me.

He rested his head on my breasts. "Damn, Robyn. You're amazing, baby."

I smiled. "I love you, Maxwell."

"I love you, too," he replied, squeezing my body tighter until he fell asleep in my arms.

I rubbed the nape of his neck and stared at the ceiling fan. His soft breathing was so melodic that I soon drifted off to sleep, too. Moments later, the room shook from the door slamming against the wall.

Click. Click.

On cue, a voice shouted the words I knew too well.

"Welcome to L.A., motherfucker! You know what time it is."

I provided my usual best performance, screaming with my hands in the air at the sight of a Glock pointed at us.

Before Maxwell could react, his hands were swiftly cuffed.

"Leave her alone," he hollered.

My dress smacking my face put an end to my screaming.

"Roslyn, put your damn clothes on," the voice commanded.

I looked at Goldie—my accomplice—fully masked as Batman, his favorite superhero since we were kids.

Maxwell squirmed in the cuffs as if he could escape them like Houdini.

"Roslyn? Robyn? Who the fuck are you?"

Goldie deepened his voice. "I'm motherfuckin' Batman."

When Maxwell finally realized what was going on, he started yelling obscenities. Having been called every name in the book, I tuned him out while slipping into my dress.

"Did you bring my Chanel?" I asked.

Goldie pointed to the doorway, then placed a towel over Maxwell's face. The room suddenly fell quiet.

"What did you do to him?" I asked.

"I put his ass to sleep."

"With what, Inspector Gadget?"

"Chloroform. And I told you, I'm motherfuckin' Batman."

We walked swiftly to Maxwell's master closet, where I collected the hidden cameras I had used to get the combination to the safe. It was payday for my full month of work in this gig. Goldie and I stepped over last week's laundry and emptied his safe, tossing the neatly stacked bills into my Chanel luggage.

As Goldie and I bolted out of the closet and through the spacious master bedroom, I stopped to take one last dreamy look at my latest victim.

"He was the best kisser."

"He was business, Roslyn. Now let's go."

We ran out the front door and down the long driveway. Maxwell's house stared down at us, looking like a piece of modern art alone on a hill.

I smacked my lips. "That's not my name."

Goldie opened the passenger door of my white Corvette.

"I can't keep up with who you are anymore," he shot back and ran around the car to jump in the driver's seat.

"You're Batman, and I'm Robyn, nigga. It's not hard."

He laughed while starting the car. "Damn, that's funny as hell."

Goldie put the car in drive, and we sped off. The car zipped down the narrow, sharp streets until we hit Interstate 405. Goldie tossed his Batman mask into the backseat. After turning on Dr. Dre's *The Chronic*, I snatched off my Halle Berry pixie-cut wig. Goldie let down the Corvette's top, and I tossed my fake eyebrows and lashes into the wind. Then we high-fived because Maxwell was our biggest score.

This was how we welcomed suckers to the wild Westside. It's kinda like what Tupac and Dr. Dre said in the song "California Love." Goldie and I were untouchable in Cali, and in Compton, we kept it rockin'.

My name is Pearle Monalise Brown, and I grew up deep in the CPT, Compton, lit by the deceptive gleams of sunshine during the day and weeping candlelit vigils at night. The youngest of three, I had two stepbrothers, Goldie and Nike. My mother, Claudia Jones, and my stepfather, Niles Brown, married in 1979 when I was a toddler. My biological father, Devin Davis, was killed in a car accident when I was one year old, and Nike and Goldie's mother died of cancer when they were also toddlers.

Niles had adopted me when I was too young to remember, and he and my mother were the only parents Nike, Goldie, and I had known. So, we were raised as blood in a loving home. Claudia was a beautiful, soft-spoken, nurturing woman who worked as a secretary until she was laid off a few years ago. She was Black but had been raised by a kind Mexican family. She spoke fluent Spanish and taught us to speak it, as well. Handsome, strong, and protective, Niles had been an auto mechanic and our financial support.

Mommy and Daddy loved each other and showed it, which grossed us out as children. Now, I wish I could watch them kissing in the kitchen again. They'd both grown up in a more suburban Compton when middle-class minority families dominated the neighborhood, whereas I grew up at the height of the crack era when the CPT became the straight-up hood.

I didn't realize my life wasn't typical until I got accepted by the Los Angeles Visual and Performing Arts Academy in the sixth grade. The kids I went to school with walked around with no concept of time or danger; their conversations were frivolous and carefree. They were inviting and much too trusting. I initially thought they were prisoners of the suburbs, but I soon realized I was the one living behind a metal fence and barred windows.

In my neighborhood, everyone's feet moved quickly and eyes stayed open, always on alert for the lurkers and jackers waiting for someone to get relaxed and caught slipping. Our family slept on the floor many nights to avoid gunfire. Our parents bought us neutral-colored school clothes and shoes to make sure we didn't get caught up in gang affiliations. As children, we would hear gunshots on the next block while playing outside and rode our bikes past gang fights in the streets. Everyone had been in at least one physical fight and countless cuss-out matches, and every kid had one male family member in or out of jail.

Where I lived, it was inevitable that someone's mama, auntie, uncle, cousin, or daddy would become the next neighborhood crackhead. There was often talk about a family member or friend who was murdered. We all had at least one gang-affiliated cousin who was only a phone call away to fight on our behalf. Teenage sex and pregnancy were no big deal. Basically, no one gave a shit about the beauty of palm trees.

Once I experienced life on the "outside," I wanted a one-way ticket out. An acting career was my passport, or so I thought. I had wanted to be an actress for as long as I could remember. Teachers selected me to perform in all plays in elementary school. Now at the Visual and Performing Arts Academy, I was surrounded by creatives and theater lovers. Life could be different. I was sure of it.

My talent was undeniable, and my family embraced it, showing their support by attending every performance. I loved the art of it and needed the escape, too, even though the getaway was only temporary. I poured my soul into the characters I played and continued to do so until I, Pearle, no longer existed.

Daddy was supportive of us all, but he also taught us to hustle, survive, and thrive. He dreamt of owning an auto shop. Every morning at 5:30 a.m., he would drop me off at the bus stop on his way to work. I'd catch two L.A. Metro buses and arrive at school by 7:30 a.m. My voyage home was longer because of traffic and an extra bus added to my route. I didn't mind the commute, but Daddy hated it. Ultimately, he wanted the family out of the hood, and it's what I wanted just as much, if not more.

When I was sixteen, everything changed. Daddy and his childhood friend became involved in armed robberies of stores and banks. My older brother, Nike, soon joined the crew, and the money grew even more. During one heist, they were caught, though. The consequence of the crime was a fifteen-year bid for my father, but worse, Nike was shot and killed by an armed security guard. The emptiness in our family's heart would never be filled.

Before my mother had gotten laid off, her secretarial wage didn't cover rent, and now with my father behind bars, the financial strain became even more unbearable for her. So, Goldie and I quit school to work. Goldie was happy about it because he hated school. I, on the other hand, was devastated and hated working at the mall. I auditioned whenever I could, but the streets of Compton sucked me back in like a vacuum, and I got trapped somewhere between the lint and dust.

After two years of drowning in sorrow, Goldie and I decided to step outside of Compton and found glitter inside a random strip club in Hollywood. That night, I wore a wig and switched my makeup to create a new fun look.

Goldie was surprised when I jumped in the car.

"Damn, Pearle, you look completely different. I almost didn't recognize you."

"*Me llamo Teresa*," I replied playfully.

We laughed, and I became the Teresa character nicknamed Ri-Ri for the night.

At the club, I got the attention of Enrique, a gangster from Oakland. After a few drinks, he whispered in my ear that he had a house he rented near the beach in Malibu. When I noticed his duffle bag full of cash for the strippers, I convinced him to end his night early so he could take me to his place and show me the ocean.

I met Goldie by the restrooms. We set it up so that he would follow us, and I'd distract Enrique so he'd leave his bag in the car. Once the coast was clear, Goldie would break into his vehicle, and we would walk away with the cash.

At first, my protective big brother hated the idea.

"I don't have time to argue," I told him, speaking firmly. "*Me gusto este hombre*. I'd fuck him *for free*."

The thought grossed Goldie out, but he finally complied.

Enrique and I drove to his Malibu rental home as Goldie tailed us. Enrique was sexy with his golden, tanned skin and dark, wavy hair. The way his lips moved, I couldn't wait to feel them on my body. We talked and laughed the entire way down the beautiful Pacific Coast. When we pulled up to his gorgeous house on the beach, I noticed cars in his driveway.

"Enrique, is someone here?" I asked.

He licked his pink lips. "Yeah, Ri-Ri, but it's cool. We have a private room."

Right there in the car, I straddled him in the driver's seat and stuck my tongue in his mouth. His eyes widened at my aggressiveness.

I grabbed his hands and pulled him out of the car. "*Vamanos, papi.*"

Entranced, he led me to the bedroom, leaving his duffle bag vulnerable. Within seconds, it was in Goldie's possession.

Enrique and Ri-Ri had an unforgettable night. The next morning, Enrique was upset about the robbery but never suspected his sexy *mami*, Ri-Ri, was responsible. Goldie and I walked away with fifteen thousand dollars each, and our underground operation began.

From that day forward, I got lost in characters, experiencing the same high from the cons I executed as I did when I performed onstage during my school days. I had no close friends and spent many nights alone. I carefully chose the men I slept with and robbed. I liked and had fun with them most times, but after my performance ended, I disconnected.

People knew me as Pearle Brown, the cute, lowkey, around-the-way girl from Compton who owned a hair salon in the hood. Goldie was my funny, more flamboyant brother who owned a strip club. We both loved and took care of our mother and visited our father, who had a decade left to serve in the penitentiary.

What people didn't know was how our businesses gave us immediate access to targets for our next heist. My quiet facade was how I listened undetected in the salon while women discussed the latest gossip and talked about the out-of-town celebrities and ballers who were visiting L.A. Goldie's club swarmed with unknowing prey as they carelessly threw endless cash from backpacks, duffle bags, and briefcases.

Initially, jobs were quick and easy. Greed was a seductress to us. Although we made sure each robbery was more lucrative than the last, they became more dangerous, too. Word spread underground of a dynamic duo who could easily steal candy from a baby. During the late 1990s, cell phones became more common, which made my job—the sneaking, the disappearing—harder, not easier. Still, I craved the escapism, the money, and the free feeling. So, foolishly, I ignored the red flags.

CHAPTER 2
IT WAS A GOOD DAY

MAURICE "GOLDIE" BROWN

AFTER A VICTORIOUS nighttime robbery, nothing felt better than waking up on top of Benjamins, sandwiched between two beautiful bodies with warm breasts on my back and a juicy ass positioned right in front of my thighs. With a payout of one hundred and fifty thousand dollars, the Maxwell job should have been Pearle and my last. However, greed is destructive, and later that day, my indulgence in that sin would change the trajectory of our lives forever.

My stomach growled loudly, expressing its anger at being empty. "Damn, I'm hungry."

Alyssa smiled and slipped from behind me. "I'll make our usual."

I moved to sit on the side of the bed and slapped the hundreds stuck to her thighs as she slid into her purple fitted dress.

Alyssa was sexy and the best dancer at my club, with her big breasts, tiny waist, and nice booty. She had smooth, chocolate skin and long hair that was either natural or a weave. I couldn't tell, nor did I care. She danced to get out of Compton and clung to me like dryer sheets to get what she wanted. I liked her, and she liked playing her position. So, our arrangement worked perfectly.

Tina, my ride-or-die alibi, main boo, and top bartender in the club, slid into my tank top and then sat on my lap. "I'll make us Tequila Sunrises," she offered.

I wrapped my arms around her waist. "What did you, Pearle,

and I do all night?"

"Smoke, drink, and play Tetris."

I kissed her neck. "And what time did Pearle leave, boo?"

"Six o'clock."

"Dang, I missed all the fun!" Alyssa yelled from the kitchen. "The club was jumping till daylight, so I had to get that money."

Tina and I smiled.

I played with her cropped curls. "I like the Jada Pinkett look on you."

"I didn't think you noticed."

"I may not always say shit, but I always notice the sexy shit you do."

She pulled my face to hers, and we kissed again. Tina had been in my life since middle school, and our shit was complicated. She was thick, brown, and beautiful and changed her looks randomly, which always held my attention. I was digging her new vibe. It highlighted her cheekbones and pretty eyes.

I couldn't figure out why Tina put up with my ass. I guess it's because we'd been through so much. Eventually, I would marry her if she was still down with me. I loved her and wanted what my parents had, but monogamy wasn't going to happen anytime soon. Marriage scared the shit out of me. So, the women in my life had a choice to either love me as I was or leave me the hell alone.

Tina handed us drinks, lit a blunt, and took a hit before passing it to me. "It's a wake-and-bake kind of morning."

I inhaled and passed it to Alyssa. "Shit, that's every morning."

After we ate and played a little Nintendo, Alyssa cleaned the kitchen and prepared to leave. While heading to the door, she stopped and turned to me.

"Goldie, I need to go shopping and get my hair done."

With no hesitation, I slid a bankroll into her cleavage. She pecked my lips in response.

"Thanks. See you at the club, Mr. President."

When I turned around after closing the door, Tina was standing behind me, holding a garbage bag in one hand and a bright pink letter in the other.

"How late am I?" I asked.

"Late enough to lose your mother's house."

"Shit. Can I take out a second mortgage on my crib? How much equity do I have?"

"You've done all that." She took another pink letter off the end table. "This one is from the mortgage company about your house."

"What about the club?"

She turned over the garbage bag, and pink letters dropped to the floor. "Baby, you have nothing else to rob from Peter to pay Paul."

"Shit!"

She grabbed my face. "It's time to tell Pearle."

I shook my head. "She will beat my ass. I promised her and Pops I would handle Mama's bills."

"Well, what are you going to do?"

"I'm going to handle it the way I handle things."

"Rob niggas?" she asked.

I nodded. "But I'll have to do it solo."

"No, you don't." She placed her arms around my neck. "I'm your partner for life."

"No, I need your eyes on the club." We kissed. "You know a nigga knows when to be serious and stop fucking around."

"I know."

I grabbed her face and admired her natural beauty. "I love ya, boo."

"I love you, too, Goldie."

Still exhausted from the previous night, Tina went back to bed to get some more sleep. So, I smoked a blunt while separating the stolen cash equally for Pearle and me. I grabbed a few stacks to give Mama and stuffed the money inside a Louis Vuitton bag I bought her from the mall. Bills were past due, but I couldn't have Mama looking broke, rocking a swap meet knock-off.

When my brother, Nike, was killed and my pops was sentenced to fifteen years in prison, I went numb. I promised Pops I would protect Pearle and Mama, and I didn't want to let him down. Shit was getting hot since the streets were talking, but no one suspected us. Despite the rumors swirling around about a thieving pimp and his bottom bitch, I believed Pearle and I were untouchable.

After walking out the door of my mother's house, I stopped on the walkway to deeply inhale the fresh air. The visit with my mother was nice, like always. She was appreciative of the cash and loved the designer bag. Sure, I felt guilty whenever she looked me in the eyes and expressed how proud she was of me. It would've killed her if she ever found out that Pearle and I were thieves, but her losing her house would've killed me. So, I did what I had to do.

My thick gold chain, watch, and earrings gleamed in the City of Angels' sunshine. I wiped the smudge from my brand-new purple and gold Kobe Bryant Adidas and then jumped in my car. It was calm in Compton, so I dropped the top on my old-school black Deville, or what I called the Batmobile. As the birds chirped, I hit the switches down Rosecrans Avenue. Feeling fresh in my new Sean John fit, I looked up at the heavenly sky and smiled, sensing Nike's spirit around me. I cruised slowly while bumping some Ice Cube as my people showed me love. Who knew Maurice "Goldie" Brown, the class clown, would end up a stick-up kid who jacked niggas?

Growing up, I'd slipped through many fights, gang affiliations, and typical hood shit by making niggas laugh. Pearle and I had seen so much over the years. We navigated the streets like Marco Polo, dodging bullets along the way. Being funny was my hood survival tactic. I now owned Gold's Room, the hottest strip club in South Central L.A. I loved to crack jokes and make people laugh there, too. I stayed neutral and kept niggas entertained with the finest, most talented dancers in the area.

Before I bought the place, dudes would ask me, "Goldie, how did you pull that fine-ass girl and you're broke?"

My answer was, "I made her laugh right up outta her panties."

I'm handsome, but fuck that sexy shit. Pretty women loved me because I made them laugh, and I loved making pretty women smile.

I parked in front of my spot and walked immediately to the bar. Tina fixed my favorite drink, Crown and Coke. She poured herself a small shot and lifted her glass.

"Cheers," she said, and our glasses kissed.

The sweet burn from the alcohol massaged my senses as I looked around, admiring my accomplishment. The mist in the air, flashing lights, and women dancing on poles never got old. Gold's Room maintained high standards, providing illusions of seduction and fantasy, and I respected my dancers as the talented entertainers they were.

I inhaled the mixed fragrance of weed, vanilla, and baby oil. I loved the aroma. The stronger the scent, the more money the club made, and I needed every dollar. I was high and floating like the dollar bills on a good night when we kicked the fans on full speed to make the dancers' hair blow like the fine ladies of Destiny's Child. I was relaxed but alert. The day was the closest to perfection I'd experienced in years.

After my drink, I was ready with my duffle bag full of cash for Alyssa. I reclined on the couch in the President's VIP room and watched the lights hit the chandelier, causing rainbows to dance around the room. Suddenly, three nicely dressed Hispanic men appeared in the room with scowls painted on their faces.

"Hey, this room is taken!" I yelled as I sat up. My jaws tightened, and the veins stuck out like spider webs on my neck. Where is my security guard?

Ignoring me, the men spoke Spanish as if I wasn't there. People assumed because I was black and from the hood, I didn't know the language.

One dude stood at the door, and another sat on the couch in front of me, stroking an all-black velvet cat with a triple-strand diamond collar. The other man stood next to the couch. I had no gun or security; my buzz was fading fast.

I stood up. "*Hablo Espanol*, motherfuckers. *Que quieres?*"

The two men standing pointed their guns directly at me. The one seated, who appeared to be in charge, snapped his fingers. The weapons disappeared. He slowly massaged the back of the cat, and the scowl on his face vanished. As my mind raced in circles, he signaled me to sit back down, but I stood on guard, not looking afraid.

"Dude, this is my shit."

"Goldie, *mi nombre es Matias Escobar*," he said, crossing his legs. "These are my brothers, Felipe and Tomas. I run a cartel, you might say, and I've been told that you and your sister, Pearle, might be able to assist me."

"The Matias Escobar?" When he nodded, I continued, "I'm sorry for your loss."

It was recently on the news that Matias's twin brother, Miguel, was killed like his infamous uncle by the Columbian police.

Matias's eyes watered. "He was murdered right in front of me."

The cat's eyes glowed green and purred in sadness on cue.

"He was my twin, so when he died, I died. My heart stopped beating, and I had no breath left. Then, beautiful Pussy, this cat, hopped onto my lap and saved me. I believe when my brother was killed, his spirit leaped inside this cat, and now, his soul lives on in Pussy."

The cat nodded as if in agreement and gave a loud meow. I made the mistake of laughing, and two gun barrels kissed my face.

"*Lo siento.* I'm so sorry. I mean no disrespect," I said, putting my hands up. "My only brother, Nike, was murdered a few years ago, and I have to go to the cemetery to feel his spirit. So, *Señor*, you are lucky to feel your brother's presence anytime you want. I wish I had a Pussy."

His disdain washed from his face. He snapped his fingers, and once again, the guns disappeared.

I was not going to show my fear. No one wanted to be on the bad side of an Escobar. Their reputation for limb removal and other heinous consequences for enemies dated back to the 1980s.

"*Señor Escobar*, you mentioned you needed services from me and my sister. Do you need dancers for an event and hair and makeup? You're in my place of business, and my sister owns a hair salon."

He smiled and replied, "No. I need your other service. I was outbid in an auction for a Jean-Michel Basquiat painting by a man named Blaque, who recently moved here from Atlanta. I want to hire you and your sister to get that painting from Blaque and bring it to me where it belongs."

I put my hand up slowly in protest. "*Señor Matias, por favor.* My sister and I are business owners in this community."

I will never forget Matias's next words.

"*Señor Goldie,* I will pay you two million dollars for this. Wouldn't you agree that is enough?"

At the sound of that number, my body jerked like I had been hit by the Holy Ghost.

His two brothers raised their weapons at my sudden movement. Matias snapped. For the third time, the guns disappeared.

"Nigga, are you asking me to steal a painting, and the payout is two million?"

His face brightened. "Actually, it's one million for the Basquiat painting and one million for Blaque. Whether he is alive or dead doesn't interest me."

I'd never killed or kidnapped a person before, but I would do anything for that amount of money.

"Tell me more about Blaque."

Matias took his time telling me everything: how Blaque was an arrogant asshole who wanted to open his own operation in L.A., how he was disrespectful to Matias's people, and how Blaque had bought the painting just to irk Matias. One thing was clear—Matias hated Blaque.

At some point, I tuned him out. I only wanted to know where Blaque lived and the location of his painting, but Matias didn't know. He didn't have the most important details because that bad motherfucker, Blaque, had two armed bodyguards and was securely protected by a bunch of black crime family members. Still, I knew Pearle could easily infiltrate that operation without danger to herself.

It sounded like movie shit. Either way, a two-million-dollar payout was worth the risk and enough money for my entire family to be set for life.

"Señor, how did you find out about us?" I asked.

"A general always knows who the best soldiers are on the battlefield."

Our cover had been blown, and with all the niggas we'd jacked, the exposure would be dangerous. I knew Pearle and I needed to retire immediately and reject Matias before word hit the streets, but that two million clouded my judgement.

"If you're the boss motherfucker of the cartel, why don't you just take Blaque and the painting yourself?"

He laughed as if I had told a joke. "I like you, Goldie. You know, part of running a business is hiring the right people, and you're supposedly the best at the art of—"

"Robbing niggas?" I interrupted.

He laughed again. "I was going to say theft. We specialize in producing and selling cocaine, not committing theft. This is why we contract jobs outside our specialty. I've heard Blaque is a gentleman, and his weakness is pretty black women. Your sister is beautiful. I hear she's his type."

"My sister might not like his ass."

Matias put up his hand. "I really don't care how you do it. As I said, it's not my expertise, so I'll leave it to you."

Doubt slithered into my mind. "Too easy. What's the catch?"

He signaled for his goon to drop a briefcase in front of me.

"None. I've told you everything I know. Here's one million. Once you take this money and shake my hand, you're locked into a contractual agreement with the Escobar brothers. Everything you need is in this briefcase. I'll need the original Basquiat painting and Blaque for you to get the other half. This painting is very important to me—Basquiat was my brother Miguel's favorite artist, and he loved this specific piece the most. So, if you fail, I'm sorry, but you and your sister die. It's that simple."

"Die? Can't we just return the money?"

"We would not be having this meeting if I thought you'd fail."

He was right. My sister and I held a hundred percent robbery success rate. This was a once-in-a-lifetime opportunity, and I needed to seize the moment.

"Is there a time limit?" I asked.

"You've got one week."

"We need more time. Our last job took a month."

Matias stuck out his hand. "Alright. Two weeks. I hate this country and don't want to be here longer than necessary."

Before I knew it, I'd shaken hands with the devil.

"There's a phone, a photo of the Basquiat painting, and photos of Blaque. I don't want to hear from you until you have both of them," he said, then added, "He goes to a club called Red Light every night."

As if teleported, he and his goons vanished, and Alyssa appeared. Her ass was suddenly a distraction I didn't need, so I bolted out of the room. Sweating, I ran down the hallway to my office, locked the door, and once seated behind my desk, I opened the briefcase. The scent of new money hit my nostrils, and I inhaled deeply.

The geometric arrangement of a million dollars was like the perfect woman, and I was aroused. I needed that money. I needed to catch up on past bills without Pearle's knowledge, so I thought it was God's blessing. But I should've known greed is a gift of the devil's delight.

I gave the money one last look. "You are the sexiest thing I've ever seen."

When I opened my office door, my security guard was standing there with his hands on his stomach and beads of sweat dripping down his face.

"What the hell happened to you?" I asked.

"I'm sick. I think I have a stomach bug."

"Damn." I couldn't tell if he was lying, but I found his sudden "illness" too convenient. "That's fucked up, but you're fired."

With that, I ran down the hallway, kissed Tina at the bar, and stuck a bankroll in her cleavage.

She removed it and whispered. "Keep it."

"Trust me. We're all good, boo."

I gave her another kiss and raced out of the club.

I sped home and rolled a blunt. As the weed cleared my mind, I saw the plan like my favorite Nintendo game, Tetris. I controlled the pieces to ensure they'd quickly fall into place to keep the board clear. I pulled out the pictures of Blaque, who was GQ and Pearle's type. Piece number one was like the line block, which was the easiest to fit: Get my sister on board. One million was enough to entice her even if she wasn't interested in Blaque. Piece number two was like the flexible T block: Steal the painting. We were expert thieves, so we'd execute this flawlessly once Pearle agreed. Piece number three was like the oddly-shaped Z block that barely fit any other piece: Kidnap, trap, or kill Blaque. Pearle would not be down with that, so I would collect all the information I needed about him from her to deliver him to the cartel. Piece number four was like the tricky L block: Keep the fact from Pearle that our lives were on the line. Her head needed to be free for everything to work. Being an expert Tetris player, I knew the goal was to keep the blocks falling in the right places with speed to avoid a pile-up. Before Pearle and I could lose, I'd turn the system power off, and we would walk away rich.

I was high as hell, lost in thought, and the remains of the blunt burned my lips. I took one last hit of the purple haze, then called Pearle to get our real game of Tetris started.

CHAPTER 3
IN A SENTIMENTAL MOOD

PEARLE MONALISE BROWN

On MY WAY to visit my brother, I rode with my Corvette's top down and let the wind kiss my face. Unlike me, Mommy and Goldie were Compton residents for life. They lived in the same neighborhood on a better block where we had grown up.

I loved and appreciated many parts of Compton. At its core, there was clarity and shine under the smut. Once you've survived it, you attained a hunger that kept you focused and driven. You would devour anything in your way. I respected my city and knew from her life's lessons that before I hit Tam's at Rosecrans and Central, I needed to close my drop-top, open my eyes wide, and stay alert.

Strangely, it was a quiet afternoon. Goldie sat comfortably on his couch, playing a game of Tetris on his Nintendo 64.

"What's up, Goldie? What's so urgent that you had to text me 911?"

He launched his throw pillow toward me. "Mama said you better come see her today, or she's going to beat your ass."

"Liar."

"She said it in English *y Espanol*."

"Stop lying."

"We gave her a Louie and a few stacks."

I shook my head. "I told you to lay low on the cash until I cleaned it."

"Too late. Start shampooing, Vidal Sassoon."

I coughed. My eyes were watering from the marijuana smoke that filled the room. Goldie was high. He tossed me a backpack full of cash, which landed on the floor near my feet. When I bent down to pick it up, I noticed a bright pink envelope beneath the coffee table.

I fanned a cloud of smoke drifting towards my face with it. "Is this a late bill notice?"

Leaping off the sofa, he snatched the envelope from my hand.

"No. Mind your business," he said, then reclined back into the coach. "We've got a new mark."

I had burned the Robyn character I played for the Maxwell job and wanted to lay low. However, Goldie immediately started pitching this new gig, and we pulled at each other in a tug-of-war.

He looked serious. "Pearle, after this, we will be set for life and can actually retire. All of us."

"No new jobs right now, Goldie."

He handed me an envelope. "Check out this dude named Blaque, a big-time drug dealer from Atlanta. He's rich and recently moved to L.A."

The first picture was of two muscular men in black suits.

"Which one is Blaque?" I asked.

Goldie peeped over my shoulder. "Those are his bodyguards."

I was confused. Blaque didn't sound like our usual target.

Not interested, I handed the envelope back. "No, thank you. That's too much security to worry about. Maybe I'll take Mommy to the spa," I said, attempting to change the subject.

Goldie was stressed, which stressed me. Ignoring him, I started thinking about my ninety-minute hot stone massage.

He snapped his fingers to snatch my attention.

"Sis, focus. This dude has an original Basquiat worth one million."

I whipped around. "What do *you* know about Jean-Michel

Basquiat? And we don't steal art. We take cash and jewelry."

Goldie's lips moved, but I had stopped listening to what he was saying. My mind was drifting from the contact smoke. All I could see was Goldie and I getting caught by the police, looking dumbfounded while holding a big-ass painting in our hands. I giggled at the thought.

His voice got louder; he wasn't giving up.

"Sis, this is serious. We have someone interested in purchasing the painting from us already. They'll give us cash."

"Cash?"

This made me suspicious, but the temptation of a million in cash got my immediate attention. Goldie had stopped begging and pleading. He didn't have to because I was hooked. I was already thinking of a new character needed for the job.

"How did you find out about Blaque, Goldie?" I finally asked. "And who's willing to pay us one million for this painting? That's a lot of cash."

I snatched the envelope back and waited for his answer.

Goldie hesitated before saying, "Matias Escobar and his brothers came to the club. They want to hire us to get the painting."

I stared at Blaque's pretty face. The news was disturbing. I had stopped breathing.

"They *who*? The fucking Escobars? How the hell do they know about us?"

Goldie's voice was slightly shaky. "He wouldn't say, but it's cool—"

"Cool? I don't think so."

Goldie touched my hand, which calmed my fear a little.

"We're not in any trouble, Pearle. The infamous Escobars hired us because they know we're the best for the job. I promise that after this job, we are done. It'll be easy money. It's what we do—what *you* do. It's just a lot more money. We can do this."

I'd die for Goldie. I trusted him with my life, and he knew it.

Now calmer, I took a closer look at Blaque's photo and was pleasantly surprised. He was gorgeous.

"What else do you know about this dude? Why did he move to L.A.?"

"Blaque is part of a crime family in ATL. He wants to be an L.A. boss."

I laughed so hard my chest hurt. "So he wants war with the most gangster city in the country? He's fine, but I don't want that smoke. He sounds crazy."

My comment didn't throw Goldie off, though.

"He may be feeling himself, *and* he may be crazy, but the Escobars know his weakness—beautiful black women. Find out whatever you can about him, Pearle. Locate the painting, and I'll take care of the rest. Don't forget we're professionals. We're experts at what we do. We can do this quickly and easily."

He put a fist in front of me for a reassuring fist bump. My fist met his, and we were locked.

"How much was the good faith payment?"

"The what?" he asked blankly.

"The job pays one million. How much did the Escobars give you for a down payment?"

"Oh, we shook on that shit. Bada bing, bada boom."

"Bada bing, bada what? Are you high?"

"Yeah, I'm high—high as hell, but the handshake is the true gangster contract. Godfather shit."

"That's dumb as hell. What if we do the job and walk away with nothing?"

"Sis, the contract is locked. Trust me."

I smacked my lips and got distracted by Blaque's picture.

"This man doesn't look gangster. He has soft eyes and a pretty face."

"Pearle, Blaque's dangerous. He's a bad motherfucker if Matias Escobar is willing to pay us major cash to steal a painting from him. Remember that Blaque is strictly a one-million-dollar business contract for us—too big for anything else."

I didn't agree. This looked like pleasure, too, and the mysterious mix of Blaque as both business and pleasure aroused me.

"Yes, I know. So when do I make my move on this Blaque character? Who do I need to be for him?"

Goldie laughed out loud. "Shit, be your damn self. He's been at Red Light, your boring jazz spot, every night."

My mouth dropped. "A pretty-ass man with swag who loves art and jazz is a dangerous thug?"

"You're a dangerous, pretty-girl thief from the hood who loves artsy shit. So what's your point?"

We laughed, and I shrugged.

"*Touché*. I'll get dressed and head over. I'm looking forward to his one-million-dollar ass showing me his *collection*."

"*Yuck.*"

I kissed the disgust from Goldie's face and was gone.

I stopped by Mommy's house to give her a big hug and kiss. She looked beautiful with her new hairdo from my salon and clothes from her shopping spree at the mall. She modeled the new gift from Goldie and showed me how she would proudly parade the bag in front of her friends.

I would love to keep her happy and buy her everything she deserves. One million will indeed be a life-changer, I thought while looking at her smile as she talked with me.

When I passed Rosecrans, I let the Corvette's top down, allowing the breeze to run its fingers through my hair. The palm trees danced as the sun dipped behind the mountains. After pulling into the garage of my private condo in the hills, I walked through the door, turned on my retro record player, and let the sounds of Miles Davis' trumpet move through me while I grabbed a glass of wine. Then I went out on my terrace to relax and use the Hollywood sign in the distance for inspiration.

Who will my new character be? Who should I be for Blaque at Red Light?

Goldie had told me to be myself, but who was I? I'd never played myself on the job.

How do I play me*?*

I went to the closet and picked out a long, flowy black dress. As I sipped my wine, a white, off-the-shoulder, fitted mini dress called my name. I bought myself that dress years ago and had never worn it. I matched it with red pumps, a long double-strand of pearls, and ruby lipstick. While looking for a wig, I stopped and decided to rock my natural hair, which was tossed by the wind and hung to my breasts.

I stared at myself in the mirror and felt beautiful. This was me, and it felt good.

After finishing my wine, I headed out.

Club Red Light was small and intimate. It was another place where I could escape. I drifted with the rhythm, the music freeing me. Though I hadn't been there in a while, I was a regular—the owner and staff knew me well. A part of me hated the fact that Blaque went there. It was *my* place, wasn't it? My favorite place in L.A. I always disappeared after a heist, and Red Light was my refuge. It's where I could be myself again. I could stop the acting.

The atmosphere was thick, hot, and smoky, and the small dance floor stayed packed. Everyone danced and rubbed against each other, carefree in a music bubble. It was sexy and steamy with the best damn live jazz sessions you would ever hear.

I sat at my favorite table near the bar, where I could see Blaque when he walked in. I closed my eyes, feeling Coltrane alive and flowing through me.

The sound of a glass being placed on the table jarred me from my reverie. Looking up, I smiled at my favorite bartender.

"Tommy, are you hooking me up tonight?"

He smiled back and pointed toward the bar. "Nah, baby. That cat in the back treated you. He asked me if I could guess what type of drink you liked. I told him I *know*—martini, extra dirty."

"What cat in the back?"

I turned to my right. It was Blaque. He was standing at the bar and looking even finer in person. Our eyes locked like magnets.

Without turning back to Tommy, I told him, "Yes, you make the best drinks in L.A., and you definitely know what I like. Tell him I said thank you."

I had to take a sip to calm down. *Damn, he's fine. How did I miss his sexy ass at the bar?*

Blaque was gorgeous with his beautiful tan-brown complexion, hazel eyes, chiseled face, smooth skin, and bright white teeth. He wore a Gucci fitted, black button-up shirt with the top buttons undone. His hair was brown with deep waves, like an ocean. He had thick eyebrows and long eyelashes. His lips looked luscious. He stood about six feet and had a strong chest, shoulders, and arms. He was accessorized with two huge diamond-studded earrings that sparkled in the light and a diamond Rolex I could see from across the bar.

Before walking to my table, he studied me and then was suddenly towering over me.

"May I sit with you?" His deep baritone was melodic.

He watched, waiting for me to respond as my eyes traveled up and down his body. His smile gave me chills.

"Yes, you can. Thank you for the drink."

He pulled his chair closer and kissed my hand. "My name is Blaque. What's yours, beautiful?"

I couldn't help but smile. "Mr. Blaque, I thought men only kissed women's hands in movies. Where are you from?"

He flashed his perfect smile. "It's just one name, baby. B-L-A-Q-U-E, and I'm a southern Jamaican gentleman from Atlanta who knows a rare gem when I see one."

Heat rushed between my legs. "Pearle," I blurted, then kicked myself for using my real name. Then again, wasn't I supposed to be myself? How could I do that with a fake name?

He touched my necklace. "Wow. Pearle at Club Red Light. I knew you were special, and I didn't have to dive deep into the ocean to find you."

The man gave me butterflies, ones that danced up my dress.

"How did you get the name Blaque?" I quickly asked.

He laughed. "You'll have to ask my mama. It's from her."

His game was too strong, like he was playing a staged character, but I loved it.

I looked into his eyes. "And what do you do for a living, *Blaque*?"

"I run shit," he replied coolly, then sipped his drink while staring directly at me.

I damn near choked on my martini. "So…you run a company of some kind?"

In a sexy, natural Jamaican accent, Blaque answered, "No, my lady. I'm a criminal from a family of criminals—the don dada of all the dons."

His honesty took me off guard and turned me on even more.

In my best Jamaican accent, I finally said, "Are you a…rude boy?"

His sexy eyes narrowed as he seductively said, "No boy. *Mi da bad* man."

His lips were so close to mine I could smell his peppermint ChapStick.

"This woman likes *da bad man*," I whispered.

He grinned, and his finger danced on top of my hand. "Pearle, I like you. Would you dance with me?"

Our hands securely locked, and Blaque helped me up. He guided us to the little wooden floor, where we entered the intimate dance orgy. With bodies all around us, we moved slowly while staring intensely into each other's eyes. Blaque turned me around, and I lifted my arms above my head, locking my wrists around his neck. His hands traced down the sides of my breasts, waist, and hips. As we swayed to Coltrane's "In a Sentimental Mood," his warm breath set my insides on fire. Heatwaves shot up and down my spine when his lips grazed my shoulder and neck. Although he was much taller, our bodies were somehow perfectly matched. We moved in harmony.

We talked, drank, and danced for hours. I didn't want our time to end, but suddenly, it was *very* late.

I grabbed his hand and looked at the time on his Rolex. "Blaque, I should get home."

He placed his other hand on top of mine. "Okay, beautiful, but let me walk you to your car."

We interlocked our fingers again—it felt so natural—and were followed closely by the two handsome bodyguards I had seen in the photo earlier.

Following my gaze, Blaque told me, "Don't worry about them. They'll hang around us from time to time."

"Are you saying you want to see me again?"

He opened my door. "Pearle, I would love to take you to dinner tomorrow night if you're available."

I laughed. "I see you don't waste time."

He ran his fingers gently along my cheek to my chin.

"I don't play games, baby," he said. "I told you I like you."

I wrote down my phone number and put it in his shirt pocket. Then I stepped closer, wrapped my arms around his neck, and planted my lips on his. Our mouths opened, and our tongues moved like our bodies on the dance floor. His hands traveled down my back and firmly gripped my ass. My body loved how he responded naturally to me. My arms locked tighter around his neck, and we kissed passionately until he took my last breath. He smiled.

"Blaque…it was wonderful meeting you. I'll see you tomorrow."

I floated into the driver's seat, started the engine, and immediately turned the AC on blast. I was *so* hot.

He stood at the door, biting his lip. "The pleasure was mine, Pearle. Can I call you tonight to make sure you made it home safely?"

I nodded, and he smiled. Then he kissed me sweetly on the cheek before closing my door.

I saw him waving in my rearview as I drove off.

Shit, I think I'm in love.

CHAPTER 4
ANYTIME & ANYPLACE

PEARLE MONALISE BROWN

I WAS CONSCIOUSLY AWAKE, but the day after Blaque had entered my life, I moved vicariously as if in a dream—every emotion and feeling gigantic. Every part of me wanted to feel him, which was unusual because I had never felt like this about a man. He was dark and mysterious, with an inner glow that sparked my curiosity.

Blaque and I had stayed on the phone the previous night until after sunrise, so I slept till noon. Upon finally waking up, I called Shay, my master stylist at Top of the World Salon, and she immediately answered the phone.

"Hey, boss lady!"

"Shay, I need to get my hair done."

"My Aaliyah masterpiece from yesterday is already destroyed?"

"It was beautiful, but after Club Red Light, my hair is a sweaty monstrosity. I want braids for my date tonight."

"Poetic Justice will take hours, so come now."

I grabbed my Chanel bag and headed toward the door. As I was leaving out, I was greeted by a tall delivery man wearing a Kangol.

"Pearle?"

"Yes?"

He handed me a large floral bouquet. "These are for you."

"Thank you," I told him and proceeded to close the door, but before I could, he stopped me.

"Wait. There are more."

Like marching soldiers, men walked in with bouquets, suddenly transforming my home into a tropical oasis filled with every exotic flower in the colors of the Crayola spectrum.

"Sign here to confirm receipt of the delivery, please."

After my signature, he tipped his hat and left.

I immediately yanked the card from the envelope.

> *To my precious gem, Pearle,*
> *One bouquet for every hour that you've taken my breath*
> *away. I can't wait to see you tonight.*
> *Blaque*

I inhaled the sweet aroma that filled the air and said aloud, "Don't do it. Don't you go falling. Remember the task at hand, Pearle."

My only concern was ensuring my heart and mind stayed on the same accord.

With a late start to my day, I rushed to get ready. While applying my makeup, my house phone rang repeatedly. I ignored it, but then my cell phone started buzzing and chiming like an alarm.

"Damn, Goldie, what's up?"

"Rude."

"My bad. I'm in a hurry for my date with Blaque."

"Cool. Do you need me to follow you? Does he have more than two bodyguards? Where are you going? Where does he live?"

I looked out my bedroom window. A black Bentley, followed by a black Escalade and Benz, rolled up like a presidential motorcade. The shiny exteriors and custom rims made me tingle in all the right places.

"*Ay, Dios mío*! He has a Bentley. Don't follow. Two guards. Roscoe's. Don't know yet, but I will find out after I fuck him tonight."

"Ugh, and Roscoe's? All the fancy restaurants in L.A., and you asked a rich nigga with a Bentley to take you out for damn chicken and waffles?"

"Blaque likes a real around-the-way girl, and this hood chick has a taste for chicken and waffles."

Goldie laughed. "Whatever. I guess you know what you're doing."

When we hung up, I realized for the first time I didn't know what the hell I was doing. I wasn't playing a different persona; I was free to be myself. I took one last glance in the mirror at my sexy, Lisa Bonet-bohemian look, grabbed a soft denim jacket to prevent L.A.'s nightly windy kisses from chilling me, and ran out the door.

Blaque was walking up my driveway, and when he saw me exit my home, he ran to help me down the stairs. The warm wind lifted my skirt and caressed my thighs. My Poetic Justice braids danced while the breeze gently pushed me toward him. Unlike the night before, Blaque was casually dressed in FUBU, Air Jordans, and an Atlanta Falcons fitted cap. The diamonds that decorated his ears, neck, and wrists were clear as ice.

I smiled. "Hey, handsome. Thank you for my beautiful flowers."

He smiled back and opened my car door. "You're welcome, and you still take my breath away."

"Don't you have a driver to open doors?"

He gently grabbed my face and kissed my lips. "I do, and his name is Blue, but I'm selfish. I want to be the first man to lay eyes on you before you get in the car. You look beautiful, baby, and I love the braids."

He closed the car door, and I slid onto the warm leather seat. The wood panels on the interior were accented with silver aluminum. After removing my sandals, my feet sank into the plush rug. I inhaled deeply, and the fresh smell of leather flowed through me. Before the partition went up, I caught a glimpse of the navigation system as it rose gracefully from the dash. When Blaque sat next to me, I got goosebumps.

As we rode to Roscoe's, we joked like old friends while Janet Jackson sang softly through the speakers. She wanted it "Anytime, Anyplace." As Blaque massaged my feet, I fantasized about what I'd do to him.

"There's going to be a line at Roscoe's, so tuck your diamond chain inside your shirt," I warned.

"I don't do lines, and I never hide my jewelry," he replied, then pressed his thumb into the soles of my feet. The sensation caused me to melt into the seat.

I laughed. "It's peak dinner hours, so we'll be dealing with the tourists. Get ready."

He slipped my sandals on my feet. "I'm getting ready to see if L.A.'s Roscoe's can compete with my ATL's Paschal's."

When we pulled up to the restaurant, the entire block was empty. It looked like a ghost town.

Disappointed, I smacked my lips. "Dang, it must be closed."

Blue opened my car door and offered his hand. I took his hand and got out of the car. Blaque exited right behind me, and we started walking toward the entrance.

"What are we doing?" I asked, confused.

Placing a kiss on my cheek, Blaque responded, "I told you I'm selfish."

Suddenly, a chef opened the restaurant door. "Welcome to Roscoe's."

Stunned speechless, my mouth dropped open. That didn't stop Blaque from kissing my lips, though.

"I told you I don't do lines, baby."

He helped me to the table, and I floated to the chair. Not

only had he rented out Roscoe's for the night, but all the tables, except for one, had been removed from the restaurant. Blaque sat across from me, grabbed my hands, and blessed the food. Candle flames flickered while we ate. The Red Light jazz band serenaded us, making the night more hypnotic.

I devoured my food in minutes. "Roscoe's or Paschal's?"

Blaque took another bite and laughed. "Damn, you eat fast."

I laughed. "It's a habit I formed growing up with brothers who loved to steal food from my plate."

"I love a woman who can eat." He smiled. "And Paschal's all day, baby. Now, I want to know more about you. Let's start with your last name."

Taken off guard, I responded, "Pearle Monalise Brown," offering my full name.

He smiled, and his eyes glowed. "You have a pretty name. Monalise. That's different."

I took a sip of my drink. "My mother said I looked like a baby Mona Lisa when I was born."

Blaque lifted an eyebrow. "Hold up. You are named after Mona Lisa, the Da Vinci painting? I get a gem and a work of art in one woman? You're the one, baby."

"You say all the right things." I searched for the truth in his eyes. "Your game is trump tight."

He moved in so close that our lips almost touched.

"Games are for boys. I'm a man who is not afraid to say exactly how I feel, and with you, everything feels right."

I grabbed his face. "Tell me how you feel right now."

"I feel like laying your sexy ass across this table, 'cause I'd rather eat you than Roscoe's."

Seductively, I slid across his lap, turned his hat to the back, and slowly sucked his lips while his hands gently rubbed the skin around my waist. As we kissed, I felt a bulge rising in his pants, and I was quite pleased with the size. He stood up and wrapped my legs tightly around his waist. With no directive needed, the chef opened the restaurant door, and Blaque carried me to the car, where Blue was holding open the door to the Bentley. Blaque carefully laid me across the backseat. I pulled him on top of me. After the door slammed, the partition rolled up, and wasting no time, he created a pathway of kisses from my forehead to between my thighs. He lifted my skirt and stared hungrily. The cool breeze from the open moonroof tickled my exposed bare skin. I arched my back in response, and Blaque licked his lips.

Looking up to the stars, he whispered, "Thank you, God."

His warm mouth engulfed the bare lips between my legs. Then his tongue began a treasure hunt.

Once he found my pearl deep inside my ocean, I snatched the hat off his head, placed it over my face, and screamed, "Dammit, Blaque!"

He kissed my ear and replaced the hat on his head.

"Damn, you taste as sweet as you look. I can't wait to get you inside."

When I awakened from my orgasmic daze, I slowly opened my eyes and saw we were parked. With Blaque holding my hand while leading the way, we entered his contemporary-style Santa Monica home. The entire first floor had an open layout with a view of a small pool in the backyard that led to the ocean. The marble floor gleamed bright white, and the decor was sleek and modern, with black and white furniture. Eccentric, colorful art pieces were focal points. My eyes scanned each wall like the Terminator. Where is the Basquiat? I wondered as we walked up a silver, textured staircase to the second floor.

"Blaque, your house is amazing. I need a full tour."

Just then, my phone chimed and buzzed loudly, making my purse an annoying distraction.

"I know it's my brother. He worries about me when I'm on a

date with a man he doesn't know."

"I understand, baby. Go ahead and answer."

"*Que paso?*"

"I'm up the street. Where's the painting?"

"*No, vete a casa, porque no se.*"

"You don't know? And why are you telling me to go home? Is his security there?"

"*Si. Tres.*"

"He has three guards now?"

"*Si.*"

"How long will you be there?"

I told him about thirty minutes and then ended the call, not wanting Blaque to become suspicious.

We continued to the third floor, and at the end of the hallway, Blaque called me to him with his eyes. As I stood in front of him, he slipped his strong arms around my waist.

"Pearle, you need to call your brother back and tell him that Blaque is going to have you here till *manana*." We walked inside the bedroom, and he closed the door. "'Cause I ain't no thirty-minute nigga."

"*Hablas Espanol*, Blaque?"

His deep, low voice entered my ear. "*Si, mamacita. Yo quiero y necesito la cocha pronto.*" His teeth grabbed my earlobe. "*Por favor?*"

"*Si, papi*," I said, then fell to my knees, unzipped his pants, and took every inch of him into my mouth.

He moaned and grabbed my freshly-braided hair. The slight pain from the tug at my sensitive scalp stimulated me. The way he felt inside my mouth, I didn't want to pull away from the pleasure.

"Not yet, baby," he told me, lifting me to my feet.

We kissed intensely while removing each article of our clothing until we were completely naked. We connected in a mystical place beyond what our eyes could see. The moonlight illuminated the bedroom, and the sound of the ocean waves in the background serenaded us softly.

My finger caressed the artistic details surrounding the word "Savage" tattooed on his shoulder. A mystical lion was soaring across his muscular chest, lunging toward a beautiful cross.

"*Ay Dios mio.*"

Blaque lifted my body in the air effortlessly and placed me face down on the bed, my breasts and stomach sliding across his silky Egyptian sheets. His wet kisses started at the back of my neck and traveled down my spine. When he spread my cheeks, I grabbed the feather pillow with my teeth and used it to muffle my scream as his tongue and fingers created a volatile earthquake within my body.

In one fluid motion, he flipped me over, and I wrapped my arms around his neck. When he entered me, his kiss captured the sound from my mouth. I was helpless in rapture as he stroked deeper, and our bodies quivered.

"Damn, that feels so good," he uttered, his lips close to my ear. "I want to stay right here forever."

He was swimming in unexplored territory, and my body didn't want to let him go.

"*Si*, papi," I moaned. "Stay right here."

We locked limbs and rocked until his pinnacle reached my ecstasy's waterfall. We were soaked with passion, unable to move. Our hands gravitated together, and we interlocked our fingers. When I reached up to wipe the sweat from his forehead, his anticipation rose again.

"Blaque, *hola otra vez.*"

He smiled and whispered, "I told you I ain't no *triente minuto hombre.*"

The sweet smell of cinnamon and maple nudged me out of peaceful sleep. The bed faced the ocean, and the open glass doors welcomed a gentle morning breeze. I walked naked on the balcony to catch the view. In the daylight, the magnificence of the bedroom demanded my appreciation. The black and white modern décor was consistent throughout the house, and brightly-colored art pieces dressed the walls and tables.

I slid into Blaque's white t-shirt and inhaled the scent of his Issey Miyake cologne. Mmm. I danced in the mirror as if under a spell. Then I stopped. I had to remember the reason I was there. I tiptoed out of the bedroom and down the open hallway. From the third level, I looked down and saw Blaque standing shirtless in the kitchen. I peeked into the game room, theater room, and guest room—no Basquiat.

The smell of the hot breakfast screamed my name, so I walked down the three flights of stairs to see what was cooking. Blaque's skin glistened from the sunshine beaming through the window. Pancakes, French toast, bacon, sausage, and hash browns were beautifully arranged on plates that damn near covered the entire kitchen island, and a bottle of champagne and orange juice were chilling on ice.

Standing behind him, I wrapped my arms around his chest, and my lips grazed his muscular back. "Good morning, handsome."

"Good morning, my Monalise. Do you like plantains?"

"I love plantains. Blaque, I can't believe you cooked all this."

He laughed. "Nah, baby, my chef cooked everything except these."

A sweet peppered plantain entered my mouth and slid down my throat.

"Damn, that's good."

He took a bite. "I don't like anyone's plantains but my mama's. I'm close, but hers is the best. You'll see next weekend. Want me to fix your plate?"

"Your mother is coming to town?" I asked.

"No, woman," Blaque replied as he loaded our plates with the food. "*Wi a guh Jamaica.*"

Composure intact, I grabbed two champagne glasses and made mimosas.

"You expect me to go out of the country with you and meet your mama when I don't even know your real name?"

"Christian Laurent," he replied casually, then squeezed my ass and whispered, "Savage."

My eyes popped open despite the feeling of pleasure as his lips traveled around my neck.

"Savage?"

He grabbed my face and planted a kiss on my lips. "*Si.* Savage is my last name, baby. What else do you want to know?"

Spellbound, I followed him with our drinks to the outside patio. "I'm...good."

As we ate, the spectacular view of the calming ocean enthralled me.

"Blaque...Christian...Laurent...Savage. What do I call you?"

He laughed. "In the streets, call me Blaque. Behind closed doors, call me whatever you want."

"Well, Blaque, I don't have a passport."

"No worries. I've got you. What do you do for a living?"

I placed the champagne flute to my lips and took my time to answer. "I own a hair salon in Compton called Top of the World."

He stopped eating and stared like he was expecting me to say something else, so I added, "And as a side hustle, I use my salon to clean dirty money."

I looked into his eyes and waited for a response.

He smiled. "Wow, I have an entrepreneur and Gangsta Boo in one. Do you know any good barbers?"

I exhaled and reached across the table to run my fingers along his nearly perfect hairline.

"The best barbers in L.A. are the ladies who work in my salon. But first, I will need to conduct a team meeting to make sure they understand you are my man."

"Is that right?" he whispered. "So you're ready to claim me?"

I licked his maple-sweetened lips. "Yes, and I'm very possessive."

"That's good, baby, because I'm all yours."

We leaned in and locked lips; our sudden relationship felt contractual. Now, I was in double jeopardy.

How can I satisfy my obligation to the cartel without breaching my commitment to my man?

CHAPTER 5
LIFE WE CHOSE

CHRISTIAN "BLAQUE" LAURENT SAVAGE

BEFORE STEPPING INTO the shower, I inhaled her sweet scent. Although Pearle had left, her fragrance lingered on my skin, and the scalding hot water couldn't wash her away. She was like a flower; I was a bee thirsting for her nectar. Closing my eyes, I reminisced about her unforgettable entrance into Red Light. I never expected her to be naturally beautiful. *And why wasn't she in disguise?* She was a brickhouse with the prettiest smile, face, and smooth shea butter skin. Her long, straight hair puffed into the sexiest afro while on the steamy dance floor. The way she danced with confidence had turned me on.

Why did Pearle Monalise Brown give me her real name? Maybe it was the same reason I wanted her to meet my mother. Pearle was the only woman from the hood I'd ever met who loved the sounds of Coltrane, Duke, and Miles *and* could spit every line of *Reasonable Doubt, Illmatic,* and *Straight Outta Compton.* She was cool like that, comfortable around me, and it made me want to be in her presence always. And the freaky shit she did with her body? Hands down, it was the best sex I'd ever had. There was only one major problem, though—she wanted my Basquiat. But I had fallen in love with her, so I couldn't let her have it.

Bankhead Highway and 285 is where I spent most of my childhood—in the great city of Atlanta nicknamed Hotlanta, the Black Mecca, and Black Hollywood. Atlanta is a vibe, and you would have to experience it personally to appreciate all its glory. Sexy, beautiful, and successful black people from across the world in one city filled with endless opportunities and surrounded by green—money, tall trees, and mountainous hills.

Peach Grove Park, a predominately black community built in the 1980s, is where my life's foundation was built. Because my mother and father grew up in ghettos, they worked hard to be able to raise me and Chloe, my older sister, in a nice neighborhood. Eventually, all my uncles and aunts bought houses in Peach Grove.

Chadwick Savage—my father and idol—came from a big family; he was the middle child and had six brothers and two sisters. The Savages dominated the streets. However, in the late 1980s, our middle-class neighborhood became the hood overnight. The city closed many projects, and part of Peach Grove Park transitioned into Section 8 homes. Like ants, kids from different areas in the city flooded into one school and one neighborhood. New kids tested and challenged our strong family bond, but we fought and won every time, rolling deep to beat their asses if necessary.

After being told by a teacher that I was gifted and had a talent for art, my mother was so damn excited that she forced me into Solomon Academy, an expensive and prestigious all-black private school near Decatur. My sister, Chloe, went willingly. Dudes often made the terrible assumption that because I was a light-skinned pretty boy and wore a uniform, I was somehow weak. They were wrong. The constant tests made me more vicious and created my reputation for having hard, quick hands. My father and uncles were either gangsters or criminals, and the OGs in my family taught us survival, loyalty, and how to fight.

In the early 1990s, crack hit the streets like candy, and my dad and uncles opened the dope fiends' candy store. By 1992, the Savages moved from the hood in Bankhead to luxurious mansions in upscale Buckhead.

Our legacy began with my great-grandfather, Major Savage, who started a profitable numbers operation in Harlem in the 1930s after he fled Atlanta during the Great Migration. The Depression stripped him of his blue-collar job in the New York City promise land, but he became rich from his underground gambling and illegal banking operation. He taught the rest of the family the game, and everything took off from there. He gave black families opportunities through jobs or winnings from his successful operation. He paved the way, providing generational wealth that we continue to reap. The Savages became one of America's most ruthless and affluent crime families, with empires in New York, the Midwest, and Atlanta. Los Angeles was part of our enterprise expansion.

My mother, Lillian—a beautiful, light brown-skinned, Jamaican-born woman—came from the Laurent family in Kingston. She and her three brothers grew up in 1950s Trench Town, The Hollywood of Jamaica, before the guns, drugs, and political violence consumed the impoverished streets. They were raised poor, but by the time I was born, my mother's brothers— Henry, Winston, and Delroy—were don dadas who exported Jamaican sugar to the U.S. and transported drugs throughout Jamaica. While growing up, our innocence was shielded by the intense security detail and armored trucks that escorted us everywhere in Jamaica when we visited during the summer. My uncles were feared but equally loved and respected in Kingston.

We danced to reggae, shared much laughter, and enjoyed feasting on the jerk chicken, aunties' famous ackee and salt fish, my mama's plantains, tasty peas and rice, and beef patties. My aunts and uncles lived in mansions on hills surrounded by gates and palm trees. Each home had a swimming pool in the backyard with easy access to the beach, where the kids played all day. My cousins looked to me for the newest American music, clothes, and trends they saw featured in The Source and Word Up magazines. We smoked ganja, ate the freshest fruits and fish, and partied for hours at the dancehalls with the prettiest island girls. I grew up in true gangster paradise in Atlanta and Kingston.

I loved everything about my life, including my early years in Bankhead. My teenage years were the best, surrounded by unlimited money, foreign cars, and the finest girls. I had to rock school uniforms; however, my jewelry stayed iced, and I rarely wore the same shoes twice. My mother was strict about our education, but I owned the night and stayed on the streets.

Chloe and I learned a lot while attending Solomon Academy, including Spanish and French, which were required curricula. The Spanish came in handy as I later dealt with Mexican and Columbian distributors.

My mother always wanted me to go to college to become a doctor like my older sister had planned, but my heart's passion was art. Around my junior year of high school, she gave up hope. The bad man genetics in my DNA was too strong and overpowered me.

A Savage man was born with an uncontrollable hunger and lust that took a special woman to tame. I spent most of my young years wild and reckless, on the hunt with more testosterone than I knew what to do with. Now, I was calculated. Time was money, so a woman was like an investment to me. My schedule was only reserved for a fine-ass woman like Pearle, who had the right balance of street and intelligence.

With blessings from the Savages and Laurents, I quickly became the leader of both family empires. I loved my job, but with double the power came quadruple the stress. The responsibility for two legacies fell on my shoulders, and the decisions I made impacted us and future generations. Once my powerful energy source, the pressure had become my Kryptonite.

My life had cruised like a plane at the perfect altitude, only hitting a few bumps in the sky, until a strong surge of wind caused turbulence. One night changed my life's course forever.

I was standing outside in Atlanta, welcoming the crisp night air and savoring the taste of the kiss from the fine-ass woman I'd just met while at Justin's, Puff Daddy's new restaurant. We had a wonderful evening together, and for a few seconds, I got lost in my thoughts.

Do I want to see her again?

Before I could answer myself, I felt a quick prick followed by a burning itch at the nape of my neck. Thinking it was a mosquito, I smacked at it. Then all of a sudden, I got dizzy and blacked out.

I don't know how much later, but eventually, I awakened in a fog as if I was coming out of a dream. The pulsating throb in the back of my head and the loud ringing in my ears caused me to pray to God immediately for both to stop. I tried to move my hands, but my wrists were tightly cuffed. As my vision cleared, I could see a sack of some sort over my head, and from the tightness around my neck, I would guess it was secured with a noose.

My lungs struggled to fill with air; every breath echoed deep and heavy like Darth Vader's. My mouth was parched and permeated a nauseating staleness.

"Fuck," I grunted through clenched teeth.

I replayed the moment I had turned around and dismissed my security team right before stepping inside that woman's condo. Regret punched me repeatedly in the stomach.

When the ringing in my ears finally stopped, I heard tires rolling smoothly over the road. Next, there were subtle movements in the background, keyboard tapping, feet shuffling, and a chair creaking, indicating I wasn't alone. My heart raced, and my adrenaline pumped.

Maybe that chick from Justin's set me up. Was I taken for ransom? Will I be tortured and killed?

I sat in my thoughts for what felt like forever until the suffocating sack was finally removed, freeing my lungs from captivity. I was inside a moving van. Quickly, I surveyed my surrounding. My eyes traveled from six small screens displaying live footage from outside to a long table covered with what looked like sound equipment. Next to that was a small desk with a computer on top of it, a mini-fridge, and a file cabinet. I was on a red leather bench. To my right and left were two white men, pale as ghosts, who looked like they'd never seen the sun. It was then that my mind processed what was going on.

Fuck! The Feds had snatched me.

An agent seated on a leather captain's chair slid in front of me. He was a young brother with swag, dressed in a nice suit and fresh Air Jordans. I was surprised. I would have expected an old, corny white dude, but he looked like a brother I would shoot hoops with on the court.

"What's up, man?" the agent asked, speaking in a mellow tone. "I want to take the cuffs off, but you have to be cool."

I nodded, and his ghosts moved swiftly to remove the tight cuffs around my wrists.

He got up, walked to the file cabinet, and pulled out a manilla folder from the top drawer. Then he grabbed two bottled waters from the mini-fridge.

"Thirsty?" he asked and placed the bottle next to me.

"No," I replied. "Am I under arrest?"

"Nah, Christian. I want to holler at you. Do you know who I am?"

"The Feds."

"I'm Special Agent David Walker with the DEA."

Knowing not to say shit without an attorney, I only raised an eyebrow in response as we stared at each other silently.

The next hour was difficult to explain. I zoned out for most of it. Walker laid out countless photos of my family members from Harlem to Gary, Indiana, in front of me. While doing so, he spat out the illegal dirt he had on me and each family member. He talked slowly and explained the potential sentence attached to each individual crime.

I was in a surreal reality, sitting stunned while he continued talking. When his intimidation tactic was complete, he looked directly at me.

"Christian, I have a proposition for you."

I rolled my eyes, and he continued.

"I know you're a very smart man. Although you don't remember me, we went to Solomon Academy together."

He was right about where I attended school, but I didn't recall a David Walker.

Walker placed a paper and pen on the bench next to me and continued.

"The good news is I'm not here for you or your family. I want you to help me bring down the Escobar brothers."

Everyone had heard of the Escobar family. They were bad motherfuckers you didn't want to mess with.

"Bring them down how?" I asked.

"Conduct your business as normal, but as a Confidential Informant for the DEA."

I shook my head. "A snitch? Hell no."

He knew street code, but he smiled and shrugged nonchalantly.

"Then you and your entire family go down immediately with one phone call."

I glared at Walker's smug ass. "I need to think about it."

He glanced at his watch. "Sure, but the only way you leave this van a *free* man is if you cooperate...or locked up if you *don't*."

He reclined in his seat and slowly sipped his water. I was disgusted with myself for getting caught and with Walker for irritating the hell out of me.

"What happens to my family after you get what you want?"

He took another slow sip. "The DEA has bigger fish to fry."

After a two-hour stare-down, I knew I would slap the bottle and then his face if I watched him take one more sip. My entire family would surely go to jail if I did that.

I snatched the pen, and once my signature was on the line, I immediately felt dirty—like a rat in the sewer.

The sun had risen by the time I was dropped off in front of my Benz, the rays cutting my eyes.

"I'll be in touch," Walker said, grinning before slamming his door, and the van sped off.

Sickened by my choice, I gagged and vomited before I opened my car door and slid behind the steering wheel, contemplating my next move.

Months later, I realized Walker had a hard-on to bring down America's most wanted criminals, the infamous Escobar brothers. It would make him famous. He had come close many times, but they had slid through his fingers like a Jheri curl.

I'd begun strategically poking at the Escobar's operation, offering lower prices with equivalent purity to get Matias' attention. Then he went into deep mourning. He had become a phantom, spotted nowhere after his twin brother, Miguel, was killed. However, Matias reappeared from the shadows after an unexpected encounter between my family and his organization.

I was at an art auction house in New York City, having flown there specifically for a Jean Michel Basquiat painting. I wasn't leaving without it. Basquiat was my favorite artist, and the artwork for sale was my favorite piece.

I'd gotten there early to observe the room. There was a Pablo Picasso worth over one hundred million for sale, attracting billionaires from around the world. The auction was open to the public, so the air in the room was vibrant. Every auction I attended had a unique personality which depended on the attendees, the type of art for sale, and mainly, the auctioneer. The best auctioneers were performers who knew how to read a room. They utilized pace, theatrics, and personality to maintain an electric atmosphere. The best had flair with the gavel, and when they yelled *"sold,"* it made every winner feel like they'd won the Superbowl.

I was anxiously waiting for the bidding wars to begin. The auctioneer stepped to the podium like a general. He paused until the room was silent.

When the hushing stopped, he smiled and said, "Welcome and enjoy."

There was a blank cinematic screen behind him. I tapped my foot, ready for the masterpiece reveal. He snapped his fingers, and the Basquiat illuminated the screen.

"This magnificent piece is an original painting by Jean Michel Basquiat. If you don't know its' worth, you don't deserve to have it."

The crowd chuckled.

He smiled and lifted his gavel in the air. "Let's start the bidding at one million dollars."

I raised my hand first.

In one quick breath, he said, "One million from the man in the fancy sportscoat and diamond earrings. Can I get 1.1?"

A Hispanic man, seated at the front of the room, raised his hand.

The auctioneer sped up the pace and looked directly at me.

"Can I get 1.2, Diamond Earrings? What about 1.3? Anybody?" I nodded, and he continued, "What about 1.4? Who wants to walk away with a masterpiece *and* a new nickname?"

The crowd chuckled again. There was a bidding war between me, a white man with long, thick, white hair, who the auctioneer called Santa, and Nice Suit, the Hispanic man seated in the front. The bids moved in increments of ten-thousand dollars and were moving at lightning speed, but not fast enough for me. Santa had the last bid at 1.9 million dollars.

"Diamond Earrings or Nice Suit, can I get two million dollars?"

We raised our hands, but I was the one who spoke up. "Four million."

There were gasps from around the room, and every head turned in my direction.

"Four million dollars. 4.1?" the auctioneer said quickly and clearly, then paused before asking again, "4.1?" When no hands went up, he slammed the gavel and yelled, "*Sold* for four million dollars. Thank you, sir."

The room cheered, and I felt like a kid on Christmas Day. Standing, I went to the restroom, walked inside, and smiled in the mirror while washing my hands. Not even a minute later, the Hispanic man walked in.

In a tone that wasn't aggressive or cordial, Nice Suit said, "Hello."

Two other Hispanic men trailed behind him. One of them closed and locked the door. At the same time, the stall door opened from behind me.

It was Blue, my cousin from Atlanta, who was also my driver, lieutenant, and best friend.

"Hello," Blue said firmly.

The lock on the bathroom door clicked and swung open. Keith—my cousin, sous chef, second lieutenant, and Blue's brother—entered with two guards behind him.

"Who locked this door?" Keith asked.

"Neither of us," Blue responded.

One of my guards slammed and relocked it. Confused, the Hispanic men asked each other in Spanish if the door was locked.

"*Si, hombre,* it *was* locked," I said.

Keith stepped closer. "And there aren't any doors we can't open."

Nice Suit redirected his attention to me. "Who's in charge?"

"Who's asking?" I retorted.

"The man I work for is offering *two* million dollars for the painting you just purchased."

"You meant *four* million," Blue said.

I stepped forward. "I don't care if you meant *forty* million. My painting is not for sale."

"Did I mention my boss's name? Matias Escobar, and a *two-*million offer from him is *unprecedented.*"

Keith shortened the distance between him and the men. "*Our* boss said, no sale. So unless you want to squabble with true soldiers, *adios.*"

Nice Suit hardened his tone. "This is what you want?" he asked me.

My posture stiffened, as well. "Repeating myself is *unprecedented.* So, *si,* tell *Señor* Escobar that Blaque said *no esta a la venta.*"

Nice Suit nodded and replied, "Blaque. *Si.* Okay." Then he and his silent partners turned and left.

Once the door closed behind them, I said, "Get ready for war, gentlemen."

Blue, Keith, and our security surrounded me.

"Say the word, and we'll end it right now," Blue said.

"Not yet. Winning a war requires a winning strategy."

I had barely gotten my painting on the wall when Walker called my cell. He had received a tip that Matias had flown personally to the U.S. to hire a team to steal my Basquiat.

I anticipated Matias would seek the most professional art thieves, and I had a list of the best.

"What are their names?" I asked.

"Goldie and Pearle."

Those names were not on my list. "Who?"

"Their real names are Maurice and Pearle Brown. They are a duo—brother and sister."

"Where are they from?"

"Compton."

I was shocked. "Compton? The Escobars went to the hood? Is your source reliable?"

Walker broke down Goldie and Pearle's tactics. I was very impressed with Matias for his attempt to outsmart me. Had I not been forewarned, Goldie and Pearle may have been his "checkmate."

Next, Walker walked me through his devised plan to get him the Escobars. All I wanted was to be unleashed from the DEA. The plan was for me to bait Pearle and allow her to get close and steal my painting. During her and Goldie's delivery and cash exchange with Matias, the DEA would ambush and arrest the Escobar brothers. They always rolled together. The problem now was the Escobars would know they had been set up. They would assume Pearle and Goldie were to blame when, in fact, the true snitch was me.

Walker and I knew cartel code. Pearle and Goldie's deaths were inevitable for betrayal. But we had our own separate reasons to let them drown—Walker wanted a promotion, and I would do *anything* to protect my family.

After Walker finished explaining the plan, he said, "Check your email."

I sighed and opened my laptop. He had sent a picture of

Goldie and a few pictures of Pearle disguised in wigs and heavy makeup. The guilt was mounting inside my stomach.

"*Damn,* this feels shady."

"The choice is yours, Christian. You can reject my offer and share a prison block with your family *or* cooperate and go on your merry way."

He knew how to convince me. There was no guilt strong enough to outweigh love, especially the love I had for my family.

"Fuck it," I said. "Let's get this shady-ass plan over with."

"Be careful. They say Pearle makes men fall in love after one taste before she attacks. She's like a black widow, so don't get caught up," Walker warned.

"I'm a grown-ass man. I damn sure don't need a pep talk from you about scandalous women."

Little did I know I would fall in love with Pearle *before* she let me taste her. I knew she felt the same about me, and there was no turning back. Her essence was permanently tattooed on me.

CHAPTER 6
SORRY NOT SORRY

CHRISTIAN "BLAQUE" LAURENT SAVAGE

HOW CAN I *protect Pearle without jeopardizing the lives of my family?*

I was still marinating in the shower, waiting for the universe to answer my question. With the bathroom filled with steam, I couldn't see in front of me. My phone rang. I fumbled to find it and slipped on the marble floor. After regaining my balance, I answered.

"Yo."

"What's up, Christian? Our plan is falling into place quickly. Pearle's brother is researching replicas, and your Jamaica trip with her is the perfect way to lure him to steal your art while you're away. Criminals are so predictable."

"Yeah, well, I need my painting back in mint condition. Also, Pearle needs a passport."

"Did she make you fall in love with her?"

"No," I lied.

Walker laughed. "Good. This should be quick and easy. You'll get her passport in the next couple of days. Once I grab the Escobar brothers, you can go back to your life."

"After this, I don't want you fucking with my family or me ever again."

"As I said, you and I are done after the Escobars' capture."

After we hung up, beads of sweat ran down my forehead and neck as I asked myself again for what seemed like the millionth time, *How can I protect both Pearle and my family?*

There was a quick pounding on the bathroom door. It was Blue.

"Hey, Blaque, are you ready?"

"Stop banging like five-o. Give me twenty minutes."

After a shot of Patrón and Miles Davis, I was back on life's tightrope. Draped in all black with a red blazer, a pair of black Christian Louboutin, and a diamond Rolex on my wrist, I was ready. I stepped outside; the fresh air was what I needed.

Blue opened the car door. "Damn, nigga, 'bout time."

I laughed. "Whatever. I see you trying to step up your suit game like me," I said, commenting on the Armani he was rocking. "Tell me about this meeting we're headed to."

Blue had an idea to hire women from a party and event promotional modeling agency known to dabble in illegal activity to sell our product. If executed, this would be part of our expansion plan. Blue had been to a few parties filled with beautiful models and bartenders who worked for a man everyone called Jules. Jules was only accessible through his assistant, but if he was going to sell my product, I needed to meet him. I didn't believe in ghosts, so there was no way I would allow one in my organization.

We rolled into Beverly Hills through the quiet streets and past tall, saditty palm trees that towered majestically over us. Overlooked by the hills and trees on Hillcrest Avenue was a flat, rectangular white house with a wooden garage that blended into its surroundings. If you blinked, you wouldn't notice it.

We pulled up to the gate, and it opened.

"We're here," announced Blue.

The exterior was sleek and simple. As we approached the door, a tall, beautiful woman appeared in the doorway. She wore all-black—a tank dress, fishnets, and leather heels that laced at the ankles.

"Welcome." On a tray, she offered cigars and Crown Royal. She had long model legs and walked like a stallion. "Follow me."

The interior was in complete contrast with the basic exterior. It was boisterous and loud; its elegance screamed, grabbing your attention. There was a long, fully-stocked bar with multiple artistically designed bar stools. The living room accommodated at least twenty with custom-made soft Italian leather furniture facing what looked like the Hoshitoshi flat screen from the TV show *Martin*. The screen and entertainment center looked so glorious I wanted to bow.

Styled head to toe like the gorgeous video vixens from Tone Loc's "Wild Thang" video were exotic women of all shapes and nationalities, beautifully colored from the world's rainbow. They were dressed in various black mini-dresses showcasing every hill and curve on their bodies, and they wore their hair pulled back to highlight their beauty. Each woman wore a different colored pair of jeweled pumps. A whiff of steak, my favorite food, made my stomach yelp in pained hunger.

We were escorted straight to the outdoor patio next to the pool. Seated at the table was a sexy, brown-skinned woman who resembled Sade. Her hair was parted in the middle and pulled into a long, wavy ponytail. Her body was silhouetted perfectly in her off-the-shoulder black mini-dress. She had thick legs and pretty feet clad in jeweled stilettos with straps that wrapped around her calves like snakes. Right above her full, pink lips was a beauty mark.

"Hello, gentlemen. I'm Jules, CEO of Precious Jewels, the full-service upmarket modeling agency for exclusive clientele."

After introductions, her eyes sexed me. "Blaque, you look better than I expected."

When we shook hands, our touch lingered.

"So do you." I couldn't deny her beauty. "I was expecting a man."

She smiled. "I don't know how that rumor started, but I assure you I'm all woman."

She slowly uncrossed and crossed her legs like Sharon Stone in *Basic Instinct*, her female evidence revealed and undeniable. I gulped my Crown Royal to drown my surge in testosterone levels.

"Blaque, do you want my Precious Jewels?" she asked.

I took another gulp. "Say what?"

"Blue says you want my employees, the Precious Jewels, to promote and sell your product."

She slowly licked her lips, and I gulped another mouthful of Crown. I turned my attention to the Precious Jewels. The women moved quickly and in silence. They were cooking, cleaning, and preparing drinks at the bar in preparation for an event or party of some kind. Their smiles never changed, like they were airbrushed on their faces. They moved so perfectly that they appeared programmed like robots.

Blue jumped into the conversation, taking over the meeting. He handled it professionally and with ease while I enjoyed the juicy filet mignon, shrimp, and arugula salad prepared by the chefs in the kitchen. Throughout Jules' conversation with Blue, she batted her eyes seductively at me. She was fine, but I wanted Pearle. With that thought, my mind started drifting.

"Blue, can I see the product?" I heard Jules ask.

I turned my focus back to her and Blue. From the black leather briefcase, Blue pulled out a small black cylindrical prism vial with a crystal top.

Jules examined the bottle. "Damn, this is pretty."

Blue said, "With your high-end clientele, I knew they'd expect something more elegant."

"How much?" she asked.

"One hundred and twenty dollars."

"I think we can sell this for two hundred dollars," she said, then called her assistant over. "Halle, try this."

"Yes, ma'am." After one hit, Halle said, "Ms. Jules, the product is very pure. I believe we can sell it for two hundred *easily*."

Blue motioned toward me with his head. "Give us a second to discuss."

He and I moved to the other side of the pool. He kept his stoic demeanor while speaking.

"First of all, goddamn, Jules and her Precious Jewels are fine as hell. Your girl, Jules, definitely wants you."

"I peeped that, but I'm not interested. What do you think about the price increase proposal?"

"I'm thinking one-fifty. What do you think?"

"I think you let her test it at one-fifty. With one gram, they get ten lines or twenty-five bumps. That's fifteen dollars per line and six dollars per bump. The market price without the packaging and purity is one-twenty, which is twelve per line or four-eighty per bump. Our profits will go even higher after I seal us as a distro. Your high-end customer should pay more for their exclusive product, *especially* since their plugs are Precious Jewels. There's nothing else like it and no competition, so you can set your market price. You feel me?"

"Yeah, bro. I should have gone with you to that private school," Blue commented with a chuckle.

While Blue and Jules continued their negotiations, I sipped my Crown. It was easy to get lost in L.A.'s photogenic views. I looked back at Blue and felt proud. The Savage legacy would continue with him taking over L.A. Maybe then I would retire.

"Blaque..." Jules wrote her number on a piece of paper. "Here is my personal cell if you *ever* need my services."

I walked past her. "You can work that out with Blue."

My stroll and diss stung her speechless.

"No problem," she finally said after regaining her composure. "You can stay for a while longer if you'd like before our event in an hour."

"No, I'm good. I have a few meetings to attend."

"You must be married."

"I'm a boss, and I stay busy running shit."

"Okay, boss. From one boss to another, I look forward to us running shit…together." She smiled, and her long lashes fluttered. "I'll be in touch." She handed the paper to Blue but kept her eyes locked on me. "Blue."

"Sounds good." He grabbed the paper. "Where do you find your employees?"

She gave a tortured smile, similar to the Joker from *Batman*. "Scarlet Entertainment. It's a full-service placement agency designed for businesses like ours that require…discretion. They have the prettiest and most professional girls I've ever worked with, and their prices are lower than any other agency." She grabbed the briefcase from Blue. "What are you guys calling the product?"

Blue looked at me.

"Pearl," rolled off my tongue.

Jules held up the fancy bottle of cocaine. "Great marketing strategy, Boss. Very elegant. My Precious Jewels will *definitely* sell this product very well. I have a feeling Pearl will make us all a lot richer."

I offered my hand. "Nice meeting you, Jules."

"Nice to meet you, Boss."

I was temporarily hypnotized by her melon lips. She held my hand tighter, but I pulled away. Pearle had already captured my heart.

When we pulled out of the driveway, Blue said, "Bro, I'm not sure if you intentionally thought of the name Pearl or if it's because you're sprung. Either way, the name is genius." He inhaled his cigar, gifted by a Precious Jewel, and exhaled. "Damn, I'm loving L.A."

Floating alongside the canyon hills, I blew a smoke cloud into the perfect wind.

"Me, too."

CHAPTER 7
L.A. MONA LISA

PEARLE MONALISE BROWN

I SANK INTO MY plush couch on the terrace and looked at the Hollywood sign in the hills. The weather was perfect for the satin sundress I was wearing, and a gentle breeze caressed my body. For the first time in years, I wasn't playing a role. I was Pearle Monalise Brown, and I loved it.

I picked up the phone, but before I could press a digit, I heard, "Hello."

Blaque's deep voice gave me butterflies.

"Hey, handsome."

His smile reached me through his voice.

"What's up, sexy? I've been thinking about you."

A strong gust of wind penetrated my dress and waltzed between my thighs.

"I was fantasizing about you. I picked up *my* phone to call you, and your fine ass was already on the other end."

"Yeah, we're connected like that. What was I doing in your fantasy?"

"*Mmmm.* You were enjoying what I was doing to you."

"Did *you* enjoy what you were doing?"

"I *loved* it, papi. Come over so I can show you."

"Damn, I have meetings tonight, baby."

"I'm a night owl, Blaque. If you want to see me after your

64

meetings, I'll leave my door open."

"I definitely want to see you. Would you mind waiting at my crib until I get home?"

"Do you trust me like that?" I asked.

"Do I have a reason not to?"

"No."

"Then what time do you want my driver to pick you up?"

"Nine o'clock. Are we having a slumber party?"

"Yes, a slumber party minus the slumber," he whispered. "So, bring some extra clothes. What I'm planning to do to you, you'll want to extend your stay. See you tonight, Monalise."

"Yeeessss!" I screamed after hanging up.

The phone rang immediately.

"Hello," I whispered, thinking it was Blaque calling back.

Goldie laughed. "Ugh. Why do you sound like a 1-800 sex line operator?"

"Oh, my goodness!" I screamed in Goldie's ear. "Blaque is *amazing!*"

"Blaque is business."

"Fuck business. He's mountains of pleasure." I gave Blaque two snaps and a circle like the Wayans Brothers from *In Living Color*.

"Damnit! I told you not to fall for him. He's a bad motherfucker. You know we can't mix business and pleasure, sis."

"I'm a bad bitch, and me and that bad motherfucker are *so* damn good together."

"Pearle, snap out of it. What's wrong with you? Most importantly, what's up with the painting?" he inquired, deflating my excitement.

"He lives in Santa Monica, and I didn't see it last night. The good news is his driver is picking me up at nine so I can stay at his place while he's at a meeting. I'll roam around and scope the place."

Goldie gasped. "Damn, that's perfect. I can't believe that nigga is letting you roam free while he's not home."

"Yesssss," I screamed. "I think he's in love with me. We're going to Jamaica next weekend, *and* I'm meeting his mother."

"Calm your whipped ass down. You sound like you're in love, too. We have to get this money. This plan is working out perfectly, so stay focused. Locate the painting. Then next weekend, when you're in Jamaica, I'll switch out his painting for this good-ass replica I ordered. Do me a favor and pay attention to his security detail. I need specifics and a thorough report. Cool?"

"Cool."

The job sounded easy if executed properly, but unlike the other jobs, I wanted to maintain my ties to Blaque after the robbery. How, though? My emotions were out of control. I knew it was dangerous, but I didn't care.

Blaque made me feel sexy and beautiful. He was gentle but rough when he needed to be. We could talk for hours, and he listened. He was honest and serious but made me laugh. I loved that he was open-minded and creative. He was adventurous and mysterious, powerful and protective. I loved how he would grab my ass and pull my hair to kiss me softly.

Being the recipient of healthy love from a man was foreign to me, and I couldn't completely comprehend how he fit into my life, but I wanted him there. At the same time, my love for my family ran deep. Did I have to betray Blaque to remain loyal to Goldie?

I checked my closet. It was crammed with wigs and dresses like a theater's costume room. My laundry was spilling over, and I didn't have any clean casual outfits. I looked at my watch—*five o'clock.*

To combat the windy day, I threw on a hooded jogging suit. Then I slipped my feet into my flip-flops and sped out the door after grabbing my Chanel bag and shades. With no traffic to get in my way, I quickly made it to Bloomingdale's in Beverly Center.

As I zipped around the designer label section like a speeding train, picking up items to try on, I noticed two men trying to blend in like they were customers. They were dressed in black suits and moving around the department inconspicuously like undercover cops. Having found several outfits I liked, I took my armload of clothing and headed toward the fitting room. While walking, I thought I felt watching eyes on my neck, but when I turned around and scanned the area, I was the only person in the department.

I loved every piece I tried on, and after tallying my bill, I had nine hundred dollars worth of outfits. I looked in my Chanel bag for a stack but had no cash or wallet. After searching every crevice of my bag, I remembered I had placed my wallet in my black Chanel. Today, I was carrying the white one. I looked at my watch; it was a quarter to six. I did not have enough time to run home for my wallet, drive back to purchase the items, drive back home, pack my bag, get dressed, and be ready when Blaque's driver came to pick me up.

There was a knock on the fitting room door.

"May I help you?" a woman asked from the other side.

"No, thank you," I responded politely.

I layered my top picks under my jogging suit, then studied myself in the mirror. I looked like I had gained five pounds. I checked my watch again and saw I had already wasted too much time. So, I decided to take the risk.

Fuck it.

I threw my shades on, ready to espionage my way out of the store. When I opened the fitting room door, a sale associate with a gratifying smile was standing directly in front of me.

"Did you find what you were looking for, ma'am?" she asked.

I smiled back. "No, I didn't, but thank you."

Extending her arms, she said, "I'll put your items away for you."

"I left them inside."

She stepped forward. I stepped back. We both looked down at the sound of cracking under my foot. I had stepped on a pile of empty hangers. We then exchanged looks. Swiftly, I slid my feet out of my flip-flops, did a Kobe Bryant crossover, and sprinted past her.

"Ma'am!" she screamed.

I ran past the register in the middle of the floor. Standing in the aisle were the two men I had seen earlier.

Shit, I thought. *They're definitely cops.*

I turned to the left and took off like Flo Jo. The problem was I had extra weight under my clothes, and my dash was more like Marshmallow Man's trot. I wasn't sure if anyone was chasing me, but I kept running. I'd learned from hood chases that once you start a race, you'd better run for your life and *never* look back. Sweat was soaking through my first layer. I was out of breath, but the door—my finish line—was about one hundred meters away. I dashed, making it to the anti-theft detector that screamed loud enough to alert anyone nearby of my crime. Red, white, and blue lights flashed like the police were pulling me over. Then, a brother holding a walkie-talkie leaped out in front of me.

"Let me help you, sister," he said.

My chest was heaving, body sweating. I raised my hands in the air.

"Lo siento, señor. No hablo ingles."

He scrunched his face. "Huh?"

To my relief, he lowered his guard, allowing me to hopscotch to his left, shove open the door, and take off like a bandit across the parking lot.

I'd escaped another robbery, but after running barefoot through Beverly Center like a fugitive from Alcatraz, I realized my glorious thieving days were just about over.

It took an hour, but I was finally released from L.A.'s death-gripped traffic and back to cruising speed. It was 7:00 p.m. when my phone buzzed and chimed inside my bag. The call was coming from my salon.

"Hey, Shay. What's up?"

"Boss Lady, Johnny just got his hair shipment, and we really need it *tonight*."

"Can't somebody else pick it up? I have plans, and I'm late."

"We are slammed at the shop, and Johnny can't deliver until tomorrow. We're opening the doors at 6:00 a.m., and we're already out of the 1B and #2 Yaki. Sisters are in here about to riot."

"Okay, call Johnny and tell him I'm on my way."

I sped to Compton, and the supplier crammed a pallet's worth of Yaki, silky straight, synthetic, and human hair of various colors inside my Corvette. Once I arrived at the shop, customers ran to my car with their hair undone to help me unload so they could finish getting their weaves put in.

By 8:00 p.m., I was back at home. I showered off the first half of my day and anxiously overpacked my Chanel suitcase. I crammed it with the most seductive items, from my sexiest noir scent to my most form-fitting dress. I packed a separate bag for accessories and shoes. Feeling like I had forgotten something, I went deep into thought.

My phone rang, startling me. "Hello."

"Ms. Brown, this is Chef Keith. I'll be cooking your meal tonight. What would you like for me to prepare?"

My heart skipped hopscotch. "What's your specialty?"

He laughed. "I cook everything like it's a specialty. Blaque likes my Cajun shrimp and grits."

My mouth got excited. "I've never had that combination. I'll try it."

"Alright, then. What about dessert? I make a bomb peach cobbler."

I smiled. "Sounds good."

We hung up, and I stood in my messy closet, surrounded by clothes. I felt something furry on my ankles and looked down.

"Meow."

A black cat with a diamond collar stared back at me. My high-pitched scream caused it to dart out of the room. Thinking I was dreaming, I chased it but froze when I made it to my living room. My eyes grew wide at the sight of two Hispanic men pointing their guns directly at me. They were the same men who had been lurking in Bloomindale's. This time, I knew not to scream. Instead, I raised my hands in the air. Another Hispanic man sat in my favorite pink chair. I immediately knew who they were.

"Stay calm, Pearle," the man said as the cat jumped onto his lap, "and the guns will go away. *Comprende, señorita?*"

"Si, señor."

He snapped his fingers, and the guns disappeared. *"Me conoces?"*

I lowered my hands. "*Si. Usted Señor* Matias Escobar."

"Yes, I am Matias, and these are *mi hermanos.*" He pointed to the men on his left and right. "Tomas and Felipe. I noticed you've been spending time with Blaque, so I wanted to make sure you knew you were my contracted employee."

"Si, señor."

"Perfecto." He paused. "You created a spectacle today at the shopping center. Did your brother let you know what's at stake?"

"*Si, señor*. What happened today will never happen again."

"I trust you are professionals. I'll let you get back to work, but this is your reminder. We are watching. Isn't that right, Pussy?"

The cat purred as if it understood, and the Escobars vanished.

Relieved they were gone, I exhaled and tried to calm myself. *Shit*.

Before I could process what had happened, there was a strong knock at the door.

CHAPTER 8
A LOVE SUPREME

PEARLE MONALISE BROWN

I GRABBED MY .22 from the front closet. "Who is it?"

"It's Blue."

I slid my gun inside my purse and looked at my watch. *Nine o'clock sharp.* My hands were trembling. I took several deep breaths and summoned my acting skills as I opened the door with a smile. Blue walked in and studied the room. He was muscular and handsome but looked like a serious professor.

"Is everything okay?"

Nodding, I replied, "Yep."

"Ms. Brown, I'll grab your bags. Do you need to make a stop before we head to Bel Air?"

"I thought he lived in Santa Monica?"

Blue quickly grabbed my suitcases from the bedroom. We hurried out, and I locked the door behind us. He half-smiled while placing my bags inside the spacious red velvet trunk of the Bentley.

"The Santa Monica house is one of his many homes, Ms. Brown," he finally stated.

"Please...call me Pearle."

He opened my car door. "Cool, Pearle."

"Are you related to Blaque?"

"Yes," he told me before shutting the door.

Once he was behind the steering wheel, I asked, "Are you a Savage?"

"I am," he answered, looking at me in the rearview mirror. "Do you have any music requests?"

"Do you have *Quik is the Name*?"

"Yep," he replied, then hit the button to raise the partition.

The city looked different through the window of a Bentley. We floated above the road as DJ Quik's "Born and Raised in Compton" blasted through the speakers. The sound system was knocking so hard it felt like I was in a DJ Quik studio session. The fresh scent of cedar wood and leather was so intoxicating that I forgot I was on a job. My fingers touched the soft leather. The toasty seats sent waves of heat between my thighs. I shook my head when I thought about how Blaque had spread my legs in that same seat the previous night. Was it voodoo that had me out of character, or was I being myself?

Enchanted by the spell I was under; I paid no attention to the route. When I finally looked out the dark-tinted windows, we were somewhere deep within the hills and guarded by a tall gate with cameras. Blue put his face to a scanner.

What the fuck? I didn't know that technology existed outside of movies.

I shook my head. *What have Goldie and I gotten ourselves into?*

Beyond the gates, Blue drove down a small road toward a white southern-styled house surrounded by a beautiful landscape.

I smiled. "That's nice."

"That's the guesthouse."

We pulled in front of a vast Greek-style mansion with tall Grecian columns. The architecture was the opposite of the boxy modern homes in Santa Monica. In front of the circular driveway was a black lion water fountain. Tall trees surrounded the mansion, with a majestic mountain as the backdrop.

After opening the car door for me to exit, Blue grabbed my

bags from the trunk and handed them to a butler who greeted us at the tall glass and iron front door. Then he got back in the car and sped off.

Blaque's butler was tall, strong, and Zaddy-handsome. His salt and pepper hair was nicely groomed in twists.

Smiling, I introduced myself. "I'm Pearle. What's your name? Are you related to Blaque, too?"

He winked. "*Ya*, Pearle. I'm his uncle, Henry Laurent."

I followed him and entered a grand foyer with the tallest ceiling I'd ever seen. At first glance, I noticed the white stone staircase that led to the second level and split into the east and west wings of the house. On the ceiling was a red and black stained-glass domed skylight. Grand chandeliers hung from the ceiling. Everything was luxurious, from the perfect eyebrow-shaped archways, eclectic art, and custom-designed furniture to the elegant décor and lush exterior. Within all the magnificence, still no sign of the Basquiat.

"This way to your room, Pearle," the butler said in his heavy Jamaican accent.

I followed him up the staircase to the right and continued along a hallway with walls decorated with black sconces.

"You are entering the master suite," he told me.

He parted the red double doors like the Red Sea. On the right was a closet with grey shelves and a chrome chandelier. On the left of the hallway was a master bathroom with dark grey and red decor.

"Is this the master closet and bathroom?"

"Yes. Those are Blaque's. Yours are this way."

We walked down the hallway and into a closet with a crystal chandelier and white doors and shelves. He placed my suitcases on the island, and as he immediately started unpacking my things, I walked across the hall to the other master bathroom. It was decked out with a white soaking tub, a long shower with multiple water jets, and French doors that led outside. I continued to the balcony and took in the nighttime view of the green hills, brightly lit pool, and hot tub on the first floor. The sky started to spin. My stomach barked. An empty stomach triggered my migraines; when they became too vicious, it was sometimes hard to reverse the symptoms.

"Pearle, let me show you the bedroom."

I followed Henry into an enormous bedroom with a seating area and wet bar to the left. There were a fireplace and king-sized bed covered with black satin linens and rose petals. I imagined all that would happen in that room later and shivered. Walking over to the French doors, I swung them open to taste the fresh night air again, hoping to calm the mounting pain.

"Are you ready to eat? Your dinner is waiting for you."

I damn near leaped at the offer of food.

"*Yes*," I replied and quickly followed Henry down the stairs.

The hallway had a trail of red rose petals that led to a candlelit table set for one. My mouth dropped. The dining area opened to the kitchen and was filled with bouquets of red roses placed all around. Miles Davis played in the background.

Chef Keith pulled out my chair. He was tall, handsome, and cocoa-skinned with facial hair and long cornrows. His looks were similar to Blue's. He was dressed in a baby blue Sean John button-up, jeans, and clean white Air Force Ones. His ears gleamed with diamonds.

"Ms. Brown, do you want a martini with your dinner?" he asked with a smile.

Speechless, I nodded. When he placed the hot plate of savory shrimp and grits in front of me, I almost cried from how beautiful the food looked. I had gobbled down everything before he finished making my drink.

"Damn, I'm so sorry, Keith," I said, wiping my mouth with the linen napkin. "I eat fast, especially when it tastes this good."

He laughed while placing the glass in front of me. "Do you

want seconds or dessert?"

"Dessert, please. I loved every morsel of dinner."

As I sipped my martini, Keith set a dish down on the table. Peach cobbler had never looked so sexy. After one bite, my body tingled.

"Oh, my goodness, Keith. Damn, this is *the bomb*. What did you put in this food?"

He laughed. "Love. I really *love* to cook."

"Your passion shows."

While he cleaned the kitchen, I listened to Miles.

Once my glass was empty, Keith brought me another drink.

"I assume you are related to Blaque. How long have you cooked for him?"

"We're cousins. When I was seven, I made him a fried bologna sandwich with white Wonder Bread. He bragged to everybody in the hood about how I made the best sandwich he ever had. He started paying me a dollar to make his lunch for school, and I've been cooking for him ever since."

Keith was sociable, the complete opposite of Blue.

"How many of Blaque's women have you cooked for?"

"You're the only one. Do you need anything else before I head out?"

I laughed at his swerve. "No, thank you. Everything was amazing. Do you have a date tonight?"

"I sure do." He smiled. "Have a great evening. Treat my cousin right, 'cause he's feeling you."

I smiled back. "Trust me, I'm feeling him, too. Have fun."

I finished my second martini and let the alcohol flow through my veins. On the island was another extra dirty martini. I looked at the time; it was almost midnight. I explored downstairs, searching for Basquiat's masterpiece. I walked through a red and oak cigar room. Across from the cigar room were a library and a sitting room near the door. Standing in the doorway was Henry.

He watched me like a statue.

"Hey, Henry."

"Are you lost?"

"I'm admiring the house. I love décor, and this is the dopest house I've ever been inside."

"The stairs are this way."

We walked to the staircase, and then he was gone. I walked upstairs and stepped into the closet room where Henry had already placed my things and chose my black silk nightie. In the bathroom, there were rose petals in the tub.

I soaked in the tub filled with roses, rinsed in the shower, and rubbed my body with the rose oil that Blaque loved. I scanned the walls, but still no Basquiat. Giving up on my search, I slid under the Egyptian silk sheets and fell fast asleep.

The warm moisture from Blaque's body and lips gently brushed against me. I turned over, and our lips locked, opening to welcome each other inside.

"Blaque, relax so I can fulfill my fantasy."

He smiled when I positioned myself on top of him. My tongue licked his lips and chin, then slithered slowly past his masterful chest to below his abs. The scent of sweet cocoa butter and coconut from his smooth body filled my nostrils. I massaged his thighs while engulfing him with my mouth, taking my time to savor every inch of him until I was ready for him to erupt.

When he did, he lay still for a moment before pulling my hips toward his face. He parted my lips and slid his tongue deep inside me. His hands massaged my back, and he sipped my candied rain until my body's tropical storm ended.

I rested my head against his chest and was soothed by the

rhythm of his heartbeat. Without words, we held onto each other and the moment. Then, he moved my braids away from my face and kissed me slowly until tears started streaming down my face.

My lips moved with no sound. He had loved me to the point of being speechless. Blaque stroked my face as his tongue moved near my ear.

"I feel the same way about you, Pearle. Just show me how much," he said softly.

My hips told him all he needed to know, and he reciprocated with the deepness of his stroke. We didn't stop until our souls melted into each other and poured down like hot lava. My tears rained on his face, and his eyes loved me back.

He grabbed my face. "Pearle, I love you."

"I love you, too."

Wet with ecstasy, we fell asleep with fingers laced and bodies intertwined.

CHAPTER 9
POISON

PEARLE MONALISE BROWN

SUNRAYS PEEKED THROUGH the blinds. I blinked, and for a moment, I wondered if I'd dreamt the entire night. Blaque had gone, and my naked body was wrapped in the sheets like a silk burrito. I didn't want to move, but I was ready to start my day. I entered the walk-in closet and grabbed my jeans and black Baby Phat cropped t-shirt. Then I jumped into the hot shower. While the water hit my body from different angles, I tried to think of a robbery plan with different approaches that would keep everyone, including myself, happy. My brain spun out of control. I needed to slow down, but there was no time. Seventy-two hours had already flown by, and I still hadn't laid eyes on the Basquiat.

After getting dressed, I followed the male voices coming from the kitchen. Blaque and Keith were sitting at the bar drinking gin and juice, feasting on Cajun shrimp and cheese grits, and smoking a blunt. I walked between Blaque's legs and wrapped my arms around him. He smelled my neck and ran his fingers along my bare waist.

"Damn, baby, you look fine as hell."

I pecked his lips and inhaled his blunt for a shotgun kiss.

"*Hola, papi.* What's up, Keith? How was your date last night?"

Keith smiled. "It was just alright. I miss ATL. Cali chicks are different."

Blaque slapped my ass. "You've been fraternizing with the help?"

I laughed. "Boy, please, it's obvious everyone that works for you is family. You have some strong genes."

Speaking in his Jamaican accent, he said, "Ya, I love my brethren."

I exhaled the smoke. "Blaque, why did you move to L.A.?"

Keith sat a delicious plate of Cajun-spiced shrimp and grits in front of me with a mimosa. I graciously thanked him. I was starved and couldn't wait to sink my teeth into my brunch.

"I'm going to run this city."

I looked Blaque up and down while I quickly finished my plate, then sipped my mimosa.

"L.A. is my city, baby. You won't run shit if people don't know you. Let's have some fun and throw a party tonight. It can be like your introduction. Let everyone meet the Savage from ATL."

He smiled. "What type of party, Gangsta Boo?"

My mind raced. "The streets are wondering who shut down Roscoe's the other night. My brother said people thought President Clinton had chicken and waffles. You need to hit the scene with a bang—a party that's different and sexy, like a yacht party. I can make a couple of calls to make that happen."

"Cool. Set it up."

I went to my Chanel bag and pulled out my phone to call my brother since he knew an event planner for the celebrities. With the right connections and, most importantly, money, we had the most lavish yacht booked for the night. As I said, L.A. was my city. So, once I called the salon and Goldie told his dancers, word started spreading like a California wildfire.

I wrapped my arms around Blaque's neck. "Keith, I'm going to hook you and Blue up with some true, fine-ass women from Compton tonight. And Blaque, I'm going to show all the hoes you are *my* Savage."

Blaque pulled me closer and kissed me slowly. "Damn right. Let 'em know, baby."

We jumped into my new favorite vehicle, and Blue drove us to Marina Del Rey Dock 69 to drop off the cash. Blaque paid the captain extra to ensure a successful night. Next, we stopped at the salon so they could get haircuts and I could get my braids freshened up. Before Blaque walked in, I announced that he was my man and the host of the yacht party everyone was talking about. Needless to say, I received a lot of jealous stares, which validated why I didn't have close female friends. Like I told Blaque, I wasn't the jealous type, but I didn't tolerate disrespect.

Tanya Walker was the newest addition to the team and my best barber, bringing in the most revenue than anyone in my shop. I wanted Blaque to have the freshest cut for the party, so I assigned her the task since she had skills. However, Tanya appeared to be getting extra friendly with Blaque. The more I let it slide, the freer she got. I closed my *Essence* magazine.

"Shay, hold up." She stopped working on my braids, and I walked over to Tanya. "If you put your fake ass titties on my man's head one more time, I'm gonna beat your ass."

Tanya laughed. "Damn, calm down. I didn't know—"

"I'm not laughing," I interrupted. "I don't play that shit, and if you didn't hear me the first time, you know now."

She stopped laughing. "As I said, calm down. It ain't that deep."

My nerves calmed, but I was ready to swing if necessary.

"As I said, calm your fake titties down."

Before returning to Shay's chair, I kissed Blaque's lips, then looked Tanya up and down. After sitting back down, I re-opened my *Essence* magazine to continue looking at the new fashions. The room was quiet. Tension was thick in the air like hot steam.

"*Daaammn,*" Shay screamed, moving her long nails in the air, enunciating all her syllables as she spoke. "Hell yeah, Boss Lady from Compton—the real C-P-T. Pay attention. *Do not* fuck with her man, or she will fuck you up. *Beeotches!*"

Everybody fell out laughing.

Looking annoyed, Tanya rolled her eyes. "Shut up, Shay. Your ass is instigating."

Shay pointed her comb directly at Tanya and said, "One more time with your fake ass titties, *bitch*, and Boss Lady is getting in that ass."

I smacked Shay's ass and smiled. "Shut up, Shay!"

"Blaque, you're done," Tanya stated, her irritation evident in her tone.

As he shoved cash in Tanya's jar as payment for her services, he turned to me and said,

"Blue and I will be in the car, baby."

We kissed, then he and Blue quickly walked outside.

Shay pointed her comb at Tanya and whispered, "Calm your fake titties down. She ain't with that disrespect."

Again, everyone was on the floor laughing. Tanya sucked her teeth and threw up her middle finger. I gave her an "I-know-that-ain't-for-me" look as she plopped into her chair to await her next customer.

Shay re-touched my braids in a design and added pizazz to my edges with swirls and pin-curls. She also did my makeup and lashes. When Blaque saw me heading toward the car after leaving out my salon's doors, he jumped out to open the door.

He kissed my cheek. "You're my Gangsta Boo for real, with your fine ass."

I grabbed his face. "They know I don't play. Let's go shopping."

During our shopping spree, I went in and out of boutiques searching for the perfect swimsuit for the yacht party. I needed to stand out and look on point. After all, Blaque wasn't some ordinary Joe I was dating, so I had to represent him properly. I started panicking, thinking I wouldn't find the right one, until my eyes landed on a white bikini accented with pearl and diamond straps. The sheer cover-up dress had a plunging neckline and back that fit my curves as if it had been custom-made just for me.

Thank goodness, I thought as I exited the boutique's doors, but then I remembered I needed shoes to complement my outfit. So, I ran back inside. The saleswoman came out with a pair of Jimmy Choo clear wedged heels and a cute pair of flip-flops. She also found a Chanel beach towel that matched the white Chanel tote bag I had purchased. After sliding her a cash tip, I dashed out the door and ran toward the Bentley parked a few stores away. Suddenly, a sharp pain shot through my arm from my wrist being yanked. My body, followed by my bags, hit the concrete.

"Not so fast, bitch." Maxwell opened his flip phone with his free hand. "Where's Batman now?"

"Batman? Let me go, you fucking psycho!"

My hand was numb from the tight grip around my wrist. I was no match for the six-foot-five-inch mountain that towered over me.

"I'm Batman, motherfucker!"

Maxwell's body flew in slow motion and crashed into the store window. Blaque lifted me off the ground while glaring at Maxwell.

"Nah, partner, you're too tall to be Batman. So, unless you had something to do with the hundred and fifty thousand stolen from me, you need to walk away."

"Motherfucker, I don't fucking know you!" I screamed, my performance good enough to win an Oscar.

"You don't know me, Robyn? Or is it Roslyn? Up until last week, that pussy knew me *very* well."

Blaque's fist catapulted across Maxwell's jaw. He wobbled, fighting to regain his balance, and then charged towards Blaque like a taunted bull. Out of nowhere, Blue punched Maxwell, knocking him to the ground, and started laying the smackdown on him like a UFC fighter.

From behind, I heard two officers shout, "LAPD!"

One quickly snatched Blue from off Maxwell and cuffed his wrists. Maxwell, now irate, charged toward us like a Raiders linebacker. Blaque dodged him, and the other cop took Maxwell to the ground.

Blaque pointed at Blue. "He's with us, officers."

"You're going down, bitch!" Maxwell shouted.

Struggling to cuff him, the officer warned, "Hey, you need to calm down."

Nosey onlookers tried to hide their delight from the untelevised drama.

"Officer, he didn't do anything," I said, pointing at Blue. "He saved me from that man over there who attacked me."

Ignoring my plea, the officer looked at Blue and told him, "I'm going to keep you restrained until we figure out what's going on. Okay?"

Blue grunted through his teeth. "Yes, sir.'"

Through the tears I conjured using my acting skills, I explained the events to the officer.

"I *guarantee* she spent *my* cash—the money she *stole* from my safe—for her purchases today, officers!" Maxwell shouted. "Check her receipts."

"He's crazy, officers. My man bought these things."

Maxwell's officer walked over and collected our IDs. "He's Maxwell "Deep Well" Covington. He filed a police report Thursday morning about an armed robbery. He claims she was there with a man disguised as Batman."

"Officer, I've *never* seen that man before. He keeps calling me the wrong name and accusing me of things I didn't do or would never even think of doing. I'm a business owner in South Central L.A."

"And my woman was with *me* all week," Blaque added. "She practically lives with me. He's accused the wrong woman."

The officer's eyes shifted to my shopping bags. "We need to sort this out at the station."

Maxwell laughed hysterically. "Hey, partner, Bell Biv Devoe tried to warn us, dawg. 'Don't trust a big butt and smile.' That bitch is poison," Maxwell said, serenading the lyrics to BBD's song to Blaque.

Suddenly, three men in black suits moved swiftly toward us like ninjas. They looked like vampires whose skin had never been exposed to sunlight.

Maxwell started singing the theme song to *Cops*. "'Bad boys, bad boys. What you gonna do? What you gonna do when they come for you?'" He laughed harder. "Poison, one hundred and fifty thousand is a felony. That's the Feds coming for your ass. You robbed the wrong one, bitch."

My heart Crip-walked in my chest. Was Maxwell right? Beads of sweat started to form in my perfectly designed baby hair and trickled down the sides of my face. *Shit!* My mouth was dry, and my eyes burned, desperate for some Visine. I slowly blinked, and like magic, the three vampire ninjas were gone.

The officer quickly removed the cuffs from Blue's wrists and handed us our IDs.

"Sorry for the mix-up. This is a mistaken identity. You guys are free to go."

Still handcuffed, Maxwell yelled, "What?!? Y'all letting Poison go? Hell no! Partner, trust *me*, not that butt and smile."

His obscenities were soon silenced when we got into the Bentley. The partition went up immediately.

Blaque had not given me eye contact.

I touched his hand. "Blaque…"

He quickly pulled away and cut his eyes at me, his stare slicing through me like a knife.

"Pearle, I need a minute."

The blare of the sudden silence was deafening. Once we arrived at the house, Blue opened the car door. He also had not given me eye contact. In the master suite, Blaque went into his bathroom and slammed the door. Thank God for the separate spaces.

An hour passed, and we still hadn't spoken any words since the incident in Beverly Hills. I ran inside the closet, crouched down, and pulled out my phone to call my partner in crime. He listened in silence as I broke down the eventful confrontation.

"Goldie, that nigga kept calling me Poison…you know, the song by BBD."

Goldie erupted into laughter. "Oh, my God. Now that's hilarious, 'cause we both know *you* ain't got *no* booty."

"Whatever, Goldie. Stop playing. Do I tell Blaque the truth?"

"Have you lost your damn mind? As far as he knows, you told him the truth. So, leave it at that."

"But, Goldie, I think Blaque knows something is up. What if he's a Fed?" I said, becoming paranoid. "He even told the cops I was with him all—"

"Like the cops said, mistaken identity," he interrupted. "We'll talk at the party tonight. Cool?"

I knew our conversation was over when he hung up in my face. Then something dawned on me.

Wait! If those were the Feds, there's a good chance our phones are tapped. Fuck!

CHAPTER 10
RUMP SHAKER

PEARLE MONALISE BROWN

I PUSHED MY BRAIDS to the side, along with my anxiety. My makeup was flawless, and my swimsuit and cover-up dress fit like a second layer of skin. Before going downstairs, I stopped to look at my perfectly round ass in the floor-length mirror and smiled. *Poison.*

As I cautiously descended the staircase, my heels clicked against the marble. Pausing midway, I could see Blaque, Keith, and Blue smoking a blunt while waiting in the foyer. The three men together looked like a male version of a *Jet Magazine* fashion spread, oozing sexiness and class. Blaque wore a black Versace button-up with the top buttons undone and matching board shorts. His ears, neck, and wrist were decorated with diamonds.

His hazel eyes locked with mine, and I got nervous, unsure how he would react. When he smiled, I exhaled, finally feeling like I could breathe again.

"Let me help you, baby," he said, rushing to grab my hand and walk me down the remaining steps.

I flashed my "poisonous" smile, and the glow returned to his eyes. "Thank you."

When we reached the bottom, he grabbed me around my waist from behind and spoke softly in my ear. "Before leaving, we have a meeting in my bedroom first."

I gently took the blunt from his mouth and inhaled. "We *need* to be on time, boss man. I want to give you the rundown as people file in."

Blaque kissed my neck. "Blue, my man, how long will it take us to get there?"

Blue looked at his watch. "It should take thirty-five minutes, but with L.A. traffic on a Saturday night, it could take an hour and fifteen. I'll try to get us there as quickly as possible, though."

This time, Blaque kissed my ear before speaking in his sexy, bad-boy Jamaican accent.

"No worries, mon. Me and my woman 'gwan *talk* in the backseat."

I shook my head. "You're crazy."

During the drive, Blaque ended up falling asleep. Although confused by how his vibe drastically changed—going from not speaking to me to wanting to sex me, I was also relieved we never had the "talk".

When the car stopped, Blaque woke up in a good mood, ready to party. After we got out of the car, he spun me around, pulled me close, and planted a kiss on my lips.

"Oh, wait. I almost forgot. I bought you something."

He ran to the trunk and returned holding a black velvet jewelry box. I opened it, and my mouth dropped at the sight of the thick diamond and black pearl necklace.

"Blaque, baby, it's beautiful," I said as he placed it around my neck. "I love it."

He fixed a couple of my braids, kissed my cheek, and looking me deeply in the eyes, he replied, "To match your beauty. Blaque Pearle forever."

As the hired event planner, Goldie had arrived much earlier. The entertainment and bar were already set up, and Tina was fixing all-black and all-white cocktails. Party planning and management was Goldie's side hustle, so at the last minute, he added a few bottle girls and servers from his club.

He walked over and handed us drinks in pretty martini glasses. "Hey, sis. You're missing some clothes."

"And you look like winter in the summer."

He laughed. "You know I don't do water. Anyway, one Blaque Business and one Pearle Harbor. Drink up. I have no idea what's in either of them, but my boo, Tina, did her mixology thing, and they taste good as hell."

Goldie turned to give Blaque dap.

"Blaque…the man who shut Roscoe's down for my sister. Nice to meet you."

My brother pulled him in for a hug and mouthed to me, *Let's get this money.*

Blaque smiled. "Anything for my queen. Thanks for setting up everything at the last minute. It looks dope."

"It's all good," Goldie said as he looked around at the lively atmosphere. "You're cool with my sister, so you're cool with me. That payment you dropped off at the club was extra lovely, so I'll do an event for you any day."

I shook my head at the vicious game we played. We were criminals who smiled in our victim's faces one day and stabbed them in the back the next.

"Blaque, I need to holler at my brother. I'll meet you at the bar."

"Cool." He kissed my lips and then looked at Goldie. "Nice

to meet you," he told him before walking off.

Goldie touched my new necklace. "Sis, that nigga's whipped as hell. You have nothing to worry about."

"You don't think his behavior is weird?"

"Hell no. God created us with that flaw."

"Created who? Men?"

"Hell yeah. It started with that nigga Adam. He had no worries or stress but ate the forbidden fruit because of Eve."

"You can't call Adam the n-word."

He burst into laughter. "God made Adam out of clay from the earth, right? Have you *ever* seen white clay?" I laughed, and he continued. "So, I'm not surprised your man ain't mad at you, and I'm not surprised by Maxwell. No man—not even Adam—can resist the power of the P-U-S-S-Y. It's the way God created us. Women hold *all* the damn power. It's just most of y'all don't know how to use it.

"Whatever! You're going to get us struck by lightning."

"You know I'm right, *Poison*."

"What about the Escobars?" I asked.

"What about them?"

"They broke into my fucking house with a creepy-ass cat."

"Shit. Really? What happened?"

"They wanted to make sure I knew about the contract."

"Oh, that ain't shit. They're just crazy as hell."

"Goldie, they pointed *guns* at my face."

"Sis, that's *Godfather* shit. That's why we gotta get that painting. Bada bing, bada boom."

"But what if the Escobars and Blaque are with the Feds to set us up?"

"Hell no. Maybe they're watching Blaque's ass, or maybe it was your lucky day. I don't know. Just keep your eyes open, but stop being so damn paranoid."

"Alright," I told him.

"Put that Maxwell shit behind you," he continued. "It's over. Blaque is the new job, and everything is going according to plan."

"I'm really falling for him, Goldie. I can't shake my feelings."

"Remember, you're the queen on the board and have all the power. That nigga is feeling you, too, but he ain't as perfect as you think. I can tell he's a player. Game recognizes game."

"You're right," I said, conceding.

"I'm always right. And I can already tell his party is going to be live as hell. I'm about to get my pimp on."

"Boy, please! Nobody wants you but Tina."

He smiled and slowly pimp-walked with a limp.

"Shiiiiit, you're crazy as hell if you believe that." He threw up the peace sign. "Let's get this money, *Poison*."

I shook my head and walked to the bar. *Legacy*, our yacht for the night, was immaculate and white. The bar was illuminated with blue and purple lights and faced the dock. Anyone who boarded was greeted with a complimentary signature drink: Blaque Business or Pearle Harbor. I sat on a barstool, and Blaque stood between my legs. We faced the pier. I whispered the low down in his ear on the locals, gangsters, and hustlers as they strolled in.

"If you want to run L.A., you need to know all the major bosses go by their city's name—Hollywood, Compton, Pasadena, Englewood, and Watts. Hollywood is the oldest and a quiet OG. Pasadena is loyal and speaks Spanish. I'll introduce you to Compton Leonard. We grew up together, and our mothers are cool."

"Baby, how do you know so much about everybody?" he asked.

"The wives, sidepieces, aunties, and mamas tell all their business at the salon. They feel it's neutral territory. At Goldie's strip club, niggas use strippers as therapists. His girls tell him everything."

I knew everybody from the hood, although most didn't know me. Blaque listened intensely while sipping his drink and puffing on a cigar.

He rubbed my legs. "Damn, I can't keep my hands off you."

I didn't say it out loud, but I loved that shit.

I introduced Blaque to important people and possible competition or connections. Every player was part of the game. You couldn't trust anybody. Hell, I was in love with Blaque and planned to steal his painting behind his back. I was low down, but a part of me knew he had kept something from me, too. Goldie was right. No man was as perfect as he portrayed. Blaque made all the right moves, which at times felt calculated. But until I figured him out, I would play the love game because the thrill of it felt like the right play.

"Hey, boss."

Blaque and I turned to the right. In front of us stood a tall, brown-skinned wannabe Sade dressed in black boy shorts, a bikini top, and diamond hoops. Her hair was parted down the middle and pulled into a wavy, fake ponytail.

He didn't move. "How are you, Jules?"

"I'm fabulous." Her eyes traveled up and down my body. "I came to scope my competition."

I sat upright. "What bi—?"

Blaque quickly interrupted. "Jules, meet my woman, Pearle. Pearle, Jules owns a promotional event company."

I searched her eyes. "Sup."

"Sup." She smiled. "Pearle, I *love* your name." Then she gave Blaque a weird look. "Blaque, my Precious Jewels could've provided better services at a discount, considering we do business together."

I gave him the side-eye and stared at Jules. "Excuse you. My *brother* has the best women in the industry."

"So Goldie's your brother?"

"He sure is." I stood up from the barstool. "And there ain't no competition."

Like Superman, Blue swooped between us and handed Jules a Pearle Harbor, relieving Blaque's sudden uneasiness.

"Hey, Jules. Are you here for business?"

"Hey, Blue. You can keep the cute little cocktail because I don't drink. I was here for business and pleasure, but I've seen enough. I'll call you tomorrow to discuss my revised projections." She turned to leave, switching as she walked away. "Apparently, folks can't get enough of Pearl."

"Damn right, they can't. Be gone."

Blaque pulled me towards him. "Gangsta Boo, calm down. Jules' models sell our product."

"Well, you better check your little employee. I don't like her ass."

"She's working with Blue, not me."

"What is she talking about, 'folks can't get enough of Pearle'? She better keep my name out her mouth.'"

"Pearl is a product I named after you."

"What?"

He kissed my neck. "It's sexy, the best on the market, highly addictive, and rare."

"Uh-huh. What else?"

"It's the highest quality and protected by a hard, black exterior. Apparently, folks can't get enough of it," he whispered. "And it's mine."

He spun me around, and our lips locked. Deep down inside, I knew something was wrong, but Blaque's wrong always felt so damn right.

CHAPTER 11
THE AFTER PARTY

PEARLE MONALISE BROWN

"**P**ARTY OVER!" THE DJ announced. "Also, someone left their ponytail at my booth! Please make sure to stop and claim it on your way out!"

Laughter erupted from the crowd, as well as some booing from those who weren't ready for the yacht to dock. Security peacefully moved them to the parking lot until the boat was finally empty.

Goldie came by where Blaque and I were standing with Tina on his arm.

"Bye, Pearle," she said, smiling. "Nice party, Blaque."

As Goldie and I hugged, I whispered in his ear, "I told you nobody wants you but Tina."

He pulled out a pocketful of phone numbers. "And I told you you're crazy as hell if you believe that." He turned to Blaque and gave him dap. "Party was live."

"Thanks again for pulling it together."

Blaque was given love and respect from new foes on their way out. We waited for security and were the last to leave. Once we finally made it to the Bentley, we relaxed on his heated leather seats and talked about some of our favorite highlights of the evening. The party was like a hood episode of *Baywatch*—several drunken people forgot they couldn't swim and jumped into the water, someone else's ponytail was left unclaimed in the hot tub, and there were countless water rescues. Blaque and I laughed for an hour. We were having so much fun together that I didn't even notice the car wasn't moving.

Suddenly, there was a knock on the window, and Blue opened my door to help me out of the car.

"Follow me."

My mind raced, not knowing what was going on. We followed him back onto the yacht, past the bar, and up two flights of stairs. The ship had been cleaned, and security had swept for potential stragglers.

Once on the top deck, Blue opened a door and dropped a set of keys in Blaque's hand.

"This whole floor is the master."

They hugged, and Blue walked away. After locking the door, Blaque swept me up into his arms.

"You've officially entered the matrix. Are you ready?"

I wrapped my arms around his neck. "Absolutely, Neo."

The master hallway was like a maze filled with several private rooms. One room was a large closet with shopping bags on the floor. Another was a sauna.

He opened the door to an arcade and smiled. "What do you know about Pac-Man?"

I laughed. "I bet more than you. Goldie and I are video game masters."

"Bet up. We'll see tomorrow."

The last door on the left was the master bathroom. He carried me past a large Jacuzzi tub and an enormous shower with multiple jets that spanned the length of the wall. He closed the door, put me down, and turned on the shower. Sexual steam immediately filled the room.

Blaque traced around my lips with his finger. "A life with me is truly like living in the matrix. Do you want that type of life… with me?"

It was too late. I loved Blaque by fate, not choice.

I kissed him with everything in me and replied, "Call me Trinity, Neo."

After an intense night of passion that started with a sultry shower, I woke up alone, the bright sun's rays licking my face. I searched for my clothes but forgot I hadn't packed a bag since I didn't expect to be out overnight. In the bathroom, I was greeted by a white Versace sundress on a hanger. I shook my head. *He can't be this perfect.*

In the shower, the streams massaged my body from all angles. Once dressed, and now filled with energy, I went outside to receive the sun's love. A few minutes later, the phone in the cabin rang.

"*Buenos dias, mamacita.* Keith is almost done with breakfast. *Tienes hambre?*"

"Good morning, and yes, I'm starving."

After hanging up, I touched up my edges and applied lip gloss for the perfect shine before leaving the room.

Downstairs, Keith, Blaque, and Blue were engrossed in a deep conversation in the outdoor kitchen. The scent of maple sausage, cinnamon, and brown sugar filled the air. Blaque spoke to me with his eyes, and I waved.

Shay and Keisha were seated under an umbrella at a table outside, wearing their "men's" t-shirts and chatting nonstop. Shay, my hairstylist, was tall and cute with a slender shape. She was also very much a party girl. Keisha, on the other hand, was quiet, but only with people she didn't know. She was a sexy schoolteacher and extra thick in all the right places.

As I approached them, I noticed Shay grabbed her jaw like she had been hit.

"Hey, ladies. Shay, what's wrong with your mouth?" I asked.

"I think I have lockjaw," she replied with a painful expression while moving her jaw in a circle.

Keisha shook her head. "Damn, sounds painful as hell. How did you get that?"

"I got extra freaky with Keith's fine ass and jacked up my jaw."

"Shay!" Keisha and I yelled in unison, then started laughing.

We toned it down to giggles when the men looked over at us.

Keisha shook her head. "Hell, I can't judge. Blue brought out the Adina Howard in me last night."

I laughed again. "You two are crazy."

"Boss lady, don't act brand new," Shay said. "We heard your ass last night."

I gasped. "Oh my God. Was I that loud?"

"Yesss!" they both said.

"The whole damn universe heard you calling Blaque's name," Shay added. "Where the hell did you find these niggas? Who are they?"

I took a deep breath and exhaled. "They're Savages."

Looking concerned, Shay grabbed my hand. "Wait a damn minute. What does that mean? Is that their name?"

I nodded. *"Si."*

"No wonder they're turning bitches out," she said, and laughter erupted amongst us again.

This time, however, we didn't care how loud we were.

Like always, Keith's meal was delicious. He had cooked French toast, omelets, steak, and home fries. After eating, Blaque and I returned to our room. Pulling out the bags from our Beverly Hills shopping trip fiasco, he handed me a black Versace one-piece with a plunging neckline and cut-outs along the waist. It fit my body perfectly.

"I love it. I would never have picked this one."

He stood behind me in the mirror and touched the side of my face. "You are so beautiful. I love you."

I smiled. "I love you, too."

Blaque moved my braids from my face and kissed my cheek. Then he took my hands in his and kissed the back of each one.

"Come," he told me. "Let's go take a dive in the ocean."

"Dive in the ocean?"

After getting life jackets and snorkeling equipment from the lifeguard onboard, Blaque grabbed my hand, and we dove into underwater heaven. Blue, Keith, Keisha, and Shay decided they would rather stay on board to enjoy each other's company while drinking. I think Keisha and Shay's decision had more to do with them not wanting to get their hair wet.

A family of fish with electric blue bodies, red stripes, and yellow fins welcomed us to their paradise. Hundreds of tiny silver fish danced around us. An exotic group with turquoise skin, black stripes, and purple beauty marks moved past us with saditty attitudes like they ruled the kingdom. The large group of orange fish with blue dots invited us to follow them through the pink coral reef. Holding my hand, Blaque swam strong and steady like a real shark, holding me beside him. It was the best adventure of my life.

When we came up for oxygen, the lifeguard signaled us back,

but before we could do so, a heavy wave crashed over us. The Pacific Ocean shoved us forward with mighty strength like she wanted to fight. Blaque tightly wove the fingers of his right hand with my left. I reinforced his grip with the muscles in my hand.

"Baby, take a big breath and relax," he said calmly. "Don't let go of my hand."

We deeply inhaled. Suddenly, the ocean yanked our ankles and dragged us straight down. She held us under, then pushed us backward. Before she released her hold, she aggressively tossed us around like laundry in the dryer. We tumbled as underwater gymnasts until she got bored. Salt water filled my nasal cavity and burned my nose, throat, and chest. I opened my eyes, but Pacific stung them shut with icy fingers. Finally, the bully left us alone, and we floated to the surface. Once oxygen refilled my lungs, I started coughing nonstop.

Blaque kissed my hand. "You're okay, baby."

I closed my eyes and took deep breaths. He guided us swiftly with the calm currents back to *Legacy*. Never releasing his grip, he pulled me up the ladder. Two lifeguards helped us onboard. Blue, Keith, Keisha, and Shay stared at us like we were ghosts.

"What?" I asked.

Shay threw her arms around me and began kissing my face over and over. "Girl, we thought y'all were dead! We prayed to tiny baby and grown man Jesus."

"You too, Blue and Keith?" Blaque asked.

"Yeah, man," Keith said.

"A couple died last week in that undertow by the reef," one of the lifeguards said. "That's why I called you back."

Blaque placed a towel around me. "We were already in it."

The lifeguard took our gear. "We went out but couldn't find you."

Keisha shook her head. "That shit was scary. That's why I only swim in a pool or stay where it's dry."

Blue handed me a blunt. "How are you, Pearle?"

I took a hit and passed it to Blaque. "I'm *good*. My man is a fucking shark."

Blaque smiled and exhaled. "The top of the food chain, baby."

After the Pacific gave Blaque access to her beauty below, she overheard him confess to me that he was still in love with the Caribbean Sea, which he said was calmer and prettier. The Pacific was like most women who knew her worth but were told she wasn't good enough. She made us recognize her splendor and taught Blaque that he had better respect a bad bitch from the West Side.

CHAPTER 12
FIFTY CANDLES

PEARLE MONALISE BROWN

IT WAS LATE afternoon when we returned to the dock. Once Blaque and I got in the backseat of the Bentley, we relaxed to the sounds of Boys II Men's "50 Candles" while he masterfully massaged my feet. I thought of the roughness of his hands. *He could knock a man out with one punch.* I thought of the gentleness of his lips when they would lightly sweep across my skin and the light in his eyes whenever he saw me or the darkness whenever he got angry. His calmness had kept me unaware of the danger, and the strength of his body had pulled us to safety.

As the car floated along the highway, I fell fast asleep on his lap, only to be awakened to the strong scent of hamburgers and dirty grease. I quickly sat up and saw the familiar Rosecrans Avenue sign from the back window.

"Blaque, why the hell are we in Compton?"

"Relax, baby. Blue wanted a burger, and I told him to get you a chili cheeseburger."

"Where is he?" I asked, scanning our surroundings with my eyes.

"He's in line."

"Blaque, we're sitting in the hood in a new Bentley at the most dangerous intersection in the country."

"Again, relax. You watch too many gangster movies, *Miss*

Compton. Plus, all my rides are bulletproof."

"Damn right. Compton is *my* hood, so I know how niggas move out here. And Blue is outside unprotected. I wouldn't go to Bankhead and act like I know your hood."

Just as I said that Koran, a stick-up kid who ran with Goldie a few years back, walked quickly past the car. He wore jeans with a grey hoodie, and his hair was cornrowed. As he walked in the direction of the take-out spot, he pulled the hood over his head.

"Shit." I quickly slid into my sandals. Blaque grabbed his Glock, and we bolted out of the car.

Koran's right hand went towards his waist, and I instantly feared the worst.

"Koran!" I called out.

Stoic at first, he slowly turned around but then quickly smiled.

"Pearle! What's up, boo?" He gave me a long embrace. "Damn, you look fine as hell."

I felt Blaque's glare on the back of my neck; I could only guess he wasn't happy about Koran's innocent compliment. To avoid any misunderstandings, I made introductions.

"Thank you. This is my man, Blaque. Blaque, this is Koran. How's Porsha?"

"She's good. We're about to have a baby, so I'm out here busting my ass, hustling."

"Congrats on the baby and the wedding."

"Thanks, boo. By the way, we got your wedding gift. You're the only person that actually got us something from our registry."

"You're welcome. I'm sorry I couldn't make the wedding, but my schedule wouldn't allow me. Saturdays are usually a busy day at my shop."

"No worries. So, what are you doing here? Grabbing something to eat?"

"Blaque's cousin, Blue, is in line."

He gave Blaque a handshake. "Shit, y'all come with me. I'll hook y'all up."

"Hook us up with what?" I asked.

"Food. That's why you're here, right? I need to clock in first before I'm late. Then I'll take your order."

My mouth dropped open. "You work here, Koran?"

"Hell yeah. This is temporary, my side hustle. I'm a manager at the YMCA, but I'm stacking extra money for the baby. Goldie's greedy ass didn't tell you? He's up here almost every day."

Koran talked for thirty minutes about all the positive changes in his life while he swept and picked up trash with a smile until our food was ready.

When Blue took out his wallet to pay, Koran told him, "Nah, Pearle is family. The meal is on me."

Before we left, Blaque placed a rolled stack neatly bound with a rubber band in Koran's hand. "Keep doing what you're doing. We need more positive brothers like you. Congratulations on your wedding and baby."

"Wow, I truly appreciate you, man. Y'all have a blessed day. Come by whenever. And, Pearle, things are better around here."

When we got in the car, Blaque touched my face. "What did I say? You watch too many gangster movies."

With my belly full of food, I yawned and stretched across the backseat. "You were right *this* time."

My phone rang loudly, waking me. I didn't remember how I got in the bed, but my body was recharged and ready to roll like a race car in the Indy 500.

I ran to the closet and answered quietly so no one would hear. "What's up, Goldie?"

"What's the 411? Why haven't you answered your phone?"

"We've been out to sea. I just got back."

"Don't forget your mission, sis. I need those deets."

"I got you. Bye."

After hanging up, I ventured to the west wing. There were more guest rooms, a theater, and an empty room, but no Basquiat. I tipped down the marble staircase and crept through the foyer.

"Pearle."

I jumped when Henry appeared from nowhere.

"Are you looking for Blaque?"

"Yes, sir," I replied, fighting to slow my heart rate after being startled.

"Follow me."

Behind the stairs was a hidden door. He pushed the wall, and it slid to the left.

"He's in his office. Downstairs and to the right," Henry said, then disappeared.

My feet tapped like Savion Glover's on the marble floor as I walked down the dimly lit, winding staircase. In the basement was an indoor pool with a cascading lion fountain. Crown molding outlined the ceiling and gold-accented walls. Blaque lived lavishly, like people featured in Robin Leach's *Lifestyles of the Rich and Famous*. I turned to the right, passed a giant Buddha sculpture, and approached a closed door. I knocked lightly.

"Come in, baby."

When I entered, I was surprised to see Blaque meditating, seated like a yoga master on the floor on a black and gold rug with candles and sage burning around him. Against the wall were another Buddha statue and a sand-filled Zen garden.

I sat on the rug in front of him. "How did you know it was me?"

"'Cause everybody else knows when my door is closed, I don't want to be disturbed."

I tried to get up, but he held onto my hand. "Stay. I was just talking about you."

I turned my head, searching around the room. "With who?"

"God."

I stared into Blaque's eyes. No man had ever told me he talked to God about me. I was speechless.

"Pearle, your boy Koran had me thinking."

"About what?"

"True happiness."

He confessed that he admired Koran—how he had changed his life and found happiness in simplicity. I was shocked to hear this since nothing about Blaque was simple. Everything about him was complex and extravagant. Anything he wanted, he could get. Every time I felt I had him figured out, he switched it up.

"Pearle, wake up," he said, snapping his fingers and smiling. "Do you meditate?"

I shook my head. "No."

He grabbed my hands. "Why are you so quiet?"

"I didn't imagine you being the meditating type," I answered.

"I have to Zen out every day, or I'll go insane. So many people depend on me for their survival. That's why I keep the right energy around me. My life is different than Koran's. I must approach my life like the game Jenga. If I move too quickly or take away the wrong piece, *everything* my family and I have built crumbles. You feel me?"

"I do."

As his eyes pierced my soul, he laced our fingers together. We closed our eyes, and he instructed me to close my eyes and take deep breaths with him. The room went completely silent except for the popping flames from the candles. With my eyes shut, all my other senses heightened. I inhaled sage, salt, and peppermint. The water trickling down the Buddha statue sounded more like a river stream. Our hearts pulsed through our palms. The peaceful intensity lifted us spiritually above everything around us, and in our state of meta-tranquility, my love for Blaque was elevated.

When I opened my eyes, he kissed my hand.

"Do you want to see the rest of the basement?"

I nodded, and we walked across the hallway to a spa room with two massage tables, a sauna, an open shower, and a hot tub. The whole room screamed serenity and smelled like eucalyptus and lavender.

I marveled at the room. "This is amazing, but why is your house so big? It's just you."

"I'm a country boy who loves open, spacious houses."

Past the indoor pool was a room secured with a large steel door. I watched as he entered the code, committing it to my memory. We walked into an art gallery filled with paintings and sculptures. Like the entire floor, the room was dimly lit.

"This is my favorite room in the entire house. I'm passionate about my art."

There was a painting that was so magnetizing that it brought my steps to a measured pace, pausing to admire the seamless lines and intricate details.

"This is so dope," I said, running my forefinger along the canvas. "Who's this artist, baby?"

"I made it in an art class in Kingston."

"What?" Shock punctuating my one-word question. "Are you an artist?"

"I wish I could call myself an artist and create all day. Tattoo art is my true passion. When I get inspired, I find time to do tattoos for the family."

I unfastened the top buttons on his shirt. "Did you tat the lion on your chest?"

He kissed my finger. "I did."

"It's beautiful, and I may want one," I said, gliding my fingertips across his tatted pec. "That is if I inspire you." I brought my focus back to him, gazing into his eyes. "Do I inspire you?"

As our eyes locked, a slow grin spread across his lips. "Of course."

We basked in the moment briefly before I gently grabbed his hands and asked, "Which is your favorite?"

He led me around the room and called out details and things I wouldn't have noticed on each piece. We stopped in front of the Basquiat. "Jean-Michel Basquiat is my favorite artist, and this is my favorite painting," Blaque said.

We stared at it for what felt like hours. He turned to me, but I couldn't look at him.

Then he said, "I love all of Basquiat's work for many reasons, but this piece is my most valuable possession because Basquiat tackled our history and social injustice. He used the crown in his work to show the world that black men are kings. Our royal roots come from Africa. We were stolen, enslaved, and then thrown into a world with nothing and expected to thrive. Most of us do what we need to do to survive in a place foreign to us. My great-grandfather, Major, went to Harlem to make a better life for our family. When his job ejected him on the street with nothing, he learned those streets and became a hustler in the Black Lottery. He pulled a bunch of men out of the ghetto, and our families thrive from his foundation. People judge men like Gramp Major, but I say fuck them. He was the shit and deserves his crown. He taught us to be kings, too, no matter if we live in the hood or suburbs, America or England. I paid four million for this one piece in an auction. I was the only black man in the room bidding, and as always, they underestimated the brain of a real nigga. They were so busy looking at my hand that I walked away paying half the value. Art appreciates over time, baby, so think of how much it will be worth years from now."

I walked behind him and wrapped my arms around his chest. "I get it, baby."

He stood there for several more minutes in silence, studying his painting with pride in his eyes. At that moment, I knew there was no way I would steal it. Goldie and the Escobars could kiss my ass.

The next day, Henry grabbed my bags, and we walked to Blaque's car.

Blaque moved my braids from my face. "Stay with me another night."

"Blaque, I need to go home."

His lips grazed my ear, and he kissed my chin. "I'm addicted. *Necessito mi cocaina a mi casa.*"

I smiled. "Blaque, you have a meeting, and I have work to do at the shop."

"Please?" he begged while holding open the car door.

I almost fell under the spell he cast with his enchanting eyes, but I needed to be in my space to think. The rules of engagement had changed significantly over the previous days, and I needed to develop a new plan. He finally shut the door after I got in and waved goodbye as the car slowly pulled off.

Blue looked in the rearview mirror. "Do you want to listen to music in the back?"

"No, I'm good. Do you like Keisha?" I asked, hoping there would be a love connection between them.

"Yeah, she's cool," he replied, smiling before rolling up the partition.

My mind raced about the weekend. Blaque was like a puzzle with a few missing pieces that I couldn't put together. I switched my thoughts to the conversation I would have with Goldie. I had to let him know I wanted to abort the robbery, even though I knew it wasn't that simple since we were contracted with the cartel. Every time I tried to focus, a strong urge to feel Blaque raced through my veins. He was magical, and I couldn't break the spell.

Damn, I love my brother. I just hope he loves me enough to understand.

CHAPTER 13
BORN AND RAISED IN COMPTON

PEARLE MONALISE BROWN

ONCE AT HOME, I fell back into my routine—Miles, drink, and soak. In the tub, I floated above the drama with the bubbles—my mind clear and my thoughts quieted. I deeply exhaled. A loud banging on my door suddenly disrupted my tranquility. Jumping out of the tub, I slipped into my robe, grabbed my gun, and cautiously approached the door to peer through the peephole.

"Dammit, Goldie. Why are you banging on my door like the damn police?"

"Put some clothes on, thug," he said, looking at my pink .22 as he stepped inside. "I knew you were here but not answering your phone."

I laughed. "Godfather shit, and I was in the tub. What's up?"

"Did you see the painting?"

"Yep."

"Great. Bada bing, bada boom. What's the report?"

"It's not happening, captain."

"Whatchu talkin' 'bout, Willis?" Goldie replied, quoting Gary Coleman's famous line from the show *Different Strokes*.

"Blaque's mansion is secured with indoor and outdoor cameras, face recognition for the front gate, and an espionage uncle who blends in with the house."

"Well, we'll move to plan B."

"I can't."

"Why?"

"Because I have real feelings for him."

"Fuck your feelings."

I jerked my neck back. "Excuse you?"

We stared at each other then he gave me the middle finger.

"Get out," I told him.

He didn't move.

I stepped closer to him, getting up in his face. "Goldie, get your ass out."

Without saying another word, he turned and left.

I poured a glass of wine and sighed deeply. Seconds later, there was a soft knock on the door.

I swung the door open with an attitude, thinking it was Goldie coming back. "What?"

Blaque stood in my doorway, looking like he was about to win an ESPY award.

"Hey."

My mouth dropped as I slowly opened the door wider, inviting him inside.

"Damn, Blaque, you look so fine."

He smiled. "Thank you, baby. I'm on my way to an important meeting and needed a good luck kiss from my woman."

I grabbed his face, and our lips connected. His kisses traveled down my body until he was on his knees.

I smiled. "Just a kiss, huh?"

"You have two sets of lips, right?"

"*Si.*"

He smiled and slowly French-kissed between my thighs,

taking his time, and then finessed his way back to his feet.

"Thank you, baby," he said while tying the belt on my robe. "Sorry I came unannounced, but I needed some sugar for good luck."

"You can come over *whenever* you want."

He grabbed my chin. "I'll call you after my meeting, beautiful."

"Blaque, I love you."

With a quick peck on the lips and a wink, he replied, "Love you, too."

When the door closed, I leaned against it and clenched the diamond necklace around my neck. *Damn.*

As soon as I slid into my jeans and fitted tee, there was another knock on the door. *Who is it now?* I wondered as I went to open it. There stood Goldie.

"Sis, I'm sorry."

"You should be," I told him, placing a hand on my hip.

"I don't want to fight anymore."

I removed my hand from where it had been resting and relaxed. "Me either."

"Cool. Can you ride out with me?"

After I slipped into my Air Jordans, we headed out the door. Once in his car, he dropped the top on the Batmobile, and we drove without a care. I couldn't remember the last time we talked without purpose. Back in Compton, we stopped at a gas station.

"Hey, sis, you want some hot chips and a red soda?"

"Hell yeah. Get me a red, not cherry, Blow Pop and a hot and spicy dill pickle, too."

"Okay! I see you still have a little hood left in you."

The gas station was jumping. The humming of vacuum cleaners, the hissing of the air being pumped into white wall tires with Sprewell rims, and the blasting of songs from hip-hop and R&B filled the air. There was a small line at the payphone for those who still used pagers or couldn't utilize cellular minutes until after seven p.m. Girls walked around in tight jeans, short shorts, and fitted sundresses while admirers ran over to ask for their phone numbers. I inhaled the smell of weed, jasmine car freshers, and gasoline. I was home, and it felt *so* good.

Suddenly, my door swung open, and Goldie pushed me onto the floor, covering my body with his as gunfire erupted around us.

After what felt like an eternity, he whispered. "Are you okay, sis?"

I nodded. "*Damn.* Koran said shit was better around here."

As he got up from off of me, he said, "It is, but some shit never changes."

I waited for Goldie to get in the car to drive off.

"Goldie?"

Goldie whistled at the pump. "*Que paso?*"

I turned my body to look out the rear window. "*Vamanos!*"

"Man, I'm getting my five dollars' worth of gas."

"Five dollars?

"Yep."

"Man, let's go!"

He fanned his hand. "Why you acting scared? Them niggas been gone."

"Them niggas are gonna be the least of your worries if you don't get your ass in this car."

He hollered, doubled over in laughter. "Damn, I love fucking with you," he said as he got in the car and threw a thin, black plastic bag filled with goodies in my lap before pulling off.

After one sip of my red soda, I looked up and saw we were at the intersection of Greenleaf and Central. We turned into Woodlawn Memorial, the cemetery where Nike was buried. Goldie navigated the dirt road, twisting and turning past beautiful oak and palm trees until we arrived at the tallest tree in the park. We had picked that spot because Nike loved to climb trees as a kid. We imagined him climbing that tree to heaven.

I sat on the grass in front of the grey marble headstone that stood two feet above the ground. I deeply inhaled the smoky wooded scent of green earth. When I turned around to see where Goldie was, I found him towering over me with a blunt in his hand.

"Really, Goldie?"

He exhaled. "Hell yeah. I smoked and drank with my brother when he was alive, so I come here every day to talk, smoke, and drink like we always did."

He passed me the blunt. I deeply inhaled and exhaled. The smoky cloud drifted toward the sky.

"Damn, you come here every day?"

"Yeah, man, but I didn't want to come alone today for some reason."

We blew purple haze into the purple sky while eating hot chips, pickles, and Now and Laters like we had done as kids. I felt Nike's presence and wanted to linger in the peaceful atmosphere.

Goldie looked at his watch. "Sis, it's time for me to take you back."

"Do you want to stay over tonight and watch old movies?"

"Not tonight, sis. I have a date with a *fine* sister. She might be the one."

"The one for life?"

He laughed. "What? *Hell no.* I was thinking a girlfriend, but now that I've said that shit out loud, I take it back."

"You love running from commitment."

"Aren't you the kettle calling a nigga black. You've been running since we were kids."

"Whatever, Goldie."

"You know I'm right. You love running."

"No, I hate running, but I can't help it. I run from the good because it makes me feel bad, and I run to the bad because it makes me feel good. I wanted to be a famous actress, Goldie, to get us out of the hood, and I feel like I let everybody down. So, I rob niggas to escape my real life. I'm all fucked up."

"Human beings are fucked-up individuals. Our sins are imperfections that make us who we're designed to be. You're talented as hell, but you grew up in Compton, not on a stage. We're not actors. We're family, and we need to stick together. Robbing niggas is our survival tactic that has kept us and Mama safe from the real hood shit. I promise you'll know it's time to change your life when the bad doesn't feel good anymore."

He crip-walked to the car and opened the passenger door. "Time to go."

I got inside. "I love you, heathen."

After hopping into the driver's seat, he blasted "Space Age Pimpin'" by 8Ball & MJG until it sounded like we were inside a live concert.

"Pearle," he yelled over the music, "until God reveals otherwise, don't run. Lean into your sins." He hit the switches and leaned to the left and right. "It will set you free. And I love you, too, *Poison.*"

Like old times, we got lost in our laughter.

"I've missed this," I said.

"I'm always here." He put the car in reverse and looked in his rearview mirror. *"Shit."*

"What?"

I turned around and saw a black limousine had crept up behind us. Tomas and Felipe were standing outside the limo with one of the rear doors open. Goldie turned off the car ignition. My heart was thumping so loudly I felt like it was in my ear.

"What in the hell do they want?"

He grabbed my hand and squeezed it. "It's more scare tactics, sis. We haven't done anything wrong, so be cool."

We got out, and Goldie walked around the car to grab my hand. Then we walked to the open door. Goldie got inside first.

"Let Pearle go, and I can relay any messages you have," I heard Goldie say.

It was Matias's voice that responded. "That won't be necessary. Come inside, Pearle."

Goldie extended his hand, and I grabbed it. It was wet and clammy. I slid next to him. Seated across from us was Matias, with Pussy sitting on his lap. A Hispanic man dressed in a nice suit was on a long, leather seat to our left. Matias was wearing a Cheshire grin and stroking Pussy with one hand while holding a champagne glass in the other. The other man grimaced, showing his fear as he clenched his champagne glass with both hands like he was holding on for his life.

Tomas and Felipe shut the door. Immediately, the interior was pitch black. I couldn't see anything around me; the darkness was suffocating. I felt like we'd been shoved inside a small closet. The only sound heard was the slow rhythm of Pussy's deep breaths, followed by sporadic, soft purrs.

There was a click, and dimmed lights illuminated like tiny spotlights.

Maita's smile hadn't changed. *"Hola."*

Goldie and I responded like twins. *"Hola."*

"Were you visiting your brother?" he asked us.

"Yes," we said.

"My brother is not physically with us, but as I've said, his spirit hopped inside Pussy, and his soul lives on. We are twins, you know. I really miss seeing him."

Pussy purred like it agreed.

"Today is our birthday," Matias continued.

Again, we responded in unison. "Happy Birthday."

Matias looked at the man in the nice suit. "My guests are Goldie and Pearle. I had to hire them to get my painting to correct *your* fuck up."

"*Por favor, Señor* Escobar, I can fix this."

Matias only smiled. "We are here to celebrate." He paused and continued, "Goldie, please, grab two champagne glasses for you and your sister and pour the two of you a glass."

There were two fancy glasses in front of a crystal bowl. A bottle of Don Perignon was inside and surrounded by circular ice cubes.

Goldie obeyed, and Matias asked me, "Pearle, would you mind saying a toast?"

We lifted our glasses, and I cleared my throat.

Taking a deep breath, I said, "*Feliz Cumpleanos* to you and your brother. God Bless."

He smiled. "Very nice. Amen."

Our glasses clinked together, and we drank. Suddenly, the Hispanic man's glass dropped from his fingers onto his lap. He crossed his arms over his chest, grabbing his left arm with one hand and clenching his fist over his heart with the other.

"Are you okay?" I asked him.

He sipped the air twice like a fish out of water before his head bowed and his arms dropped like dead weights onto his lap. Immediately after, his champagne glass fell to the floor. The entire time Matias kept drinking and stroking Pussy with a smile.

"*So*…thank you, *señor*, for inviting us to your celebration," Goldie said as we placed our glasses down. "But Pearle and I will…"

"*Tu y tu hermana* will stay and drink until your glasses are empty," Matias snapped.

We picked up our glasses, exchanged nervous glances, and threw back the contents like a shot of vodka, then placed our empty glasses next to us. Matias knocked on the partition; seconds later, Felipe opened the door.

I scooted out first; Goldie quickly followed. Felipe took our places in the backseat and closed the door. The limo sped off, leaving Goldie and me standing hand-in-hand like two lost kids.

"Goldie, what in the hell just happened?"

"Godfather shit."

CHAPTER 14
SAY HELLO

CHRISTIAN "BLAQUE" LAURENT SAVAGE

 F OUR MISSED CALLS *from Agent Walker. I wish he would stop calling. I don't want to talk to his ass.* His voice irritated me. Plus, I despised his fake games. More than that, we weren't friends.

I had no respect for him. He was willing to let an innocent woman and man die to help his career. He referred to Pearle and Goldie as small casualties in a big war—the war our government started when they flooded black communities with cocaine to fund the CIA's guerilla army overseas. Now that underworld chemists had figured out how to rock up the government's product to gain more profit, there was a need for the DEA to end the drug war. Who was the real author writing this tragedy?

It was my first official meeting with other crime kings. Pearle had already given me the lowdown, but we arrived thirty minutes early to peep out my surroundings and potential employees. I needed to flawlessly present my product and become the new connect for L.A. The market would be free with the Escobars out of the way in a week, and if the deal went through, my Jamaican family would become L.A.'s new plug. The players in this game were only loyal to money. My product was better and cost fifteen percent less.

Blue, Keith, and I sat in my car across the street from BLACK, the cigar bar on Sunset Boulevard I had purchased. BLACK, my newest business venture, was neutral territory and where we would hold business meetings. The first to arrive was Englewood, a young brother dressed in Sean John. Next, Hollywood strolled in rocking a tan suit with a gold grill and pinkie ring. He was the OG in the game. Pasadena, an Afro-Latino, entered the bar dressed in a cream Ecko jogging suit. Compton, Pearle's boy Leonard, was a tall brother. He arrived in a black and red Nike jumpsuit. Watts, the last invitee, was the youngest. He was dressed in FUBU and red Dopeman's. Every king was draped in diamonds, gold, and platinum.

I pressed the intercom. "Y'all ready to roll and get this money?"

We confidently crossed Sunset Boulevard, stopping traffic with swag that dared anyone to hit us. Blue and Keith held briefcases filled with product samples.

Nova Savage, my cousin, was like a sister to me and also my manager at BLACK. She had hired a very attractive all-female staff that rocked short black dresses with red pumps and matching red lipstick. A pretty, dark-skinned woman from Peach Grove Park, Nova was a tall, stylish, and intelligent businesswoman who didn't take any shit. She sported a short diagonally-shaped haircut, a red dress, black pumps, a diamond necklace, and hoop earrings. She embraced us with love when we walked in.

"What's up, Nova? The place looks amazing," I told her.

"Thanks, Blaque, and thanks again for getting me out of Atlanta. Maybe now I can keep a boyfriend without my daddy and uncles running them away," she stated jokingly while being serious at the same time.

I pointed at Keith, Blue, and myself. "Your man still has to meet *our* approval, though."

Blue gave Keith dap. "Damn right."

Shaking her head, she replied, "I can't stand the men in this family."

According to Nova, not much had changed in Atlanta, which was great news. That meant my ATL operation was running smoothly without me. I had left my cousin, Arion Savage, who led our Midwest operation, in charge.

We had another three weeks before the grand opening. Half of the bar was still under construction, but the VIP room was finished. Nova gave me a quick lay of the land since construction started. The floors were black and white marble. The walls were textured, and the black ceiling was outlined with white crown molding. The bar and seating areas were almost finished. There was an empty space intended for a small stage that would feature live musical performances and entertainment. Overall, the atmosphere was dark and sexy.

"Keith, when are you cooking?" Nova asked.

"Tonight. Come over after you close. You can meet my lady, Shay."

She smiled. "Cool. Hopefully, she meets my approval."

We hugged, and Nova helped her employees gather cigars, lighters, and whiskey. Then we followed the ladies inside the VIP room secured with an electronic code, a facial recognition panel, and a red, heavy, bolted door that would prevent fire and bullets from entering.

A heavy haze that smelled of sweet cedar wood and whiskey filled the room, and a crystal chandelier hung from the black ceiling, glistening against the dark mahogany walls. A black leather sectional gave the perfect view of the large-screen televisions strategically placed around the room.

The men sat around the large circular red table in the middle of the room, puffing cigars, sipping whiskey, and listening attentively. They were the five kings of the hoods surrounding L.A. We had all started as paupers of the ghetto, descendants of survivors. We were now street strategists—fathers, sons, brothers, and husbands making dollars out of dimes.

Our swag was unique, but our purpose was the same. We rocked stereotypical societal labels like designer clothes—menace, thug, and criminal—but like any other business, we provided a product to customers who demanded it. In our communities, Koreans supplied hair care products and weaves, the Vietnamese supplied nail salons, and Arabs provided gasoline and snacks. There was a political war against drug dealers and hip-hop because we were the truth-spitters of our neighborhoods. We got paid for telling the truth. Why were they mad at rich niggas?

Drugs arrived at our hoods like a special delivery from an anonymous admirer. The streets were flooded with addicts who wanted that crystal rock to shoot them to the moon. No one knew our customers and streets better than the men at the table. If we didn't feed our customers what they desired, someone foreign would monopolize the industry like everything else in our communities. Then we would be left scratching our heads like, *How the hell did that happen?*

"We sit equally at this roundtable as kings," I started, addressing the three men. "How we got here doesn't matter because everyone here is in this business to make money. I'm presenting you with an opportunity to make an additional fifteen percent for every kilo, which is, on average, a savings of six stacks per brick. We have different international distribution channels on lock, so you never have to worry about shortage issues like you've been having."

Watts shook his head. "Fifteen percent sounds too good to be true."

"What country distros L.A.?" I asked him.

"Columbia."

"In Columbia, cocaine costs four dollars per gram, which is four thousand for one kilo," I responded. "Compton, how much do they charge you per brick?"

"Forty to fifty stacks, depending on the market," Compton replied.

"So, at the lowest cost, the Escobars—your Columbian distro—

makes thirty-six thousand per brick, and the product has gotten shitty. When was the last time any of you bought one brick?"

Hollywood shook his head. "Never."

"They make millions off us daily, and our soldiers end up in prison," I told them. "Why not keep the hood dollars black like Black Wall Street in Oklahoma did? I spent months in Columbia as a tourist. They didn't know this nigga *hablo Español*. So, I know shit they don't think I know. You feel me?"

Blue and Keith passed out samples in plastic bags stuffed inside custom black velvet bags.

I translated in Spanish for Pasadena, and he tasted the pure snow.

"Blaque, I can't speak for everybody, but nigga, you had me at 'We are kings of our hoods.' You are a smooth motherfucker."

All the kings laughed and gave each other dap.

Compton smiled. "Hell, you had me at saving six stacks per brick."

We were foes who laughed and joked as friends, but the bottom line was everyone was down and ready for business. The best news was my family would become the main L.A. distributor. We would rack fifty-seven billion per year.

"Blaque, what's up with Pearl?" Hollywood asked.

I had two pearls, my woman and my product, so I had to be clear on which he was referring to.

"What are you talking about?"

"The hundred-and-fifty-dollar per gram product in the pretty bottle. Do you know the supplier?"

According to a conversation I'd had with Blue, Pearl was exclusive and not ready for introduction to the mass market.

"I've heard of it," I replied.

"I have some celebrities and models interested," Hollywood informed me.

"Like Blaque said, we've heard of it," Blue interjected. "So there's no need for us to discuss it."

Watts got back to business. "When will you be ready to move major weight?"

"Next week," I told him, and just like that, I had five new markets. As they walked out to return to their respective hoods, I shook their hands and told them, "I'll be in touch."

Nova stood at the door, handing each a black leather and wooden cigar box filled with our best cigars. Yeah, we conducted ourselves with class in these parts and would stand out from the rest.

After Blue, Keith, and I got in the Bentley to celebrate our major power play, I took a moment to call Pearle.

"What's up, beautiful?"

Pearle had the sexiest voice, but I could tell something was bothering her when she answered.

"Hey, I need you to come to my house after you finish business."

"Are you asking or telling me?"

"I'm demanding."

I smiled. "Gangsta Boo, I need to handle business early in the morning—"

"Blaque," she interrupted, sounding melancholy.

"What's up? You cool, baby?"

"Yeah. Goldie is here but will be leaving shortly, and I don't want to be alone tonight."

"I'll come get you, but you'll have to stay at my crib. I've got a bunch to handle before we go to Jamaica."

"That's cool," she replied, then hung up.

As we traveled down Sunset Strip, we passed the bright lights and people searching for the next spot or bar to patronize. The meeting ended quicker than I had planned since it didn't take much convincing from me; everyone was ready to make money. With my real-life Jenga game stacking up perfectly, I was ready to celebrate with my queen. She was my lucky charm and had accelerated my expansion by introducing me to all the major players.

There was so much that needed to be done. I instructed Keith to secure a large warehouse to store our product and for Blue to schedule our meeting with the Port of L.A. connect within the week. I exhaled as Keith rolled a blunt. He must've sensed I needed to relax.

As we were pulling up to Pearle's condo, Goldie was leaving. He threw up the peace sign at me before driving off. I barely reached the steps before she ran into my arms. The look on her face was a mixture of fear and sadness. I moved her braids behind her ears and kissed her forehead.

"What's wrong, baby?" I asked, grabbing her bag as we walked to the car,

"I'm better now that you're here," she said.

Blue, waiting at the trunk, took her bag from me and placed it inside.

"What's up, Pearle?" he asked her. "Are you okay?"

"I'll be okay."

"Do we need to kick somebody's ass?" Keith yelled from the passenger seat.

Smiling slightly, Pearle replied, "No, I'm good."

I pulled her into the backseat, and she sat on my lap.

"How was your meeting, handsome?" she asked.

"Way better than expected, thanks to you."

"I'm glad to hear that. How do you want to celebrate?"

"I want to do whatever you want to do. I'm free all night." I lifted her chin. "But first, tell me what's bothering you."

Suddenly, she broke down crying while in my arms.

"Goldie and I went to see Nike today. It was the first time

I'd been to visit his grave since he died, and it was hard, Blaque—extremely hard. I miss him so much."

"Look, how 'bout we chill tonight? We can pop some popcorn and find some good movies to watch?"

She looked relieved. "Are you sure? I know tonight was a big night for you. I figured you would want to celebrate with Keith and Blue?"

"Babe, watching *Coming to America* while holding you in my arms sounds like a good evening spent together to me. Besides, you could use the laughs."

She wrapped her arms tightly around my neck. "Blaque, you're so perfect."

"Nah, I'll never be perfect, but I'll love you as perfectly as I can. Will that be enough for you?"

"It already is," she replied, sealing it with a kiss.

CHAPTER 15
TOP OF THE WORLD

PEARLE MONALISE BROWN

BLAQUE'S INTIMATE PRESENCE was the vacation I needed to escape my troubles, but our prism of serenity was temporary. My afro danced naked in the wind with my Corvette's top down as I sped down Compton Boulevard to my hair salon. Kenya Gruv's hit song, "Top of the World" from the *Menace to Society* soundtrack, was the inspiration for my salon's name and my favorite R&B song. The soundwaves and bass penetrated my car's speakers as I pulled into my VIP parking space.

To an outsider, Top of the World was no different than any other sanctuary for black women. The atmosphere was eclectic yet tranquil, with the calming colors of baby blue, pale green, and white. Every client was served tea, white wine, or mimosas, which balanced some of the ratchet conversations.

The salon was where we relaxed, networked, and gossiped. Historically, female Freedom Fighters used the salon to beautify *and* strategize undetected. So, since its creation, we have used the beauty shop to escape and solve real-world problems.

Secretly, Top of the World was an integral part of my and Goldie's criminal operation. Having a premier salon staffed with master stylists and sexy female barbers had given me direct access to drug dealers, celebrities, and athletes. The loose lips of their wives, girlfriends, and side chicks revealed conversations and incidents meant for pillow talk. I had dirt on all the L.A. shot callers, and my salon was primarily how I had gained access to the whereabouts of unsuspecting out-of-towners and robbed them of their cash and valuables.

Gold's Room, Goldie's strip club, and Top of the World were cash-only businesses, so I easily cleaned all the dirty money we stole. We had the perfect cover, and until Blaque, our operation was flawless.

I busted through the doors, ready to be transformed.

"*What* did you do to your head?" Shay screamed. "Hurry up and get your ass in this chair so I can fix it."

I took off my Chanel shades and twisted my hand. "Whatever. My afro is gorgeous."

Shay shook her head. "No, what makes an afro gorgeous is when it's neatly groomed and styled like Pam Grier's. Your hair is windblown from your topless Corvette and poofed from your man, Blaque, sweating it out. You *cannot* fool a real beautician, sweetie."

Everyone laughed hysterically, but I couldn't dispute it. "Whatever, heffa. Hook me up."

We decided on a natural look with a twist out, a cornrowed design on the left, and loose curls that dangled to my shoulder. Once Shay washed, conditioned, and styled my hair with her magical fingers, we high-fived at the African Goddess look she had created.

She smiled. "Now you're ready for the world, boss lady."

I slid the much-deserved hundred-dollar tip into her pocket and then scanned the room with my eyes until they locked with Tanya. She immediately looked away and continued meticulously sweeping up the hair in her area from her last client. Just from the way she avoided eye contact with me, I could tell she still felt some type of way from our previous interaction when I checked her about Blaque.

I cleared my throat. "Ladies, first I would like to publicly apologize to Tanya for my behavior last week when I accused her of pushing up on my man. That is not like me. I set a bad example and acted very unprofessionally. So, my bad."

Tanya looked at me as she kept sweeping. "It's cool, boss lady. Don't worry about it."

"No, Tanya, it wasn't cool. So, again, I apologize. I also want to acknowledge that you are the highest producer in the shop, always on time, and your barbers are on point. Therefore, I'm promoting you to manager. You are more than deserving. I have some things to finish up first but meet me in my office in a couple of hours so we can discuss the details."

Shay cut her eyes and muttered, "Oh, *hell* nah."

I ignored Shay's displeasure. She and everyone else knew Tanya deserved it. Shay was my girl and an excellent stylist, but Top of the World was a business, and I was the boss. Tanya was the best fit for the position because she was the first one at the shop every day and the last to leave. Plus, since I had started spending less time at the shop, I needed a manager to oversee the staff and operations. Regardless of how things turned between Blaque and me, I needed to make sure my investment was taken care of during my absence.

My cell phone chimed and vibrated on my desk. I looked at the screen and saw it was Goldie calling.

"Hey, brother."

"Where are you?"

I sucked my teeth. "Damn, can I get a hello back? I'm at the shop finishing up things before I head to Jamaica."

"My bad, hello. Okay, I'll be there in five."

Minutes later, Goldie busted into my office wearing a big smile.

"What up, sis?"

I got up and walked around my desk to hug him. "Why do you keep busting up in here like your five-o?" I said. "What have you been up to?"

I returned to my seat, and he relaxed in the chair across from me.

"Nothing new. I'm ready for you to outline the plan so I can handle business like we planned. It's bada bing, bada boom time."

I shook my head. "Goldie, I told you that I can't steal from Blaque. I'm in love with him."

"So, you're choosing a nigga you've just met over family? After all the shit you, me, and Mama have been through?"

Tears fell down my face when I thought of Nike's death and Daddy being locked up.

"We could pay off Mama's house and set her and Pops up for retirement when he gets out," Goldie said, pulling my heartstrings like a professional harp player.

When he realized he had my attention, he pressed deeper.

"Pearle, the replica looks just like the original. All you have to do is keep your man away long enough for me to switch it out. His whipped ass won't know the difference."

"Trust me, he will know. He looks at that painting every day. Plus, Blaque's house has hidden doors, cameras, and extensive security."

"Does he ever leave the house unattended?"

"No, not really."

"His buff ass doesn't run or work out by himself?"

"No," I answered. "Someone is always watching him. You won't be able to do this without getting caught."

"I'm sure he chills at your house alone."

"Yeah. So?"

"I want to know how he moves in case we need a plan C."

"Plan C is me finding our way out of this mess without pissing off the cartel and betraying my man."

He got up and put his hands on my shoulders. "Pearle, I need you to remember Blaque's business and that we're under contract with the Escobars. We have less than a week left, and this is not a game of spades. We cannot renege on a Columbian cartel without consequence. Don't you remember what they did to that dude in the limo?"

"I've been trying to forget."

"Just look at the replica. We'll discuss Blaque's schedule when you get back."

He ran out of my office and returned with a long tube, placing it on my desk. I stared into his trusting eyes and pictured Blaque's trusting face. Feeling torn, I dropped my head on my desk.

"You can do it, *Poison*. Oh, and Mama said you better come see her before you leave the country, or she'll beat your ass. Love you."

He kissed my cheek and ran out of the door before I could further protest his plan. Frustrated, I stomped to my office closet and tossed the replica in the corner.

After I caught up on business at the shop, I went to visit Mommy and then went home to pack. I finished just in time; Blaque rang my condo's doorbell shortly after I placed the last piece inside my luggage and zipped it up. His muscular physique and caramel skin looked extra creamy. He wore tan shorts and a Gucci off-white, short-sleeved button-up. His smooth skin and smile glistened.

"Hey, handsome."

Blaque's eyes glowed when we kissed. He ran his fingers through my curls.

"You look beautiful. I love your hair."

Blue grabbed my luggage. "What's up, Pearle?"

"Hey, Blue. What are you going to do while Blaque is gone?"

"Work. Just because the boss is away doesn't mean I get to play," he replied, and the three of us laughed while walking to the car.

As we started on our way to the airport, my mind got lost in the palm trees while staring out the window.

Blaque gently stroked my face. "You're quiet. What's wrong?"

Guilt was overcoming me, almost to the point of being unbearable.

"Work stress," I half lied. "I promoted Tanya to manager today to take a load off."

He pulled me onto his lap and kissed me along my clavicle. "Uh-uh, remember we agreed to leave work behind. Positive vibes only on our way to Jamaica. Everyting's irie. Leave that shit here in L.A."

He let the window down, and just like magic, negative ions flew out of me and into the smog.

My trip to Jamaica would be my first time outside L.A. I realized I'd never been to the airport. Blue pulled up to a small hangar next to LAX and carried our bags to a black jet with white trim that awaited us. Wearing our Chanel and Gucci shades, we walked onto the plane like superstars.

My life with Blaque was one I'd only dreamt about; every moment felt like a fantasy. We were the only passengers, along with one flight attendant and the pilot. Blue, Keith, and his other security stayed in L.A. since the Laurent family had extensive protection in Jamaica.

Upon boarding the airplane, my feet stepped onto marble flooring that faced a fridge and bar. To the left was the cockpit where the pilot, a tall, brown-skinned man who looked to be in his late forties, sat with a beautiful chocolate-complexioned flight attendant with long, model legs. Turning right, we moved along the plush red carpet, passing four black leather seats—each with a desk. A long, black leather couch that converted to a bed faced a pole.

We sat across from each other in seats next to the window, and seconds later, the flight attendant handed us warm towels and drinks.

"One dirty martini and one Crown on the rocks. I'll be up front with Dan. Holler if you need anything," she said, then disappeared behind the cockpit door.

Blaque and I'd seen each other every day since we met, and our chemistry was stable and strong. He coached me like a new rookie since I had never flown before. Every bump and dip scared me. He laughed as I dug my nails into his hand while we ascended. After we hit cruising altitude and were finally sailing smoothly, I felt comfortable enough to roam the cabin.

Blaque followed me to the stripper pole and lounged on the leather sofa.

"There's no telling what's been on this thing," I commented, examining the pole. "Is it clean?"

He attempted to grab me, but I swung away sexily on the pole.

"Play some music. I'm feeling freaky."

Blaque pulled a wad of money from his pocket. "I have the perfect song for you. How much for a lap dance?"

I stretched my legs and arms. "You can't afford me, baby."

Through the speakers, Blaque blasted Adina Howard. As she sang seductively about her t-shirt and panties, I slowly rolled my body. His eyes followed me to the ground. I worked my way back up and swung around the pole like a professional firefighter. Then I flipped upside down in a split. Blaque popped out of his seat like popcorn, not caring about spilling his drink on the floor.

"Oh, my God!" he hollered.

Smiling at his reaction, I maneuvered and switched my body into different power holds while he created a rainstorm of hundreds. He stood mesmerized, and after a few acrobatic tricks, I placed his hands around my waist and danced slowly on his lap.

"I told you, you can't afford me, baby."

"Pearle, you got a nigga speechless," he moaned in my ear. "Do you have another profession you forgot to mention? I promise I won't judge, baby."

I turned around. "No, Blaque. My brother owns a strip club, remember? I learned a few tricks from his dancers."

"*Damn*, you're the one." Dollars flew over my head and onto the floor.

While rolling out of my dress for my finale, I lost my balance and crashed into the floor headfirst. Blaque quickly scooped me off the floor, but I ended up falling again—this time with him landing on top of me. I was in complete darkness and could not see anything in front of me; my dress covered my eyes like a blindfold. I screamed and wobbled, with Blaque as my rocky support and guide. Still blinded by my dress, I was never happier to feel the comfort of a leather seat under my ass.

"Sorry about that, Mr. Savage," the pilot's voice came through the speaker. "Please keep your seatbelts fastened. We've just entered unexpected turbulence."

Suddenly, the plane twisted, and my ass slid off the leather and crashed onto the floor. Blaque grabbed my arms and pulled me up next to him. When I felt the seatbelt secure across my lap, I exhaled. Finally, I uncovered my eyes and draped my dress around my neck like a scarf. Blaque calmly held my hand and prayed.

After he finished, I yelled, "Amen! Lord, help us!"

We were like lettuce being tossed around in a large salad bowl. The plane dipped, dove, and twisted. The seat belt secured us somewhat, but my heart felt like it flung outside my chest and flew freely somewhere within the cabin. My loose breasts flopped around carelessly; my head and neck throbbed from the smacks to the floor. Then like a California earthquake, there was a final rumble, followed by stillness as if nothing had happened.

"We've started our descent into Norman Manley International Airport," the pilot announced. "Please stay in your seats."

Blaque kissed my hand and fixed my dress. "It's over, baby. You can open your eyes."

"I'm not sure how I'm getting back home, because I'm *never* flying again."

"Baby, that was normal. We hit a small pocket of rough air."

"Well, rough air is stupid."

Once we landed, I thanked Dan for bringing us safely to the ground. When we stepped onto the hot tarmac, the blazing sun hit my face, and I deeply inhaled the pollution-free Jamaican air. I felt freer than I had ever felt before in life.

CHAPTER 16
WELCOME TO JAMROCK

PEARLE MONALISE BROWN
JAMAICA 1999

AFTER BLINKING SEVERAL times, I focused on the two black Escalades sitting in the middle of heavily-armed guards in jeeps on the tarmac. The artillery was designed for battle. Like at LAX, we were in a private hangar next to the Kingston airport. The doors of the Escalades opened, and billows of smoky haze escaped. In slow motion, two presidential-type men walked toward us—both tall, dark, and strong like Blue Mahoe trees. One man was nicely dressed in a tan linen short-sleeved shirt and matching pants with brown dress shoes. A large golden cross glistened from his thick chain necklace.

"Wha gwan! Good to see you, nephew. Who's this woman?" he asked, his voice loud like thunder as he gave Blaque a bear hug. Then he smiled and said, "No, my lady, I'm just playing with you. Nice to meet you, Pearle."

I smiled back as he kissed my hand.

"Hello, Mr. Laurent."

He shook his head. "No, call me Winston. This here's mi brotheren, Delroy."

Delroy was a slightly younger, slimmer version of Winston. He was casually dressed in khaki shorts and a light blue short-sleeved button-up, and his dreadlocked hair hung past his shoulders. The sun's rays reflected off his jewelry, which consisted of a diamond watch, huge stud earrings, and a platinum chain bearing a diamond cross.

Delroy hugged me after embracing Blaque. "Nice to meet you, Pearle. You are beautiful. What are you doing with this *ugly* man?"

They laughed, and we walked together to the car. Guards appeared out of nowhere and opened the doors, then magically disappeared.

Blaque's phone rang, but he turned it off. If I had to guess, I would say it was because he didn't want anyone drawing his attention away from me. At least, that's what I was hoping was the reason.

"Baby, don't pay them no mind," he told me, grabbing my hand. "They *think* they're funny and joke too much."

Uncle Delroy laughed. "We have fun, Pearle, and mean no harm. Not unless you are trying to harm one of ours."

I smiled, but deep inside, I was nervous, thinking about what my plans were when I first met Blaque.

"No worries," I responded. "Everyting's irie."

"Aye. I like you already," Winston shouted, then added, "Blaque, we have to take you to our sister first, or she'll kill us."

The amount of security that surrounded us was hard to digest. The guards openly carried semi-automatic rifles and machetes like we were at war. Once we started our drive, we passed brightly-colored train boxcars on the right side of the road, each covered with wood and graffiti. On rocking chairs, families sat outside in front of their makeshift doors.

We stopped at a traffic light, and peddlers swarmed the cars like bees, pushing to sell their different products from backpacks and knapsacks. When the light turned green, we cruised past several rainbow-colored shacks. Many were inhabited, although construction had yet to be completed.

"Winston, do people actually live in those houses? The roof isn't finished."

"Yeah. Once they buy the land, they build their homes in stages. As they get money, they build one room at a time until the entire house is complete. It could take years."

"What happens when it rains?" I asked.

No one answered. When I asked a second time, they only shrugged. Blaque's phone rang again, and once again, he ignored it.

We passed liquor stores, abandoned buildings with busted windows, litter-filled streets, and numerous churches. Police patrolled the impoverished streets flooded with hustlers, street vendors, and locals.

Everyone moved quickly on foot and bikes. When my head almost hit the roof from another deep dive into a pothole, my brain echoed DJ Quik, and I sang to myself, *Kingston "is just like Compton."* We zoomed past Blue Mahoe trees, rocking and swaying like seesaws on a winding red road up a hill, and arrived in a neighborhood called Red Hills. Blaque and his uncles' conversations continued unaffected with thick Jamaican accents. I was a foreigner and could no longer decipher their words. Cigar and marijuana smoke engulfed us, and my brain buzzed from the contact. The bumpiness triggered seasickness that swept over me, causing me to relive the violent turbulence from the earlier plane ride. I felt like I needed air.

My hand firmly gripped the door handle, and my mind screamed, *Where the hell are we, and where the fuck are we going?*

After a few more bumps, we rolled past large mansions and through a large iron gate that invited us in. Eight vehicles were parked on the square concrete pavement. The tan and orange Spanish-style mansion was surrounded by dancing palm trees and exotic flowers.

Blaque, Winston, Delroy, and I walked through a white iron gate and were greeted by a tall, strikingly beautiful, light, brown-skinned woman dressed in a bright purple floral dress. Blaque swept her off her feet and spun her around like a ragdoll.

"Blaque, put me down now, crazy boy!" the woman screamed in a deep Jamaican accent.

He placed her on her feet and kissed her cheek. "Hey, Mama. I missed you. You look so pretty."

She examined his face. "I missed you, too. You look skinny. Is Keith feeding you?"

A handsome, deep-voiced, older, darker version of Blaque walked over. "That man looks strong and healthy. You just want to fuss over him. What's up, son?"

Blaque and his father embraced and performed a quick secret handshake.

Blaque grabbed my hand. "Mama and Pops, this is my beautiful woman, Pearle Monalise Brown."

His mother hugged me. "Nice to meet you, Pearle."

I smiled at her kind embrace. "Nice to meet you, Mr. and Mrs. Savage."

"You can call me and my husband Lilly and Chad."

Chad, Blaque's father, kissed Lillian on the lips. "Lilly, we need to handle business for a couple hours."

Blaque grabbed my hand. "Let's go, baby. We'll drop you off at my house."

Lilly snapped. "No way. She'll stay here with me. You cook, Pearle?"

I nodded. "Yes, ma'am, and I heard you make delicious plantains. Maybe you can teach me?"

She smiled at Blaque. "I like her already. Now *go*."

"Cool, then. I'll see you later, beautiful," Blaque told me.

After lifting my chin and softly kissing my lips, he and the troops stormed out.

Our lonely footsteps echoed in the empty grand foyer. Sunrays shot through the skylights, reflecting off the three jeweled chandeliers that hung beautifully from the high ceilings. The circular staircase was black with gold details extending to the top level. Lilly and I walked past the simple living room that held three sizeable brown leather sofas in front of a fireplace.

Through a tall archway, there was an enormous open kitchen with two stoves, two large refrigerators, and an extended kitchen island and bar with multiple seating. The kitchen housed a huge wooden table with ten place settings. Blaque had told me Lilly and Chad hosted large family gatherings and parties in the kitchen.

While Lilly and I prepped large amounts of food, she explained the importance of the ingredients. She showed me how to decipher a plantain's ripeness. As we prepared to clean and filet the fish, a young boy with the cutest chocolate face and pretty eyes ran into the room.

He wrapped his arms around Lilly's legs. "Grandma!"

She kissed his face. Next, he looked at me, wrapped his arms tightly around *my* legs, and rested his head on my thigh. "Hi, Miss."

A pregnant woman, who looked ready to give birth any day, trailed slowly behind him.

"Ace, that's enough." She looked at me. "You must be Pearle. Please excuse my flirtatious son. He takes after the mannish men in this family. I'm Chloe, Blaque's sister."

"It's okay. He's so cute." His bright, innocent eyes were adorable. "Nice to meet you. He looks like his uncle."

Ace smiled and rubbed my leg. "Thank you, Miss."

Chloe grabbed Ace's hand and hugged me. "You are very pretty."

"Chloe, so are you. Your whole family is beautiful. Congratulations on the baby. Boy or girl?"

"Thank you. I think it's a girl, but we'll see in a few weeks. I'm so ready to have this baby. I walk around on fire like an oven set on broil all day."

After she hugged and kissed Lilly, we talked like old friends while preparing a large assortment of Jamaican dishes. My nerves and tension eased from their immediate acceptance. Once we placed the food in the oven, his mother showed me old pictures of Blaque and Chloe. Their family's closeness and happiness were evident through the captured memories from the photos.

Chloe and Lilly watched me while I washed the dishes.

"Pearle, you are the first woman Blaque has brought around us."

"He told me that. I was nervous about meeting you guys, but everyone has been so nice."

His mother looked at me with cautious eyes. "It takes a *special* woman to be with men like them. They are like lions and fight hard to protect us. But most times, *they* need *us* to protect them from themselves. Do you understand?"

"Yes, ma'am."

"Blaque already told us he loves you. I know how damn picky he is, so if he loves you, we love you. That's how this family gets down."

Chloe smiled. "Plus, us women need to stick together to balance all the testosterone. It's even worse in Atlanta."

I laughed. "Trust me, I understand. I grew up with two brothers; the one who owns a gentlemen's club is my best friend. We hang out with his friends, and they are the most mannish men I know."

Ace jumped around with excitement. "Ooh, I want to go to a gentlemen's club. I'm a gentleman, and I love to dance."

Chloe kissed his forehead. "When you are grown, you can go, baby."

He frowned. "Grownups have the most fun."

"*Damn*, it smells good in here. My three favorite women are in the kitchen cooking it up."

Our heads turned. Blaque led the troops in, and the room was suddenly full. He embraced his sister and rubbed her belly. Then he hugged his mother and kissed her on the cheek. His phone rang, and his face stiffened hard as a statue. He ignored it.

I kissed him and massaged the stress lines from his forehead.

"Hey, handsome. Why aren't you answering your calls?"

Curiosity finally got the best of me, and I had to ask.

He looked irritated but smiled. "We agreed to leave bullshit in L.A."

Ace ran into his arms. "Uncle Blaque!"

Blaque tossed him in the air and spun him around before putting him back down.

Lilly prepared plates. "Are you guys ready to eat?"

Blaque pulled me close and kissed my lips. "I have a *big* appetite, so I stay hungry."

His mother popped him with a towel. "You better lick your plate clean, 'cause you look too skinny."

"That's not a problem, 'cause I only eat the best ingredients *and* never waste a drop. Do I, Pearle?"

Lilly popped him in the head. "Christian Laurent Savage!"

Chloe punched him, and he laughed.

"Hey, women, stop abusing my son just because he's not wasteful. That's a good quality in a man. The youth today are uneconomical. Do you hear that, Ace? Always eat everything on your plate."

Ace sat quietly on the floor, playing with a ball, and didn't answer.

Blaque took a bite of the plantains. "But only eat *high-quality* ingredients, Ace. Make sure you understand the recipe before you taste it."

Uncle Delroy laughed. "Looks like you're *lovin'* your new recipe."

Blaque stared at me. "The best flavors I've ever tasted."

All the men cackled like hyenas. Lilly, Chloe, and I shook our heads.

Uncle Winston placed his hand on Blaque's shoulder. "Nephew, you better lock up your fine China before someone tries to run off with it."

"Bumbaclot, I'll kill a nigga if he tries to put his hand anywhere near my plate."

All the men high-fived and roared with laughter.

I grabbed Blaque's face and pointed to his quiet nephew. "Blaque, stop it, crazy."

Blaque fanned a hand. "Baby, Ace isn't paying me any attention. He doesn't know what I'm talking about."

Ace looked at Blaque confidently. "Yes, I do, Uncle Blaque."

Chloe helped Ace up. "No, you don't, little boy. Let's sit at the table and eat."

Delroy grabbed Ace's other hand. "No, we want to hear the pickney."

Winston and the men bellowed in laughter.

Chloe threw her hands in the air and rolled her eyes.

"Give my nephew the floor." Blaque stood in front of Ace. "What is Uncle Blaque talking about?"

"Uncle Blaque is talkin' 'bout... "

The room went completely silent.

Blaque got on one knee. "Say it loud like a lion."

Ace did a full body roll like a caterpillar, stomped his right foot, then left foot, and beat his chest like a drum. "The Boom-Boom."

The men erupted into hysterical laughter and performed the Boom-Boom dance.

Blaque picked Ace up, and they ran around the kitchen. "That's right! The Boom-Boom!"

Ace high-fived all the men like he'd scored a touchdown.

Lilly popped Blaque in the head with her towel.

I folded my arms. "Blaque, that's *enough*."

"Ohhhh."

The room was quiet.

"You're right, baby." Blaque kneeled in front of his nephew. "Ace, my lil' man, we must always respect the ladies. So, absolutely no more Boom-Boom talk...until you're a teenager. Then it's Boom-Boom all the time!"

The hysteria started again.

Lilly yelled. "Enough fuckery. Time to eat. Chad, bless the food, *please*."

Immediately, we joined hands.

"Heavenly Father, thank you for good food, family, love, and the quality ingredients you've brought into our lives. Amen."

Snickers of laughter filled the room.

Lilly punched Chadwick in the arm. "Pearle, do you see why we need more women around? It's always like this with these men."

"Lilly, baby, I'm just thanking God for our blessings."

Blaque and Chadwick high-fived.

The smorgasbord of food looked surreal. Our stomachs craved to demolish the ackee and salt fish, rice and peas, beef patties, and fried plantains. My plate was the first cleaned, and I sipped my freshly-squeezed lemonade while everyone else ate.

"Lilly, how did you give Blaque his nickname?"

She took a slow sip of her lemonade. "Well, the rumor is that when Blaque was younger, he blacked an eye with one punch."

"No rumor, Mama. That's actual and factual."

Everyone laughed.

"I gave Christian his nickname when he was a baby because he looked white when he was born," Lilly continued. "He had pale skin, blue eyes, and sandy hair. People didn't believe he was ours."

Chadwick laughed. "Blaque looked like a white man had eaten from my plate."

Lilly punched him in the arm, and he kissed her hand. "Just jokes, Lilly baby. Don't abuse me."

"*Anyway*, I was tired of telling people my son was black, so I started calling him Blaque."

"After baking in the sun one long summer in Jamaica, my skin, hair, and eyes permanently got darker," Blaque chimed in. "I went back to Atlanta, and Mama didn't know who I was."

She laughed. "That is true. Blaque ran up to me at the airport with a big afro and darker skin. He grabbed my leg, and I said, 'Are you lost, lil' boy?' Then he looked at me with his new hazel eyes and said, 'It's me, Mama.' I felt so bad I didn't recognize my child."

Winston laughed out loud. "Lilly called me crying and asked me why I didn't tell her Blaque was black."

Chadwick laughed. "Hell, I was relieved he got color on him, 'cause that's when he started to look like me. I was tired of beating niggas' asses for questioning if I was his real daddy."

Lilly laughed. "Chad, stop exaggerating!"

"No exaggerations, Lilly baby. I beat ass. That's actual and factual."

Blaque high-fived Chadwick. "Damn right. I get it from my daddy."

"Well, Blaque looks like you, Chad," I said. "And so does Ace. You have strong genes."

Lilly turned on some reggae, and we laughed while drinking. Ace entertained us and danced in the middle of the kitchen. After we cleaned the kitchen, Chloe kissed Ace and told us goodbye.

"Mama, thanks for keeping Ace overnight so Phillip and I can go on a date. We have patients first thing in the morning, so I'll pick Ace up after work."

Blaque grabbed my hand, and we followed with our goodbyes.

Chadwick tossed Blaque a set of keys, and we got into a black Benz with red leather interior. I had enjoyed Blaque's family, but I was ready to unwind and have him to myself.

We hit the dark, rocky, winding roads. Two armed guards in a black Jeep trailed closely behind as we shook along the dirt path a few miles up and down long hills. With no streetlights to guide us, the black iron gate in front of his house seemed to appear out of nowhere.

The gates opened slowly, and we drove into the driveway of a small, one-story beach home illuminated with spotlights. The white house was small, cozy, and cute. It was the simplest thing I had seen since I'd met Blaque.

We rushed through the house, stripped out of our clothes, and showered the day away. The house was peaceful, and after a long day, we were ready to chill. So, we slid into swimwear to bask in the moonlight. Blaque poured us a glass of Jamaican rum on the rocks, and we melted onto the hammock that hung by the pool. We faced the ocean and chilled quietly, enjoying the song of the crashing Caribbean waves while holding each other under the constellations. The Jamaican night air was countryside fresh and blew over us like a cooling fan.

"Blaque, I want a tattoo," I randomly said.

"Really?"

I was nervous and buzzed. "Yes."

He studied me for a moment before going inside the house. He returned with his tattoo equipment and a table on wheels. My heart started racing as he positioned the table at the pool's edge.

"Where are you thinking?" I asked.

"Christian Blaque Savage across your body. That would be sexy."

I grabbed his face. "You know your Gangsta Boo would beat your ass."

"Do you trust me?" he asked.

"With my life."

"I do my best work when I freestyle." He spun me around. "I need to figure out where I want to put it."

"Where's your favorite part of my body?"

"Your lips." He smiled. "Both sets."

He gently placed me on the table. "I'll let your body tell me."

Slowly, he pulled down my bikini top and sucked my breasts. His tongue traveled down my stomach. With the help of his teeth, my bikini bottom slipped to my ankles. My legs spread across the table, and his tongue steadily moved down each leg to my feet, making my eyes roll back. After flipping me on my stomach, he started massaging my back. His mouth traveled down my spine and stopped at the small of my back, where he rubbed alcohol.

"My tongue led me to the spot above that sexy ass. Are you ready?"

I nodded and closed my eyes. The loud buzzing of the equipment made me nervous. When I sensed the needle was close, I winced.

"Blaque, wait. Will it hurt?"

"It will sting at first," he whispered. "But then your body will get used to it. You mustn't move once I start *por favor*."

After my tattoo artist explored every inch of my body with his mouth, he tattooed his love permanently into my soul. The tattoo pen stung and scratched the skin on the small of my back; his steady hand etched artistry from his mind and onto my skin—his canvas.

There was a sudden stillness before he rubbed my back with alcohol.

"The tattoo is done. Baby, you are the perfect muse."

He pulled me inside and turned my back to the mirror. In the crease between my lower back were wings in the shape of a heart, adorned with a string of pearls wrapped around a cross.

Blaque kissed me gently on the lips. His finger grazed across the artwork.

"This symbolizes faith, love, and protection. Pearls are a symbol of wisdom and loyalty, and—"

Before he could fully explain his masterpiece, tears were falling down my face. I wanted to confess my devious plot. He needed to know.

"Blaque, I love you so much, but there is something I need—"

He placed a finger on my lips. "Shhh. Don't talk. Instead, let me feel how much you love me."

That night, Blaque made love to me for hours on end. Any drop of betrayal I had left vanished, and he fell asleep drenched in my undying loyalty.

CHAPTER 17
IN TOO DEEP

CHRISTIAN "BLAQUE" LAURENT SAVAGE

SWEAT POURED DOWN *my body; my heart pounded in my chest. I was running faster than I'd ever run before. I turned the corner and looked back to see who was chasing me. Before I saw his face, I tripped backwards. Before I fell, I reached up, and a strong hand grabbed my wrist. We locked eyes, and the man who saved me from falling was me. We frowned at each other, and he let go. I fell into an endless pit surrounded by darkness. I tried to breathe, but there was no air. I tried to scream, but there was no sound. I kept falling, and before hitting the bottom, my body jerked.*

I woke up and inhaled the soothing scent of roses.

Pearle stroked my face. "Babe, are you okay?"

I squeezed her tightly against my chest and exhaled. She aroused all five senses— beauty and undeniable sex appeal to my sight, honey flavor to my tastebuds, sultry voice to my ears, smell of sweet roses to my nose, and silky skin to my touch.

Her soft lips and smooth legs brushed against me. "Did you have another nightmare?"

I kissed her forehead. "I'm up now and need to get moving. I have a busy day today."

She rolled off my body and drifted back to sleep.

My phone rang, and I ignored the call. It was Walker again. After getting dressed, I stared at the man in the mirror. I had scuba dived into the depth of the sea, where everything was black, and wondered if I had enough air to rise to the surface. I closed my eyes and took a deep breath. Suddenly, Pearle's warm arms wrapped around my chest.

She smiled, wrapped in a satin sheet like a goddess.

"Damn, my man is fine as hell."

"You'd better back up before I throw your sexy ass on this sink. You're lucky I have a full workday and don't want to be late." I kissed her neck. "When I get back, I'm taking you to a dancehall downtown."

"I love reggae. Do I get cute or sexy?"

I smacked her ass. "I don't know, woman. Your cute *is* sexy."

The Benz drove like a hooptie on the rocky road before arriving at a large group of industrial warehouses. My uncles had picked the remote location tucked deep in the sugar cane fields where our enslaved ancestors had labored for hundreds of years. We planned to make millions per week in the same fields our kinsmen had shed blood, sweat, and tears with no respiration or restitution.

My family owned a transportation company that moved cargo, mostly Jamaican sugar, by the ton to and from the U.S. We had just added cocaine to the international freight since my uncles were already experts at smuggling drugs across Jamaica. Our execution plan was perfect. We had experience and access to all the major distribution channels from the legit business model.

The humidity was thick; sweat drained profusely from every pore in my body. I dabbed at my forehead with a handkerchief before pulling out my laptop and opening my report that provided initial orders, refills, and weekly and monthly projections by L.A. hood. I created a spreadsheet analysis based on in-depth conversations with the kings of Pasadena, Compton, Watts, Englewood, and Hollywood. Kilos of cocaine would be camouflaged in large cargo beds and shipped to Los Angeles for distribution.

Our total operation included Kingston, Atlanta, Harlem, and the Midwest in cities our family dominated. Our enterprise was projected to gross over $57 billion in the first year, a small percentage of the most powerful drug trafficking cartels in the world. Countries like Columbia move hundreds of billions into the U.S. every year. Like any other black-owned business, we worked harder and smarter for smaller percentages.

Staring at my laptop's screen, I double-checked the loads against the orders to ensure the weights were accurate.

My clothes weighed me down. I was drenched in sweat.

My father came over. "Blaque, what's wrong?"

I wiped my forehead. "Pops, there's no air in this place. I'm hot as hell."

He put his hand on my shoulder. "Son, what are you talking about? The air conditioner is on full blast. Look, you did an excellent job setting up this whole operation, and I'm very proud of you, but your uncles and I will take it from here. You focus on L.A. and be ready for shipment."

"Yeah, mi Lion," Uncle Winston chimed in. "Go home to your pretty woman and enjoy your last night in Jamaica."

"No, I should be here."

"Son, we've been doing this for decades. We've got you."

Uncle Delroy handed me a bag filled with weed and cigars. "Yeah, boss, get some *Boom-Boom* and smoke this ganja."

We laughed hysterically as they walked me to the Benz.

Pops slid into the passenger seat. "Son, are you sure you're okay?"

"The lack of sleep is catching up to me, I guess."

"I know that feeling. Relax and get some rest. I love you."

"Love you, Pops."

We hugged, and he got out of the car. Like a pressure cooker, the water was boiling, but I had no plans of removing the top even though the force was mounting.

When I made it home, all I wanted to do was hit the shower. I had never felt so stressed and was losing control. I started with intense, heated streams of water followed by ice-cold water. The tension was buried much deeper.

I got out of the shower and dressed in the bedroom. Then I realized I hadn't seen Pearle since I'd been home. I searched the house and pool area, but she was nowhere to be found. I continued calling her name as I went to grab my guns. Still, she didn't respond. I ran outside to where security looked carelessly relaxed in front of the house.

"Did y'all take eyes off Pearle?" I yelled, ready to kill them.

"No, boss," one of the guards responded leisurely.

Fury rose to the top of my head. Before I'd known it, I lifted my Glock and pointed it directly at them. "Then where the fuck is she?"

They both looked at me like I was a madman. "She's there, boss, on the beach."

My eyes went from them to Pearle and back to them. I flashed an uneasy smile and tucked the gun away.

"Damn, my bad."

As I walked off, my phone rang, and I ignored Walker's call for what seemed like the hundredth time.

I went to the kitchen, swallowed a double shot of Jamaican rum, and then splashed cold water on my face. The alcohol rushed through my veins, lifting the weight from my shoulders a bit.

Outside, Pearle puffed on a cigar. She was relaxed on a lounge chair in the sand with one hand above her head. Her legs glistened in her denim cut-off shorts. One leg was extended, and the other was propped on the arm of the chair. She wore a red bikini top. Her skin was sun-kissed with a golden glow.

In a state of serenity, she stared at the water, unaware of how much I admired her beauty. Her natural curls blew in the wind. Her aura pulled me toward her with its strong magnetic force. The closer I got, the more positive energy I felt. All the negativity dissipated into the atmosphere when I stood over her.

"What's up, sexy?" I said, sliding next to her on the lounge chair.

She smiled and rested her head on my shoulder. "Hey, handsome. I wasn't expecting you until later."

I kissed her lips, and she handed me her cigar filled with fresh Jamaican ganja. I exhaled the smoke into the sky.

"I told you that I'm addicted to you. I can't stay away too long. What have you been up to?"

She placed her arms and legs around me. "I've been staring at the ocean all day. It's so peaceful."

"Yeah, it's peaceful here, but where we're going, it can get chaotic, especially at night."

I helped her up, pulled out my Glock, and then moved to stand directly behind her.

"Do you know how to shoot, Gangsta Boo?"

She turned around and pressed her lips against mine. Her touch melted my muscles; I was surrendering to her kiss. Her arms wrapped around my waist, and I pulled her closer. Before I knew it, she'd grabbed my gun and made a perfect shot in the middle of the tree trunk in front of us.

"My daddy taught me real gangsters keep an extra gun in the back of their waist. You had your safety off. Very dangerous."

She put the safety on my .9mm and placed it back in my waistband.

The sound of guns cocking could be heard behind us, and we quickly turned around. Several barrels were pointed in our direction.

"Boss, we heard gunshots. Is everything okay?" a guard asked.

I smiled. "*Ya mon*. Go so I can tend to my woman."

They dipped off.

With every inch of my body turned on, I threw Pearle over my shoulder and ran across the sand, heading straight to my bedroom.

After some of the best stress-released sex of my life and a scalding shower, I threw on a black button-up and khaki shorts, then smoked the ganja Uncle Delroy gave me in the kitchen after my second double shot of rum. My phone rang. I now had eight missed calls from Agent Walker this day alone.

Pearle stepped out of the room wearing a cute black and white short skirt and a tank top, her flat abs and new tattoo on display.

"How do I look, Christian?" she asked.

I picked her up and admired the tanned glow on her face.

She smiled. "Do you like it when I call you that?"

"Baby, I like it when you call me Christian, Savage, Blaque, babe, king, *papi*, daddy, and even motherfucker," I whispered in her ear.

She screamed with laughter. "I do not call you *motherfucker*."

I placed her on her feet and kissed her. "How quickly you forgot. I can't wait to show and prove *it* again tonight. But first, I need to teach you a few moves at Top Kat," I said, handing her a .22 caliber handgun that she placed in her purse.

"*Ya mon*. I'm ready for *it*…and my dance lesson," she replied while looking down at my crotch, then strutted seductively to the door.

Hypnotized by the sway of her hips, I followed closely behind.

Since we planned to drink and smoke a lot that evening, I hired a driver for Pearle and me. During the ride downtown, we floated in the cloudy Benz to Damian "Jr. Gong" Marley's *Welcome to Jamrock* while joking and laughing.

Once we pulled up to Top Kat, a small dance hall club with nightly live bands, our two security guards escorted us inside. Bright red lights flashed, grey mist sprayed, and the strong scent of pure Jamaican green filled the room. Strings of small lights hung over our heads like stars. Top Kat was my favorite Kingston club because everyone danced. It was always thick and lively with the best reggae. Because it was a local hole in the wall, fights rarely jumped off.

The entire club felt like a hot sauna. We packed in like sardines and grooved to the drum and bass guitars. Pearle and I immediately went to the middle of the dance floor, where she started winding her hips and moving like a sexy snake. As usual, when I danced behind Pearle, my body excitedly responded to her sexy moves. She placed my hands around her smooth waist, and my mind was almost freed like my body.

My phone continuously vibrated in my pocket. I looked at the screen. Agent Walker had blown up my phone ever since I'd arrived in Kingston.

"I need to take this call, sexy," I whispered in my dancehall queen's ear.

She kissed my lips and rolled her body to Dawn Penn's "You Don't Love Me."

"Hurry back, Mr. Savage. I'm still waiting for my dance lesson."

I rushed to the club's back door and stood in the dark alley. My phone buzzed again. Annoyed, I answered. Suddenly, my face was covered with a wet cloth, and with one breath, I blacked out.

Groggy and in darkness, I awakened to deep, thick Jamaican accents. Beads of sweat dripped down my forehead, and I smelled the stench of musty funk from the nasty sack that covered my face. The bottom of the sack was tied tightly around my windpipe. My body received limited oxygen. I coughed. Finally, the sack was untied and removed. Once my vision adapted to the brightness of a surveillance van, I saw Special Agent David Walker sitting directly in front of me.

He crossed his legs. "Christian, I told you to answer the first time I called. I'm pissed because I had to leave my woman and country for you. You've compromised my operation with your heightened home security. Pearle's brother was supposed to easily be able to get in your home to steal the painting."

I hung my head with disappointment. I'd rather have been a victim taken by criminal abductors for ransom than snatched by the DEA again. The first scenario was a potential consequence for my life's chosen profession, and I would go out like a man. The other stripped away my credibility and went against what I stood for. Where I grew up, you never snitched.

"Walker, my family is going to look for me. This is hot."

Walker slowly pulled out several 8x10 photos of my uncles and cousins.

"Speaking of your family, do you remember what's at stake? Did you forget who I am and the power I possess?" He laughed and pulled out pictures of Pearle dressed in different wigs. "Or is she more important to you? Christian, I don't care about your crooked-ass family or your woman until your choices affect me and mine. You fell into Pearle's Venus flytrap like all the other flies, and your judgment is clouded. Since y'all are a package now, I own both of you."

I was infuriated. "You don't own her. I'll bring down the Escobar brothers without Pearle. If they want my painting, I'll set it up, but leave her out of it."

Walker clapped. "Fine. You have one week from today. Answer my calls on the first ring, or this will be how we communicate."

A brawny agent removed the cuffs from my wrists and kicked me out of the van like trash.

Walker laughed. "I love how *we* do shit over here. One week."

The door closed, and the van sped off. I was lost. I didn't know where I was or what to do. Walker was right about one thing—my judgment was clouded. I needed time to think.

I sat on the curb dumbfounded. Minutes later, a black Escalade followed by a line of Jeeps filled both sides of the street.

"Son, what the fuck happened?" Pops shouted. He rushed to my side to help me into the car. "Are you okay? I'm going to kill the dumb-ass guards that took their eyes off you."

I lay across the backseat. "I drank too much and passed out. Where am I?"

"Tell Lilly I found him. Call the search off," Pops yelled into the phone. Then he turned to me. "Blaque, talk to me. Are you in trouble?"

"Pops, I'm so exhausted."

He placed his arms around me. "Okay, rest. I got you."

Everything silenced, and my mind cleared. My life had become a mountain of mess since I'd been involved with Walker. He had hooked me and used everyone I loved as bait. I loved

Pearle too much to get her involved. She deserved her freedom; a life with me would keep her shackled. I painfully saw what I needed to do. Our lives were about to change forever, and I needed to bask in her love for one last night.

CHAPTER 18
THERE 4 YOU

PEARLE MONALISE BROWN

THE ROLLER COASTER dirt road and seasickness were more comforting than the loud chaos I'd just escaped at Blaque's parents' house. There was a Jamaican army of soldiers ready for battle under the command of Winston and Delroy. They hadn't figured out the enemy, but they were ready for war. Lilly was on her knees, praying the entire time.

"I knew something was wrong with him at the warehouse," Delroy said while pacing the floor.

Winston nodded. "He seemed anxious."

"I told you he looked skinny," Lilly expressed, shaking her head while still on her knees. "He was worried about something and not eating."

One of the security guards chimed in, "Boss pulled a gun on us earlier today."

Delroy was surprised. "Why the hell did he do that?"

I was shocked, as well. Blaque's mood the entire day had seemed normal to me.

The other guards pointed at me.

"He thought we took eyes off his woman," one explained. "But she was on the beach the entire time. Then we heard gunshots. Fearing he was in danger, we ran to him, but Boss told us to go away."

Immediately, all suspicious eyes turned towards me, and the interrogation began.

Winston raised an eyebrow. "Pearle, why were you guys shooting?"

"Blaque wanted to be sure I knew how to protect myself. There was only one shot fired."

Delroy looked puzzled. "Did he say you guys might be in trouble?"

"No, but he said the area we were going to could be dangerous."

Blaque's uncle moved closer to me. "Then what happened?"

I hesitated. Everyone stared.

"What next?" Winston thundered.

I cleared my throat. "We had sex."

"Then what?" Uncle Delroy questioned. "Did he seem different in bed?"

"What?" I asked, not believing he would ask me something so personal.

Everyone, including his mother, waited for me to respond.

"No," I finally replied, speaking through my teeth.

They fired off a series of questions like machine guns, yelling at me like I was a suspect.

"What did you talk about in the car? How long did you wait before you told security he was missing? How was his mood? Did he say who was on the phone? Where did he say he was going? Why did it take so long for you to tell someone he was missing? Why did you let him leave alone?"

Winston moved closer, and I started to cry. "Why are you crying?"

"I'm crying because I love Blaque," I yelled back. "I hate that he's missing, but it's not my fault. I don't ask him questions about who's calling him or where he's going. If he volunteers to share those things with me, then fine, but I'm not the type of woman who questions her man. We were having a good time dancing, drinking, and smoking. When Blaque left to take his call, he smiled and kissed me like he always does, so I didn't sense anything unusual. After I danced to two songs alone, I looked around the club in search of him. When I didn't see him, I alerted security. That's all I know."

Finally, Winston touched my shoulder and spoke with gentleness.

"Pearle, my nephew is very important to our family. He's a very powerful man, and we want to make sure nothing treacherous has happened. It's just that his behavior was strange the last *we* saw him, and you were the last person with him. What I do know is we're going to find him by any means necessary." Then he grabbed his TEC-9 and started pacing. "Whoever's responsible will pay in blood. I promise you that."

After the longest two hours of our lives, Chadwick called the house to report that they had found Blaque. When Winston hung up the phone, a wave of relief swept over the once anxious and panicked house, and Lilly immediately praised God.

On my way out, Lilly hugged me. "We both know Blaque's keeping something inside. Remember, we must protect our men from themselves. Please take care of him."

She kissed my cheek, and I jumped in the Jeep with three other guards. I knew Blaque's story had holes, but I was too ecstatic that he was safe and on his way to me.

Cars pulled into the driveway, and I ran outside immediately. Blaque walked quickly up the driveway with his father next to him. I jumped into his arms and wrapped myself around his body. When we reunited, no one and nothing else mattered. Blaque gave his father dap, closed the door, and carried me through the house while kissing all over my face.

"Take me to the bathroom," I whispered.

Once inside, I took off his clothes and walked him to the garden tub. I wanted to remove everything he had gone through. He sat quietly while I massaged his shoulders.

"Blaque, I was so scared, baby. Do you want to talk about what happened tonight?"

He shook his head, then pulled me into the tub and started sucking my hard nipples through my pink silk gown. After sliding off each strap, he softly kissed my shoulders, breasts, and neck. Each kiss lingered longer as he held me tightly in his arms. I stood up, and my drenched nightie dropped heavily into the water. Grabbing his hands, I guided him to the bedroom. He laid me down and savored every inch of my body with his lips. While holding my face in the palms of his hands, he stared into my eyes with a mixture of pain and love in his. He tried to speak, but no words came out.

I put my finger on his lips. "Blaque, I'm here for you. Everything is going to be okay. I love you."

He closed his eyes and kissed my finger. When I touched his face lightly with my fingertips, he opened his eyes and kissed both my hands, then wrapped them around his neck. When he plugged into me, our souls entered another realm, and we transferred currents of unconditional love until sunrise.

Just as I closed my eyes to fall asleep, Blaque snuggled behind me and whispered in my ear, "What are you thinking about?"

"Blaque, what happened to you?"

He kissed my back. "All I remember is stepping outside to take a call and waking up on the curb."

I turned around to face him. "Are you sure there is nothing else you want to tell me?"

"No," he replied and kissed my forehead.

"Babe, I'm so grateful you're okay. Your family was ready to go to war last night. I've never seen so many guns in my life. It was a crazy night."

He finally smiled. "Yeah, I love my people."

Blaque's phone rang, and I was mesmerized by his powerful physique when he stood to answer it. He listened intently. Suddenly, his smile and warmth disappeared. After a second call, he quickly took a shower, put on his clothes, and grabbed his guns.

He kissed my forehead and headed to the door. "I have to go. When I get back, be dressed so we can head to the airport."

"Okay. Love you," I called out to him.

The door slammed, and I was left lying there confused about what was happening. When I finally fell asleep, I could only pray I would find out before it was too late.

When I woke up, I dressed in a long floral dress with spaghetti straps and sandals, then went to the bar to make myself a rum punch before walking down to the beach. As I passed the two guards, they started following me to the outdoor patio, but I stopped them there. I wanted to be alone.

As I continued to the beach, something was different about the air. There was a crisp sweetness that hit my nose like fresh laundry. Blaque was right about Kingston's Caribbean Sea. She was prettier than California's Pacific, even though they both were fine as hell.

The spirit of the turquoise waves of the Caribbean whispered my name, calling me to the shore. I took off my sandals and sat on the sand with my rum. I closed my eyes as the waves massaged my feet, the wind tickled my skin, and the sun's rays kissed my face. I inhaled the saltwater, which purified my energy.

Kingston had its rough parts, but like Compton, I'd found a glorious shine beneath the hardened exterior. There was a strong gravitational pull to the people and culture that I connected with. Blaque's family shared a close bond, and their love for one another was as crystal clear as the native blue sea.

Fish swam around my ankles. Tying my dress around my hips, I followed the seduction. The ocean licked my thighs and sang sweet melodies in my ear. I danced in circles, with the fish nibbling at my knees. Kingston was making love to me, and I wanted more.

"Hello, my lady."

A deep voice interrupted my intimacy with the sexy sea. In front of me stood an older man with salt-and-pepper dreadlocks and beard. He floated on a tan paddleboat. He wore a green tank top, black shorts, and a seashell necklace around his neck.

I smiled at him. "Hello."

He touched the back of his boat. "Get in, my lady."

My guarded instinct would have normally told me to say hell no, but his eyes were gentle and covered with a kind wisdom that I trusted right away. So, I climbed aboard.

He handed me a beautiful peach seashell. "Look inside. There's pure ganja from Mother Earth in there."

Next, he gave me a lighter. Stuffed inside the seashell was a joint. I fired her up, and she had her way with me. He also handed me a coconut filled with rum that was so fresh it tasted like it had come directly from an oak barrel and poured through a sugar cane stalk. My body melted. Seashell Man paddled us around the corner of the island. To the left of us was the most beautiful blueish-green mountain with hills like a woman's perfect breasts. Pouring from her green forest center was a magnificent waterfall flowing strongly and steadily. As the strength of the waterfall hit the top of the ocean, foam and bubbles erupted like an orgasm at its highest peak. When Mother Earth's herbs and the coconut rum intensified my senses, I experienced Kingston's enchantment without barriers.

Suddenly, the temperature dropped, and I felt covered in ice. I looked up, and the baby blue sky had turned old navy. The boat rocked to the left and right like a cradle.

I looked around. A dark fog surrounded us, and the ocean waves were flapping in different directions. Water slapped against my legs. I froze with fear.

"What's happening?" I asked Seashell Man.

An angry wave headed towards us, and Seashell Man jabbed it with his paddle. We rode over it.

"Hold on, my lady," he commanded.

I regretfully grabbed each side of the boat and braced for a storm. *"Shit."*

A strong surge of air shoved the boat forward, and we lunged toward a dark cloud. I closed my eyes and screamed.

In a snap, the boat was floating calmly, and Mr. Seashell said, "We are here."

As I slowly opened my eyes, I saw the sun shining, and everything had returned to clear and calm.

"Where exactly are we?"

Dancing and splashing at the seaside were beautiful children in bright-colored clothing with rich, dark melanin—purified and angelic.

Mr. Seashell Man paddled the boat between a peach-colored church with a golden bell and a small yellow food cart. Enclosed around the island were tropical trees and reddish-orange dunes covered with patches of green. When I got out of the boat, a young girl placed a bright purple flower in my hair and handed me a pair of seashell earrings.

"Thank you, pretty girl, but I cannot accept those. I don't have any money," I said.

"Please," she said. "We live for Zion."

Struck by her baby face and grandmother eyes, I placed the earrings in my ears and told her, "Thank you."

Delicious aromas of sweet dumplings and spicy jerk traveled through my nostrils and distracted me from responsibility. I wanted to relish the flavors. The cook was a pleasantly plump Jamaican woman with pretty chocolate skin and a small afro adorned with a fuchsia flower. The same pretty seashell earrings the girl had given me dangled from each of her ears. She flashed a beautiful smile and spoke in a heavy accent that I surprisingly understood.

"Hey, honey. Do you want chicken and dumplings?"

My stomach growled. "Yes, ma'am."

In front of me was a plate with the biggest chicken legs I'd ever seen. They were covered in a spicy red sauce and freshly fried dumplings. I reached for it. We touched, and she snatched her hand away. The plate of food fell on the ground. Her smile turned to terror.

"What's wrong?" I asked.

"Let your gut guide your heart, my child," she whispered in a hurry, then raised her hands in the air.

Confused, I turned around. All the children were gone, and armed guards surrounded Mrs. Seashell and me. Mr. Seashell was face down inside his paddle boat and restrained with handcuffs.

I ran to the guards holding him down. "Please, let them go. They didn't do anything."

"No, my lady. Boss is waiting."

A guard helped Mrs. Seashell and me into a speedboat. Three guards and Mr. Seashell's boat roared behind us. Armed security on jet skis had us protected like a fortress.

What a mess, I thought while shaking my head.

We returned to the shore behind Blaque's house, and the guard helped me out of the boat. Blaque sprinted across the sand toward me like a track star, followed by his father and uncles in a dune buggy. I felt horrible, but the mixture of drugs, alcohol, and heat blurred my senses.

"Hi," I said, waving in slow motion.

He grabbed my face and then picked me up. "Pearle! Oh my God! What in the hell happened? Are you okay?"

"Yes."

"When we found your glass and shoes in the ocean, we thought you were pulled out to sea from that quick wind surge." He hugged me and kissed my forehead. "I thought something bad happened to you."

"I'm okay."

Blaque, Winston, Delroy, Chadwick, and a few guards surrounded me.

Blaque placed his hands on my shoulders. "Now, tell me what happened."

"I went with Mr. Seashell Man on his paddle boat."

Blaque raised his eyebrows. "You did what with who?"

"I went to an island with Mr. Seashell, and Mrs. Seashell tried to hand me a plate of jerk chicken and dumplings. Security showed up, scared her, and my food fell," I explained.

The spectators snickered, and Blaque folded his arms.

"Pearle, what in the *hell* are you talking about? Are you telling me, after what happened last night, that you got in a boat with a random seashell nigga? My mother and sister have been praying for you. My dad and uncles had the Kingston army looking for you, and I was two seconds from killing the niggas that lost you."

"Damn, when you put it like that…" I smacked my wrist. "Bad, Pearle."

Blaque pulled my face closer to him. "Are you high? Did that seashell nigga give you drugs?"

My speech slurred. "*Ya, mon.* I smoked fresh Mother Earth from his seashell and drank rum from his coconut."

Everyone except Blaque burst into laughter.

"You smoked and drank what from his what? You know what? It doesn't matter. This trip has been crazy. It's time to go."

A guard was holding Mr. Seashell by his arm, and another was standing next to Mrs. Seashell.

"Boss, what do you want us to do with them?"

"Nothing," I replied for Blaque. "They didn't do anything."

"Who are they?" Blaque asked his guard.

"Seashell nigga is actually The Healer, and Mrs. Seashell is his wife, The Seer. They are from the peninsula."

"The Healer and Seer are legends," Blaque said. "Release them."

Once the guard uncuffed Mr. Seashell, Blaque walked over to him and pulled out his wallet. He removed several bills and extended his hand. "I know of you, and I know you have saved a lot of people from illnesses, but you must be careful of who you let ride in your boat. You could've been killed today."

"Sorry, boss. Please, keep your money. God provides all we need," he said.

"At least let me pay for the food you dropped," Blaque told Mrs. Seashell.

She closed his handful of money and shut her eyes. When she reopened her eyes, her face was filled with solemnity.

"There's no need for money," she said, "We live for Zion."

Blaque placed his other hand over hers. "Please, tell me what you saw. I need to know."

She took her hand and placed it on his cheek. "Trust your gut, my lion."

"What about my heart?" he asked.

"You already know the answer."

They stood in front of each other, and she nodded before the guards guided her and The Healer to the speedboat. Blaque watched them roar away, then turned to me with a disappointed frown.

I reached for him. "She is not the Oracle, Neo. She told me the same damn thing."

He grabbed my hand. "Pearle, let's go."

When he tried to pull me away, I fell in the sand. I battled for sobriety, but intoxication won.

"No L.A. I like it 'ere in Jamaica."

Winston laughed a deep belly laugh. "So, we thought nephew got abducted, but he actually blacked out and walked for hours alone in a trance. We thought his woman drowned, but she got high and ate jerk chicken in a boat with a seashell nigga. I don't know what to say."

"Pearle, what in the hell is wrong with you?" Blaque asked.

"I'm sorry, but I'm *very* fucked up. My legs don't work anymore."

He shook his head and threw me over his shoulder.

I laughed uncontrollably. "Damn, *mi hombre es* so strong."

Making it to the car, Blaque placed me in the backseat.

"Tell Lilly and Chloe thank you for their prayers because I need it," I whispered, touching his bicep. "Blaque, I'm *Poison*."

Ignoring me, Blaque clicked my seatbelt, and I passed out.

LOS ANGELES, 1999

I blinked and felt warm leather seats underneath me. Looking over, I saw Blaque working quietly on his laptop next to me. Out the window, I noticed us gliding past 405 signs.

"Blaque, are we in L.A?"

"Yep."

"Did Mr. Seashell really happen?"

Blaque looked at my sandy feet, which had tracked Kingston onto his Bentley carpet.

"Yep."

I touched his hand. He was stiff and cold.

"I'm so sorry I embarrassed you in front of your family."

He continued typing and didn't look my way. "Yep."

"Will you forgive me?"

"Don't worry about it."

Leaning back, I ignored his rudeness for the remainder of the ride.

When we pulled up to my condo, Blue quickly carried my bags to my door and rushed back to the driver's seat. Blaque stood outside the car door on my side.

"Blaque, I don't have any shoes."

He shook his head and carried me to my door. I opened the door, and we walked in.

Blaque stared at me for a minute before pulling me to him. He lifted my chin and stroked my face. Then he planted a long kiss on my lips that jumpstarted my heart. Goosebumps raised on my entire body.

I grabbed his face. "I love you."

Without saying a word, he kissed my forehead and walked out of the door, leaving me in my foyer confused.

Blaque wasn't answering my calls and iced me the following day. He finally called me back that night.

"Pearle, I'm nearby. Can I stop by?"

"Of course."

Anticipation gave me butterflies. I hadn't seen him since we returned to L.A. Shay had hooked my hair up with a silk wrap, and I was dressed in a sexy white slip dress. When he arrived, I opened the door and could tell immediately that Blaque had disconnected from me. The inner light in his eyes was turned off, and he stood frozen in my foyer. In denial, I tried to hug him, but he backed away.

I crossed my arms. "Blaque, what's going on with you? Why are you so cold toward me?"

"You're not who I thought you were. It's over."

I stood speechless. "What?"

His gaze shifted to the floor. "I thought you were the one. I was wrong."

"Blaque, that's bullshit. Why are you doing this?"

"It happens to me with beautiful women. I fall in love quickly, and then I get bored and easily thrown off. I fall in and out of love all the time."

I was confused. "Bored? What the fuck are you talking about?"

He didn't answer or look at me.

"Look at me, dammit!" I screamed.

When he finally locked eyes with me, I started crying.

"Blaque, real love doesn't work like that. Are you telling me that you never loved me and all of this was bullshit?"

"Pearle, I don't love you. I'm sorry."

Tears fell from my eyes. "Then get out!" I screamed.

He stood still like a Buckingham Palace guard.

Blaque, get the *fuck* out of my house!"

He did an about-face and left. Slamming the door, I screamed, but my heart shattering was much louder.

CHAPTER 19
TRIGGERED

PEARLE MONALISE BROWN

THE BLAQUE GIG was the first time I had come unprepared for a role. The costly consequence was a loss of one million dollars and my heart. I'd given him exclusive VIP access to my body and a backstage pass to my soul, and he had violated his privileges.

After two days, I was permanently scarred but not damaged. At the salon, I immersed myself in work. I wore my new all-white Dolce and Gabbana shorts, blazer, and matching bra top, hoping my outfit would cover up the pain I felt inside. Unfortunately, it didn't.

Shay burst through my office door like the building was on fire and started flailing her rat tail comb in the air. "Boss lady, I'll stab his ass for you with this comb. Keith told me to stay out y'all business, but I will beat Blaque's ass for you. Hoes before bros."

"What are you talking about?"

"The client in my chair is Blaque's new bitch. I promise I didn't know. And he's in Tanya's chair getting a haircut."

"Let me guess. Her name is Jules."

Shay took off her earrings. "Yeah, that's her name. How do you want me to handle them?"

I waved my hand. "Fuck them. It doesn't surprise me that he wants to duplicate me, but it will never happen. He'd pay for strands of imitations when he had a *real* Pearle."

"Thank God. I really didn't want to lose Black Jesus of the

Hood. What do you want me to do about Jules' hair, though? I can fuck it up if you want me to. Just say the word."

"Shay, this is a business. You have a fabulous style reputation for consistency. Don't mess with your money or reputation for me or anyone else. You know Blaque is balling. So, hit him in the pockets. Upcharge his ass for every service, and call him out if he doesn't give you a good tip."

Shay laughed. "Boss lady, that is so *classy*. I'll make his ass pay," she said, then turned and walked back out the door.

After finishing my work, I approached the mirror in my office and stared at my reflection. *Is Blaque still in Tanya's chair?* My all-white outfit hugged my body in all the right places. I touched up my red lipstick and slipped on my red Jimmy Choo pumps. Then I grabbed my red Chanel bag and the shades he had bought. My silk wrap hung perfectly down my back like Aaliyah. I looked like a million bucks but felt like pennies. I couldn't believe he was intentionally hurting me, but at that moment, I only cared about what people saw. I sprayed one spritz of his favorite perfume, Flower Bomb, and switched into the salon area.

I walked over to Tanya, and we hugged.

"Tanya, you did a fabulous job this weekend. Everything looked great."

She smiled. "Thank you, boss lady."

Blaque couldn't resist me. From my peripheral vision, I could see his eyes moving up and down my body. He shifted uncomfortably in his seat.

My hips swayed side to side as I walked to the other side of the room. Tanya's other client said what I'm sure Blaque was thinking.

"*Damn*, you are fine as hell."

Smiling at my admirer, I replied, "Thank you."

Thirsty Jules from Blaque's yacht party sat in Shay's chair. She had on my exact outfit, only in black. I glared back at Blaque.

He was still staring. Our eyes locked, and I gave him a look as if to say, *Really, nigga? This is my replacement?*

Shay smacked my ass and sang. "You wear it better."

I glanced back at Blaque one last time. His hungry eyes couldn't hide his desire to consume my flesh. Mission accomplished, I threw on my shades, walked outside, and slid into my Corvette. Even with large lenses, Chanel couldn't hide the tears raining down my face.

Heartbroken, I needed my mama. I pulled my car into her driveway and felt better immediately. When I walked through the front door, a 11x14 family portrait of Mommy, Daddy, Goldie, Nike, and I greeted me. I loved that picture.

"Goldie, is that you?" Mommy yelled from the back of the house.

I walked down the hallway, past the kitchen and living room, and to the backyard where she was sitting on her white wooden rocking chair. The house looked identical to our childhood home. She was unaffected by time like she had been preserved in a capsule for Daddy's release.

"Pearle, you look like a fashion model."

I sat next to her, and we embraced. Her selfless love transmitted to me. One hug from Mommy and I was better.

I kissed her cheek. "Mommy, your beauty is timeless. You get prettier with time. Where are you going?"

"I'm coming from seeing your daddy. Today was my visitation day."

"You're glowing."

She smiled. "Thank God California allows conjugal visits."

"Mommy!"

"We're grown women. Is everything okay with you?"

I handed her a ceramic Kingston plate and a gold bracelet with a Jamaican flag charm Blaque had bought her.

"It's just one of those days," I replied while putting the bracelet on her wrist.

"Pearle, this bracelet is so pretty. Tell Christian I said thank you. I can't wait to meet him. I heard he's opening a club where people smoke cigars."

I fake smiled. "Yes, I'll let him know. How is Daddy? I'm going to see him Thursday."

The mention of Daddy made her light up. "He's good and would love to see you."

We rocked in peaceful silence. "How do you stay so committed?" I asked her.

"There's no way around love, baby. Niles made costly mistakes in the name of love— mistakes that haunt him, like when he and Nike were caught in that robbery. He lost a child, and his guilt nearly killed him. He loves all of us more than life, so I choose to stand by him until I'm six feet under."

"Is it hard to wait for him?"

She held my hand. "Of course. I get lonely, but I can't see myself with anyone else. We see each other every week, and his love letters keep me company."

"Wow! He still writes you? I didn't know that."

"Letters are how people used to communicate back in the day. He never stopped writing, even though we talk more often. When I feel lonely, I pull out a letter and experience his love in words."

My hand covered my heart. "Mommy, that's so romantic."

"I would much rather have his presence daily than his words, especially at night, but that's all we have for now."

"I want that kind of love."

"I pray your love journey is smoother than ours."

"*Te amo*, Mommy."

I'm sure she could sense something was wrong, but she didn't press me. Instead, she wrapped her loving arms around me and replied, "*Te amo,* baby."

Red Light was my faithful escape room. The smoke hit my face, and I inhaled the sweet funk of cigars and jasmine incense that filled the club. With my eyes closed, I sipped my extra dirty martini and floated on the "Summertime" sound waves from Ella Fitzgerald and Louis Armstrong. Each note of Louis' trumpet was a cloud, and Ella's voice moved me through the harmonious sky. The clouds hit my face like cool mist on a hot summer day, and the sun warmed my back. I was experiencing celestial jazzadise. Suddenly, I heard a familiar voice.

"Excuse me, Miss, is someone sitting here?"

I was slightly annoyed that I was jacked from my melodious jazz heaven, but I'd stop time for my brother.

"Goldie, do you use that line when you holler at females?"

We hugged, and he laughed.

"Hell no! I bet your man, Blaque, said that corny shit to your whipped ass, though. I use the reverse game with my women. I say shit like, 'What drink are you buying me, baby?'"

I screamed. "Liar! No, you don't."

"Shit, yes, I do. It works every time. Why didn't you call me when you made it back?"

"I'm sorry. How did you know I was here?"

"I'm a psychic."

"Whatever. Mommy told you."

Tommy walked over and placed another dirty martini on the table.

"What can I get you?" he asked Goldie.

"Hennessey on the rocks."

Tommy returned quickly with the drink, and Goldie took a sip before he continued the conversation.

"Why didn't you tell me your man, Blaque, is opening a cigar bar on Sunset?"

I sighed. "I'm already tired of hearing his name. Blaque is not my man anymore."

"Damn, what happened?"

"He broke up with me. He gave a lame excuse, but he meant it."

"He'll be back, *Poison*."

"I don't want him."

"Act like you do, and let's get this money. We have three days for you to get inside his house and switch his painting for the replica."

I shook my head. "I told you I wasn't going to rob him."

"Pearle, are you willing to die for this nigga? Because I'm not."

"I've re-evaluated the terms of our *contract* with the Escobars. I don't know any professionals that work for free, and they didn't give us any money. Therefore, we don't owe them shit."

He downed his drink. "Sis, the job is for a million dollars, and we shook on it. That's the contract."

I paused for a minute, thinking about everything at stake and what could be gained.

"Give me a couple of days to think it through. Like I said, his security is tight, and he's extra paranoid. For now, I need a break, so let me de-stress with my jazz, please."

"Cool. Two days. This place puts me to sleep anyway. I'm going to my club to watch my boo, Alyssa, flip upside down."

I shook my head. "Alyssa is your boo now? What happened to Tina?"

"Tina is my main boo," he replied while sliding Tommy a hundred-dollar bill.

I reclined in my seat with my martini and allowed Miles to groove through me. As usual, the dance floor was packed. When I closed my eyes, Blaque's face appeared. His hands were on my body and lips on my neck as we danced slowly to "Round Midnight."

I slammed my drink on the table. Blaque was blocking my mental freedom in the jazz nirvana I had created. I was held hostage and tortured by my thoughts of him.

Again, I shook my head. *Damn, the nigga took my jazz from me.*

Frustrated, I snatched my Chanel bag and headed home to dream him away, hopefully.

The next day was abnormally cold in Los Angeles. Snuggled in my sheep's wool blanket, I drank wine and ate shrimp fried rice delivered from my favorite Chinese restaurant while watching my favorite movie, *Set it Off.*

"Get him, Frankie," I screamed at the TV. "What's the *fucking* procedure when you have a *gun* to your head?" I recited my favorite line of the movie when Vivica A. Fox masterfully gets back at the detective.

My phone rang loudly in my ear, startling me. It was Goldie. "Hello."

"What are you doing?'

"Watching my favorite movie."

"*Set it Off?*"

"You know it. What's up?"

"Sis, I know you couldn't have made up with Blaque because he's wildin' out in my club *and* here with another chick. Do you want me to put his ass out?"

I balled up my fists. *Okay, nigga. First, you dumped me 'cause you claimed you were bored with me. Then you bring your fake-ass pearl— that fake Jules—to my salon. Now, you're at my brother's club actin' a damn fool? This nigga is really testing me.*

Blaque sparked a fire inside me that I didn't know existed. My anger flared through my veins and out the top of my head. Like my treasured movie, it was time to *set it off.*

"No. Fuck Blaque."

I slammed down the phone. I was so angry I couldn't see straight. He rocked my peace into turbulence, but unlike my helpless plane ride, I felt in control of this ride.

After throwing on my Tommy hoodie, loose-fitted Guess jeans, and Timberland boots, I took off my diamond studs and twisted my hair into a ponytail. Then like a race car driver in the Indy 500, I sped to Gold's Room.

The dark club was illuminated with different colored flashing lights. I scanned the room until Blaque appeared in my central vision, seated at a booth with his faux pearl. Jules was stuffed into a cheap, ill-fitting lime green dress and rocked my silk wrap but with extensions.

His dumb ass is spending money on a counterfeit.

Blaque was enjoying a lap dance with a big smile on his face. Alyssa, my brother's boo and favorite dancer, had skills like Diamond, Lisa Raye's character from the movie *Player's Club.* Jules, smoking a cigar next to him, participated in the C-notes rainstorm pouring over Alyssa.

With Blaque's security a few tables over and distracted by the girls who performed tricks and flips on the stage, I took it as my opportunity to strike. I lunged at Blaque's neck. Alyssa moved in the nick of time. Just like my daddy taught me—thumb secured with a tight fist, straight wrist, and quick punches thrown from my core and shoulder.

With his guard down, I catapulted my hardest punches non-stop to Blaque's face. I punched continuously like Laila Ali. By the time his security reacted to my attack, I had a firm grip on his shirt collar, which I snatched off in the process of them peeling me off of him. My body trembled, and my heart raced. I was infuriated and couldn't calm myself. Blaque's face was red as he stared at me stupidly.

"Blaque," I yelled, "get your disrespectful ass out and take your wannabe pearl, fake-ass Jules with you. Stay out of my city, nigga!"

Jules stood up. "Sup?"

I didn't move, praying she would jump so I could give her some of what I had just given to Blaque. "Sup?"

Goldie held me back. "Blaque, you heard my sister. Take your people and get the fuck out."

Blaque straightened his wrinkled shirt, which was now missing buttons. "It's cool. Jules, let's go. I was bored anyway."

Jules looked me up and down. "Pearle, all my jewels are real. You can verify with Blaque in the morning."

"No need, phony. You can keep my leftovers."

Blaque coolly strolled away with my replica on his arm. I couldn't believe he was the same man I had given myself to. Unable to restrain myself, I took off one of my Timberlands and launched the boot straight toward him, hitting my target perfectly in the back of his head. He wobbled forward and stopped. His guards turned quickly, but Blaque grabbed their arms.

"I hate you!" I screamed. "Don't bring your ass anywhere near Compton, or I'll fuck your world up."

Without saying a word, he turned back around and continued walking until he and his entourage were out the door.

I wish I could say I felt better, but I didn't. The few hard punches and the blow to his head didn't erase the hurt he had caused my heart.

Thursday was my visitation day at Los Angeles FCI. I hadn't seen my father in a month. When engineers designed the prison, they must not have considered visitation parking, because it was the smallest lot I'd ever seen for a facility of that size.

The main guard was gross and flirtatious. "What's your name, baby?"

"Pearle Brown."

He scanned his clipboard and checked my driver's license. "Damn, are you coming to see your man, baby?"

Annoyed, I fired back, "None of your married business. Niles Brown, please."

The prison staff conducted a thorough body and purse search to make sure visitors did not smuggle in goods from the outside. I always wore what I thought would help me get through the process quicker and not set off the metal detectors. This day, I had on a pink Juicy Couture tracksuit and carried a small clutch that held my bare necessities.

I entered the waiting room, which smelled like a combination of dirty diapers, cigarettes, cheap perfume, and baby powder. When I heard my name called, I went into the tight box with two side partitions that reminded me of a voter's booth at city hall. Daddy grabbed the phone and smiled from the other side of the glass.

His teeth shined bright white. "Hey, pretty girl. I like your hair."

I smiled back. "Thank you, Daddy. You look good, too—strong and healthy."

His skin was smooth with no wrinkles, and he had a fresh haircut. Like Mommy, he seemed unaged and in a time capsule.

"Yeah, I've been working out, and the food is not half bad. I got a new job as a librarian, so I've been reading a lot."

I was shocked. "Have you read anything good?"

"I just finished Nelson Mandela's book, *Long Walk to Freedom*. I highly recommend it. It changed my life. Life is hard in here, so you cannot allow your mind to be caged like your body."

I touched the glass. "I'm so proud of you, Daddy. I put money on your books. You can buy that book so you'll always have it."

"I heard your shop is doing well. I'm proud of you. I also heard you have a new man and are in love. Your mama said he owns a club or two in Atlanta and is opening more in L.A. Is he also a truck driver?"

Truck driver was code for drug dealer. We spoke this way because we knew all our conversations were recorded.

I sighed. "Yes, he drives a lot of really big trucks that carry large cargo, but we broke up. Mommy doesn't know, and I don't want to talk about it."

Like a protective father, he said, "Hey, don't keep that inside. I know your brother isn't any help with men and relationship issues. What happened?"

A tear escaped my eye and rolled slowly down my cheek.

"He broke up with me. One minute, it felt like he was in love with me. Then minutes later, he became icy and dumped me. Now, he's an asshole. So, it's no way I'll ever get back with him."

Daddy looked into my eyes. "Maybe he is an asshole. Or if that happened suddenly, maybe he got important information like the trucking business is going bankrupt. Or worse, a big competitor is threatening to take down his business. Either way, truck drivers know it's risky on the road, and when they break personal ties quickly, they usually want to protect the people they love from major trouble on the highway."

"Then why not tell the people they love there is possible danger instead of hurting and pushing them away?" I cried.

"Because, baby, the truck driver knows that once he tells the truth, especially if he has a devoted woman like your mother, she won't leave his side even if he begs her to. That scares the truck driver. He'd rather push her away and possibly drive off the cliff alone than see the woman he loves go down with him in the passenger seat. Do you feel me?"

Tears flowed like a river down my face. "Daddy, what should I do?"

"Baby girl, get with a doctor, engineer, or lawyer. Leave truck drivers alone. Trust me, that business is too dangerous, and their careers usually end early. So, they rarely see retirement. If the driver you love wants to roll solo, let him drive on that road alone. You deserve better. Now, pick up your pretty head. I love you. Come see me next week so we can continue."

Daddy's guard gave him the signal to end our visit.

I wiped my tears. "I love you so much, Daddy. Thank you."

He blew me a kiss and walked out.

CHAPTER 20
DANGEROUSLY IN LOVE

PEARLE MONALISE BROWN

MY UNIVERSE SHIFTED toward life before Blaque. No one uttered his name, and he was out of sight. Still, he lingered in my mind. Needing a distraction, I called Goldie about a quick job—a baller from St. Louis.

I overheard E, our new mark, brag about how he carried his diamonds and expensive jewelry in his Louis Vuitton suitcase. I sat inconspicuously at the bar in Gold's Room, dressed in sweats and a baseball cap. Like most of the out-of-town celebrities and ballers, E was in L.A. for the Tyson fight at Hollywood Arena. He asked Tina if there were any brown-skinned blondes with attitude and flavor she could send his way for a lap dance.

The thought of being someone else brought nostalgic feelings that I welcomed back with open arms. I wanted to forget Pearle. Being someone else gave me a high like a junkie. My Hollywood sign inspired me to be Natasha—a sexy, exotic video vixen from Oakland. I picked a color-blocked tank dress that dipped in the front and back. Looking in the mirror, I couldn't help but notice the tattoo that was a permanent and constant reminder of the feelings and person I wanted to vanish.

"Dammit!" I screamed and threw the dress across the room.

Blaque was like a Raider's defensive back. Even his invisible presence intercepted every aspect of my life. I was mad at myself for having a weak offense. I failed when I took my eye off the ball.

I searched for another sexy outfit for Natasha and found a hot pink, fitted, long-sleeved, off-the-shoulder mini dress. In my blonde wig and banging makeup job, I looked like a sexy black Barbie doll. With my new identity, I was ready to perform.

I took a cab to Club Zoom, the exclusive swanky spot hosting the fight night pre-party. My eyes scanned the room. The entire club was VIP, so we were granted free drinks from the bar and a table of appetizers that included iced shrimp cocktail, spring rolls, chicken strips, and roasted zucchini. The lights were dimmed, but the bright white walls made the room brighter. The deejay bumped Michel'le's "Nicety," my old school jam, in the background.

I took a seat at the bar. As planned, Goldie, who always watched my back, sat nearby. E slithered towards me within a minute of my leg cross and body roll.

With a toothpick in his mouth, he checked me out. "What's up, boo? What's your name?"

"Who wants to know?"

Removing the toothpick from his mouth, he leaned closer to my ear and said, "Me, sexy. Now, tell me your name."

My eyes explored his body before answering. "Natasha. What's yours?"

He sat down. "E. Damn, Natasha, you're fine as hell."

E was five-foot-nine, fair-skinned, stocky, and cute with curly brown hair. He wore a Ralph Lauren Polo sweater, jeans, and Timberland boots. Diamond studded earrings decorated his ears, and a platinum chain hung from his neck. He spoke with a slow southern drawl.

I knew right away I did not want to sleep with him. I wasn't over Blaque, and E didn't interest me in the least. Despite my resistance to his attempts, E was very aggressive. I signaled Goldie to the back of the room.

"Goldie, I'm not feeling this dude. Make sure you stay close. After the fight, we are going to his hotel room."

"Are you sure you want to do this, sis?"

I hesitated. "Yeah, but just keep your eyes on him."

"Don't worry; I got your back. I'll kill him before I let him hurt you," Goldie told me, and we parted ways like the Red Sea.

As people started leaving for the arena, E asked, "You smoke, right?"

"Yeah, weed."

"Cool. Let's chief in the parking lot and then head to the fight."

When we reached E's white Acura, he didn't open the door for me, but I wasn't surprised. As E got in behind the steering wheel, I noticed Goldie smiling in my peripheral. He knew I required any man I was interested in to open my door; it was one way I distinguished the men from the boys.

During the ride, I listened to him go on and on about nothingness. *This is going to be a long night*, I thought, stifling a yawn.

The arena was not far from Club Zoom. However, E continued past our turn.

"Hey, the arena is back there," I said.

His eyes searched the streets. "Yeah, I know, boo."

He continued to a sketchy area downtown.

"So, where are we going?" I asked, becoming nervous.

He flashed an evil grin. "We're going to have some fun before I take you to the main event."

I shook my head. "No, I want to go to the fight…now."

He pulled into a dark, empty lot and parked in the shadows. "I'll take you to the fight if you're nice to me."

I went for my purse, which held my .22 and cell phone, but he was able to get it away from me and threw it into the backseat.

I shook my head. "Hell no, nigga. It ain't that type of party."

As he moved closer, I panicked and reached for the door handle to escape, but he grabbed my waist. He yanked me towards him and started moving his hands up my thighs while I fought to wiggle free. I kicked, but he was strong and unaffected. Feeling helpless, I screamed. He snatched me harder, and the back of my head crashed into the door. My back smacked against the center console, and the emergency brake dug into my lower spine. A shooting pain radiated down the back of my legs. I prayed my Goldie would sweep in at any minute and save me.

E tried to kiss me. I moved my face and slapped him.

"No! Get your ass off me!"

I hit and kicked him, but like a slimy snake, he squirmed on top of me. His weight held my legs down.

I screamed at the top of my lungs and pushed him away. Holding my wrists, he continued slithering until he completely covered me with his body. My breaths became harder and shorter from the pressure of his dead weight on my chest and stomach.

"Help! Get off me, nigga!"

E ignored my resistance. I fought with all my strength but to no avail. My arms and legs turned into spaghetti. My screams silenced, and I entered a living daymare. My consciousness was shocked into a state of fear. I floated outside my body and became a spectator. I convinced myself that the woman who was about to be violated was my mannequin. E unzipped his pants, and I stiffened like a corpse, crossing my arms across my chest.

Suddenly, the driver's side window shattered.

E looked dumbfounded. "What the fuck?!?"

A fist came through the window and punched E's face repeatedly until he went limp. His body was snatched through the broken glass by his neck. As I grabbed my purse from the backseat, I heard more punches, tussling, and dragging. Then the movements outside subsided. I unlocked my door and opened it. After stumbling out of the car, I regained my balance and fixed my dress while my body shook uncontrollably. My heartbeat and breathing attempted to slow to their normal rhythms. I was safe and finally able to regain control of my speech and movements.

"Oh, my God, Goldie. Thank you. That was so scary."

A bloodied, light brown hand waited for me to grab hold.

I looked up dumbfounded. "What the fuck?"

Blaque stood strong like a king. I grabbed his hand, and he pulled me into his arms.

"Pearle, are you okay?"

I nodded, speechless.

The light was back in his eyes. "Let's go, baby."

Relief and gratitude swept over me, followed by a wave of confusion. "Blaque, what—"

He opened the door of a shiny black Maserati. "Get in, and I'll explain everything."

E lay unconscious on the ground between his white Acura and Blaque's security guard's Escalade as we pulled off.

We drove in silence for a while before Blaque asked, "Did he hurt you?"

My nerves were shot. "He scared the shit out of me, but I'll be okay. Thank you so much for your help. How did you know? Were you following me?"

His eyes were filled with anger. "That nigga, Effren, is from my old neighborhood. His bitch ass likes putting his hands on women."

I shuddered. "I thought he was from St. Louis."

"He moved there a few years ago." He looked disgusted. "I never liked his grimy ass."

We sped past my exit.

"Blaque, I truly appreciate you saving me, but we are not cool. Take me home."

As we continued our route toward Bel Air, he pleaded, "Baby, please give me a minute to explain."

"*Baby?*" I yelled. "Boy, please. I am not your baby anymore. You still haven't answered my questions. Why were you following me?"

He didn't answer. Instead, he looked at me with those puppy dog eyes that I found hard to resist.

I sucked my teeth. "Whatever, Blaque."

Irritated, I flipped down my passenger mirror and saw Natasha in my reflection. I had forgotten I was in disguise. I studied my face. Blaque watched me and tried to touch my cheek. I dodged and rolled my eyes.

He pulled the Maserati into the circular drive at his house and opened my door. He extended his blood-stained hand, but I slapped it away. We walked into the foyer, and I stood with my arms folded. When he tried to hug me, I hit him in the chest with my open palm.

"Blaque, explain. How did you know where I was? Why did you follow me?"

Blaque sighed. "I was at Club Zoom and followed you when Effren's car passed the arena. Like I told you, he's a bad dude. I knew you were in trouble from the way he looked at you."

"I didn't see you at Zoom."

"I was there for business and stayed out of your way. I didn't want you to beat my ass again." He walked toward me. "Can we please go to the kitchen? I need a drink."

He grabbed my hands.

"Please, Pearle."

Snatching my hands from his grasp, I followed him to the kitchen. I needed a drink myself; my nerves required alcohol to deescalate. He poured two drinks of Grey Goose, and we both chugged it down like water. He refilled our glasses. I folded my arms and awaited his promised explanation.

Blaque got closer, and I saw the hurt in his eyes.

"Pearle, I'm so sorry. I never should have—"

"Dumped me? Hurt me? I hate you, Blaque. You are foul for the way you treated me."

He tried to stroke my face, and I slapped away his hand again. He grabbed my hand, and I pulled away.

"Pearle, please," he begged. "I'm sorry. I've missed you so much. I'm in love with you."

"You're in love with your damn self. Call your precious *Jules*."

"Pearle, I'm in love with *you*. You're the only woman I want to be with. I can't breathe right without you."

With his every touch, I weakened and allowed his hand to linger longer.

"Listen, you saved me, but I won't jump into your arms like everything is okay. You were mean and disrespectful for no reason. You betrayed me and my trust and broke my heart, Blaque." Teardrops fell down my face as my heart cried. "I really loved you."

He gently kissed my forehead and wiped the tears from my face.

"Pearle, I know you loved me, and I'll never hurt you again. I was stupid. I love you so much. I'm so sorry, baby. Please, forgive me." His warm lips connected with the tears on my face. "Please, Pearle. I need you. I'm sick without you. Say you forgive me."

My eyes closed. I inhaled his coconut and cocoa butter scent.

I felt his charm starting to work on me. I had to be stronger.

Shaking my head, I moved his hands from my face and said, "No, you did me dirty, and you haven't explained anything. Why should I forgive you?"

"I thought I was protecting you."

"Protecting me from who?"

He looked down and backed up with tears in his eyes. "From me. I'm a CI for the DEA."

Blaque poured two more glasses of Grey Goose and started from the beginning. He explained how he had become entangled with Agent Walker to protect his family from prison.

I panicked and gulped the vodka from my glass. I knew his game had been too perfect. And the government knew about me and Goldie's operation. I was terrified.

"Are my brother and me going to prison?"

"No. They are after the Escobars."

I shook my head. "Red Light was a setup."

His eyes were glued on me. "Pearle, I fell in love with you when you walked into Red Light, and my love grew from that night. I knew your name and that you robbed dudes. I knew you planned to rob me for the Escobar brothers, but my feelings were real from the start."

"So you knew about Maxwell? The men in the black suits were the DEA?"

He nodded.

Damn. Everything suddenly made sense.

We guzzled the entire bottle. Blaque continued telling me about his phone calls, interactions, and meetings with Walker. Every time I asked a question, he would answer it slowly, adding a piece to the puzzle I had attempted to solve on my own. Most importantly, he detailed the DEA capture in Kingston and the events that interrupted the flow of our relationship. The more he explained, the faster the pieces of my heart came together and softened. My father's pep talk about finding a man with another profession was void. Blaque was my soulmate, and the danger of his ugly truth fueled my love.

One tear ran down his face. "Pearle, when Walker said he owned both of us, I felt like I was a slave in bondage, and I didn't want that life for you. I thought of my Basquiat painting and decided I would handle the Escobar brothers my way. I'd rather die a free man on my terms than a rat for the DEA. I pushed you away to protect you from all the bullshit that comes with me. I'm so sorry I hurt you. It nearly killed me, but when I saw you with that bum-ass nigga, Effren..." He punched the air like Tyson. "Damn, I should have killed his ass when I had the chance."

I grabbed his hands. "Blaque, cool down. First, you are not a rat or a slave. My daddy just told me how your body can be caged, but your mind freed. Walker pushed your buttons to mess with your head, baby. Don't make the DEA your enemy, because you won't win a war with the government." I grabbed his face. "When was the last time you meditated? You have to clear your brain and figure out a better way with that brilliant mind of yours."

Blaque's arms wrapped tightly around my waist, and he laid his head on my chest.

I rubbed the deep ocean waves on his head. "Who else knows?"

"Only you. I'm so tired, baby."

"I got you. Let's go upstairs."

"Pearle, I don't deserve you."

"You need someone to have your back while you protect everyone in the kingdom. Don't push me away again. I love everything that comes with you, including the DEA," I said while wiping the tears from his face.

Blaque took off my wig and ran his fingers through my hair.

I felt his devotion through his kiss. He swept me into his arms, carried me up the marble staircase to his bedroom, and lay me on his bed.

"I have never cried before in my entire life. Pearle Monalise Brown, there's no turning back. It's you and me. Neo and Trinity forever, baby. I will die loving you."

As our overpowering desire to make love took over, Blaque pulled my panties to the side and entered me deeply. My back arched into a backbend in response. His tongue entered my mouth to swallow my scream. After he lifted my dress over my head, removing it from my yearning body, I quickly unbuttoned his shirt. We were so close that I could feel our hearts beating in one rhythm as he laced his fingers between mine above my head. Not wanting to stop our tempo, he secured my wrists with one hand and ripped off my panties with the other, leaving nothing but heat and skin between us. We groaned and grunted in animalistic love. I clamped my ankles tightly around his waist. He pulled my arms around his neck, and we created a typhoon of passion.

He closed his eyes, and tears traveled slowly down his face. I could feel he was physically and emotionally drained.

Like the lioness who understood her king, I whispered, "Relax and let me love you."

Instantly, I felt him relinquish his power to me, his queen. I kissed the lion tattoo on his chest while the sway of my hips moved him up and down on top of me. He swam in my blissful deep sea of ecstasy and began to pulse; I slowed the pace so he could enjoy his swim longer. His nails pierced the skin on my back. I clenched, released him, and controlled his movements to the shore.

"Blaque, do you want to come with me to your island, baby?"

He bit his lip. *"Si, lo quiero todo, por favor."*

Blaque wanted all of me. So, I led him to our favorite place in my body—deep and to the right. His eyes rolled in the back of his head, and his body quaked uncontrollably. He switched from speaking Spanish to speaking French. Enraptured, I lost all control. The heat and intensity of my orgasms heightened until we created an aquatic eruption. We both trembled from the aftermath.

Satiated into serenity, I lay with my body draped across his while he stroked my hair.

"Blaque, you really know how to speak French, baby?"

He kissed my forehead.

"Oui, ma belle," he whispered before falling into a deep, peaceful sleep.

I heard my phone chime faintly and tiptoed into the kitchen to get it. Looking at the screen, I saw several missed calls from Goldie.

"Goldie, where in the hell were you?" I said upon answering, my tone laced with anger.

There was silence, and then a deep voice spoke.

"Time's up, *señorita*. If you want your brother and the money, you know what I need. You have *dos horas*."

I stood speechless for several minutes before returning to the bedroom. Blaque was out cold. *Thank God.* I quickly but quietly grabbed my hot pink Barbie dress and ran to the basement. I entered the code on the touchscreen, and the heavy door opened to the art gallery. I stared at the Basquiat painting. With my brother's life on the line, it didn't take me long to follow through on what I had to do. I lifted the painting off the wall, crept into the kitchen like the Grinch who stole Christmas, and snatched Blaque's Maserati keys off the counter. Lucky for me, the house was empty—with no signs of Blue, Keith, or Henry.

I quietly closed the iron door and moved swiftly to the car. Once behind the steering wheel, I jetted down Bellagio Road to Interstate 110.

Once home, I changed into a royal blue FUBU hoodie, a

pair of black Girbaud jeans, and some royal blue, black, and white Penny Hardaways. After pulling my hair into a genie ponytail, I stared at myself in the mirror.

There will be no more characters. This is my last performance.

Matias gave me vague directions to an abandoned warehouse downtown when I called him back. Driving slowly through an unlocked metal gate hidden by tall weeds and shrubs, I splashed through muddy potholes in the empty parking lot to the back entrance of a building covered with layers of dirt and graffiti. After parking, I grabbed the Basquiat from the backseat to trade for my brother's life.

I pulled my hood over my head to shield myself from the cold summer night's downpour and swift, cool breeze. The garage door flew open, and mildew and a sour stench invaded my nostrils. In the background, a loud fan was spinning, echoing the sound of noisy propellers. I jumped over a huge puddle and landed on the grimy concrete. My path was lit only by the moon and stars. I tiptoed slowly, keeping my eyes sharp. Guns cocked in the shadows, and I froze mid-step at the sight of two pistols aimed in my direction. Slowly, I lifted my hands.

"Walk," Tomas commanded, his high-pitched voice startling me. *"Caminas rapido."*

We walked deeper inside and entered through double doors. Goldie stood in front of me with his .45 pointed to the ground. Matias had his gun pressed to Goldie's head. Once again, I froze.

Goldie and I were in deeper than we'd ever been. This was our life's final act. Like Blaque had told me, there was no turning back. Goldie and I were like meat trapped in the lion's den, but I'd die for the men I loved.

Felipe snatched the tube from my hand and tossed it to

Matias. We stood silent. Pussy purred and nestled against my foot.

Matias pursed his lips and made kissing noises. "*Ven aqui,* *Pussy.* My brother could never resist dangerous women."

Matias smiled, and Pussy sashayed back to him, seeming to walk with attitude.

Tomas disappeared and returned out of breath. "No Blaque," he screeched.

Matias stared at me. "*Donde esta* Blaque?"

"*Señor,* you requested his Jean-Michel Basquiat, and you have it. Let my brother go. Blaque has nothing to do with this."

Matias shook his head. "*No, señorita.* Blaque has everything to do with this. *Todo.* I gave your brother one million dollars as a deposit to deliver the painting *and* Blaque. That was our contractual agreement."

My eyes narrowed, and I looked at Goldie. He pleaded with his eyes. *How could he betray me?*

Matias caught my glare. "Oh no, *su hermana* didn't know," he said to Goldie, then turned to me. "Your brother played you while you did all the dirty work. He took my million dollars. The other million would be paid when you delivered the painting *and* Blaque, but I want Blaque dead now. He stole my brother's favorite painting and my customers with his *bonita cocaina.* He messed with *mi familia y dinero,* so *lo quiero muerto.*"

Tears fell from my eyes. I was heartbroken by Goldie's betrayal and the thought of Blaque's death.

"Sis, I'm sorry," Goldie said. "I had no idea you would fall in love with him."

Matias chuckled. "You fell in love with Blaque? This whole scenario keeps getting better and better. It's midnight, so time's up. No Blaque, so per my contract, I'm killing both of you."

"*Estoy aqui,* motherfucker!" Blaque's voice bellowed smoothly like a baritone in the opera.

Dressed in all black with a burgundy lambskin leather blazer, he moved like a modern-day Shaft. He held two Glocks, one in each black leather-gloved hand.

"Let them go, and you can have me."

Goldie pointed his .45 at Blaque. "Sorry, bro."

Every gun in the room was pointed at the man I loved. Blaque stood emotionless with his two Glocks pointed at each man as if he was singing "eeny meeny miny mo" in his head.

I shook my head and stepped directly in front of him, feeling the warmth of his chest against my back.

"Pearle, move," Goldie ordered slowly. "This is not a game."

Matias snapped, "*Si*, it's no game. Your brother must kill Blaque, or I will kill all three of you. It's that simple."

I held my hands up and didn't budge.

Blaque whispered, "Pearle, move, baby."

"Listen to your man, sis. It's over. I won't let you die for him, and you know I'm not dying for his cheating ass."

My heart was torn, being pulled in a game of tug of war between Blaque and Goldie—the two men who owned my lifeline. I removed my hood and looked at Matias with sorrow-filled eyes. In a position of surrender, I begged with my hands up and tears rolling down my face.

"*Señor Escobar*, Goldie is my brother, and like you, *te adoro mi familia*. You understand? I will move out the way, but please, can I get one last kiss from Blaque? *Lo amo. Por favor*?"

He motioned his gun forward, granting my request. Turning around, I faced Blaque, touched his face with my left hand, and tasted his soul on my lips. Like mine, Blaque's eyes stayed open.

"I love you, Neo," I whispered while slowly moving my right hand under his lightweight lambskin leather jacket and around his waist.

"I love you, too, Trinity," he whispered back.

My hand firmly gripped the 9mm, then I turned and shot the

man who betrayed us. Goldie hit the dirty concrete like a bag of bricks. Standing in front of Blaque, I aimed the gun at Matias Escobar while Blaque's guns remained pointed at Felipe and Tomas.

Matias pointed his gun at me. "You tricked me."

"Matias, let her go, and you can have me," Blaque told him, then whispered in my ear, "Move out the way, baby."

Matias looked at me and replied, "Blaque, she killed her brother for you. So, you two will die together."

Blue walked in with guns in each hand. "Nah, motherfucker."

Matias stood firm with his brothers. Each of us had at least one gun pointed at the other.

"*Amigo*, we have five guns, and you have five. Drop your weapons, or we'll have an old-fashioned, bloody shootout."

Felipe pointed both his guns at me. "*Si*, motherfucker. Like the Wild Wild West."

My heart pounded in my chest.

Keith stepped from the shadows and pressed his Glock to the back of Matias' head. "Yippee-ki-yay, *amigo*."

Winston's thunderous laughter came from behind us. "And yippee-ki-yo, motherfucker."

A wave of clicks echoed through the room like falling dominoes.

Winston walked in front of Matias. "*Bumbaclot*, you can't count. We have more than five guns. Like…shit…I dunno. Henry's our mathematician. How many, brother?"

Uncle Henry held a TEC-9. "*Uno, dos*…hundreds, mother-fucker."

The room filled with laughter. Several Jamaican men moved in swiftly like ninjas, taking Matias, Felipe, and Tomas' weapons and tying them up.

"Where are you taking us?" Matias asked.

The men placed tape across the Escobars' mouths and pushed them inside a white van.

Blaque exhaled, relaxing behind me. "Damn, fam, what took y'all so long?"

Delroy laughed. "Goddamn L.A. traffic, boss."

I was frozen. Blaque wrapped his warm hands around mine and took his 9mm.

"It's over, Gangsta Boo," he whispered, his warm breath tickling my earlobe.

As I turned and grabbed his face, we kissed and tuned out the chaos around us.

"Nephew, Boom-Boom later!" Uncle Winston yelled. "Who's the dead man?"

I kicked Goldie. "He's not dead. He's my lying-ass, backstabbing brother."

Goldie coughed and pulled off the bulletproof vest from under his hoodie.

"I know I fucked up. I'm sorry, sis."

I wrapped my arms around Blaque's neck. "I need you to come to my place whenever you're done."

"Whatever you say, Trinity. Don't forget my painting."

I grabbed the tube. "I couldn't figure out how to get your Basquiat out of the damn frame. This is the replica, but it looks just like the original."

He smiled. "Damn, I love you. Rest up, 'cause it's on later."

"*Ya mon*, I know how you do. I love you, too."

We ran outside like the building was about to crumble. Goldie had Pussy and Matias' briefcase in his hands, and he and I got inside the Maserati. We sped off, followed by Keith and Blue in the Bentley. Blaque trailed us on a black Suzuki Hayabusa motorcycle until Goldie and I turned off our exit. Tingles and goosebumps ran over my body as my king of knights zoomed past us on his bike and took his place in front of the long train of luxury vehicles on the interstate.

At four a.m., I was awakened by wet kisses on my face. My eyes opened, and I saw Blaque's body glistening like fresh dew from the shower.

I stretched. "Blaque, I didn't hear you come in."

"That's because I was quiet so you could rest. Are you ready for me?"

"I'm always ready."

Given the green light, he kissed along my clavicle and pulled down the shoulder straps of my nightie with his tongue. He groaned hungrily as he engulfed each breast in his mouth. When I closed my eyes, I felt my nightie slide down my body.

I moaned loudly. "Blaque, I think you are part lion."

He pulled me up by my wrists and wrapped my arms around his neck. "No, I'm *all* lion. As your man, do you know my most important job?"

I looked into his eyes. "To protect."

He smiled and kissed my lips. "That's right, baby. Today, you almost didn't let me do my job."

"I'm sorry, but they had my brother—"

He sucked my lips. "*Shhh.* Didn't I tell you I love every part of you? Your brother is part of you. What if I didn't have a tracker on the Maserati?"

I dropped my head. He lifted my chin.

"You have to tell me everything, no matter what, so I can do my job. Do you understand?"

My tongue traced his lips slowly. "I promise it won't happen again. Now relax and let your lioness queen take care of Your Majesty," I whispered in his ear.

I kissed his eyes closed, and he surrendered. My hands and

mouth caressed the mightiness between his legs until his body went limp. He fell fast asleep soon after.

It was six a.m., and I was wide awake. So, I slipped into my silk robe and headed to the kitchen. With Coltrane playing softly on my record player, I walked outside to sit on my patio couch. My California green, wrapped in raw papers, burned slowly. I drifted high with the wind as Mother Nature blew her warm breath over L.A. and pushed the cold wind east. I stared at the Hollywood sign over the hills and saw my future clearly in the clouds. I was officially retiring from my acting career that required deception.

For the first time, I fully embraced who I was—Pearle Monalise Brown, a business owner and retired thief born and raised in Compton and in love with Christian Laurent Savage, aka Blaque.

I closed my eyes and felt the strength of Blaque's arms around me. His hard body slid behind me. The fingers on his left hand laced into mine like shoelaces. My head rested against his bare, muscular chest, and I passed him the turkey-stuffed joint with the perfect slow roast. He inhaled the herbs and slowly exhaled the haze. He joined me on a round-trip voyage on Coltrane's "Blue Train" in the clouds above the hills. Our quiet stillness was orgasmic, and we delighted in each other's presence.

He kissed my neck. "What are you thinking about, baby?"

I exhaled and moved my head from side to side. "I'm wondering where the sun will rise. I've never seen a sunrise."

He turned my head and pointed. "That way is east and where the sun rises."

We laughed and stared east. The sun popped up over the horizon quicker than I expected. I marveled at it as we held each other.

"Blaque, what are you thinking about?"

His thumb ran across my ring finger. "I was thinking about how I want to spend the rest of my life with you."

He got on one knee; my mouth dropped open. He kissed my

ring finger, and his golden eyes gazed into mine.

"Pearle, God designed you just for me. You are my perfect woman, a priceless gem with thousands of layers that can only be found in the ocean—my favorite place in the world. I'm an art junkie, and you're a black masterpiece named after the Mona Lisa. God knew I could only fall in love upon sight of a jazzy black angel, beautifully flawed and dressed in white with sexy red lips. I love you, baby. Will you marry me?"

PART TWO

CHAPTER 21
'99 BONNIE & CLYDE

PEARLE MONALISE BROWN
JAMAICA 2000

F**ROM THE MOMENT** I laid eyes on Christian "Blaque" Laurent Savage, I knew my life would never be the same. I was on the balcony gazing at a miraculous spectacle in the Jamaican sky. It transformed into a colorful layered cake with orange at the horizon, stacked with pink, purple, and navy colors. The sun was shining between the mountains over the sea, and the crescent moon had risen across the ocean. I inhaled fresh saltwater mixed with the scent of fragrant bouquets. It was winter, but Mother Nature's tropical arms were wrapped around me. A gust of cold wind interrupted our embrace, and I shivered from the unexpected breeze.

Goldie touched my shoulders. "Damn, that felt good."

I turned and saw he was drenched with sweat. He had come outside from the cabin. I turned back around to show him what I'd witnessed, but the sun had set. The moon was alone in a lavender sky.

I fixed his grey tie. "Why are you so nervous?"

Goldie was handsome in his grey tailored suit and a fresh haircut. I dabbed the sweat from his forehead.

"Sis, I feel like *I'm* getting married. Aren't you nervous?"

"Not at all."

We went inside, and Mommy smiled. While walking over

to the mirror, I watched my curls bounce happily on my right shoulder. Like Billie Holiday, a large red flower was snuggled against the left side of my head.

Mommy, aged with perfection, stood proudly in her silver satin and chiffon floor-length gown. She fixed the birdcage veil that rested over my eyes.

"You look beautiful," she said.

My wedding dress was white with a long chiffon skirt and train. The top was white lace with a deep scalloped neckline and back that accented my breasts and the tip of my winged tattoo. My neck was adorned with a diamond black pearl necklace and matching earrings decorated in my lobes. My makeup was flawless, and on my feet were red sparkle-heeled pumps. I was ready to follow Blaque to magical Oz or anywhere he wanted to take me in the universe.

With Goldie and Mommy's arms locked around me, I walked confidently out of the room.

We walked down the red velvet carpet covered with white rose petals to the bow of *Blaque Pearle*. Our new yacht floated peacefully on the turquoise waves in Kingston. My caramel king stood picturesque in a custom-designed black tuxedo jacket with silver trim and a red rose on the lapel. His pants and shirt were black, and he wore a grey vest and silver tie. His golden eyes shined like the moon and were illuminated with love as I walked towards him.

The perfect breeze caressed my body, setting my flowy, chiffon skirt free to expose my sun-kissed legs, slim-thick thighs, and lace mini skirt. With hungered love, Blaque called me to him with his eyes and pointer finger. Goldie smoothly handed Blaque my hand, and my soon-to-be husband spun me around while licking his lips. Then he grabbed the mic from our Jamaican minister.

"I do. Can I kiss my bride now?"

After laughter from our guests, the sea captain announced, "Just a few minutes, Mr. Savage."

The officiant's words faded into the background. We stared anxiously into each other's eyes and awaited confirmation that we were one Savage. Blue, the best man, proudly handed Blaque the bezel diamond wedding bands we slipped on each other's ring fingers.

After the words "By the power vested in me," Blaque lifted my veil and pressed his lips against mine. Our mouths opened, and tongues intertwined. Everyone waited and watched our never-ending kiss. When the deejay dropped Jodeci's "Love You 4 Life," our lips were still locked. Our tongues rolled, and our bodies followed. We grooved to our first song as husband and wife. Blaque's hands traveled down my back and to my waist.

"Hell yeah, son," Chadwick yelled. "Don't waste a damn drop of that sugar!"

All the men in his family jumped up and cheered us on.

"Take your time with it, Savages. Aye!"

Still locked in a kiss, I lifted my bouquet in the air, and Shay ran behind me.

"Hell yeah, boss lady! Go ahead and drop that bouquet in my hands. I know it's heavy as hell."

I tossed it backward and heard cheers.

"Keith! We're next!" Shay yelled.

With both my hands free, I stroked the back of Blaque's neck. We danced to the bass and continued our everlasting kiss.

The DJ announced, "Everybody, please join the new Mr. and Mrs. Savage on the dance floor."

After the best day of my life, Blaque and I said our goodbyes to family and friends from L.A., Kingston, Harlem, Atlanta, and the Midwest. *Blaque Pearle* was ready to hit the blue sea for our weeklong honeymoon adventure. However, security swept the

ship before we could depart and informed us of one guest who
demanded our presence.

Seated at the small bar near the rear of the dock was an attractive,
tall, chocolate man with wavy hair, a fresh razor haircut, and
studded earrings. He turned around with a joyous grin. He was
dressed in a tailored black suit with a red tie and a fresh pair of Air
Jordans. In his mouth was a hand-rolled cigar from our reception.

He clapped. "Congratulations, Mr. and Mrs. Savage. You two
make a beautiful couple. Loved the wedding, and that was quite
a first kiss." He admired the six-carat VVS round stone set in a
princess-cut double-bezel band sparkling on my finger. "*Wow* and
look at your ring. It's stunning."

Blaque squeezed my hand. "What's up, Walker? This is my
wife, Pearle Monalise Savage."

Walker had disappeared from Blaque's life, and I was hoping
he was gone for good.

I smiled and shook his hand. "Nice to meet you, Agent
Walker. Thank you for coming."

He smiled back. "I didn't get an official invite, even though
I'm the reason you two are together, but it's cool."

Blaque sighed. "Why are you here?"

Walker blew the smoke from his cigar. "This is a really good
cigar. Anyway, I'm really upset, Christian. We were supposed to
bring down the Escobar brothers, but they've suddenly fallen off
the grid. It happened hours before you told me we'd bring them
down."

Blaque pulled out his cigar, and I lit the tip with the lighter
from my clutch.

"Wow," he said. "They mysteriously disappeared? I wondered

what happened 'cause I hadn't heard from you. I thought maybe you did *your* job and took them down."

"We both know you had *something* to do with their disappearance. You probably feel like you've won, but shit doesn't work like that without serious consequences. Those men did really bad shit, and you sabotaged a critical case." Walker glared with anger. "Their capture was also the gateway to my promotion to support my wife and family."

Blaque looked surprised. "I didn't know you were married."

Walker smiled. "Yeah, I have a beautiful wife. We've been together since we were in the fourth grade."

"Damn, that's amazing. Well, if you are worried about money, we could always use part-time drivers in my family's trucking business. Some of our part-time drivers make more than double your current annual salary per month."

Walker jumped up from his barstool and got in Blaque's face. "What did you say? Say it louder so I can hear it clearly and put it on record. I'll lock your ass up right now."

The tension was thick.

I moved to stand between them. "Is there something we can help you with, Agent Walker? We were just about to sail out to sea."

"Yes, I told Christian that you two were a package, and now you are officially one. Marriage changes things."

Blaque stared at Walker. "Get to the point because we're ready to start our honeymoon."

Walker smiled. "Christian, you remind me so much of Jack Dawson. Do you know who he is?"

Blaque rolled his eyes and blew cigar smoke towards Walker's face.

Unaffected, Walker turned and faced me. "I bet your actress wife does. Don't you, Pearle? Tell your husband who he was."

I didn't respond. The end of Jack Dawson's story was tragic, and I refused to acknowledge any comparison of his fate to Blaque's.

"Blaque," Walker continued, "Jack was the lead character in my favorite movie, *Titanic*. He was an artist like you from the hood and won his way onto the unsinkable *Titanic* in a poker game. He fell in love with a pretty woman, like Pearle, named Rose."

My heart pounded like a drum as Walker continued.

"Well, Jack made it to the top level and was getting busy with Rose when the *Titanic* hit an iceberg. The ship started to sink. The people at the top were so busy thinking they were safe because they truly believed the ship was indestructible. Anyway, Jack was a third-class citizen who temporarily experienced first-class amenities before he and the *Titanic* went down."

Blaque blew smoke in Walker's face and told him, "Jack went down with the *Titanic*, but before he died, he saved his Rose—the lady he loved—*twice*. Jack Dawson was a goddamn hero. So, you're right. I'm just like him, 'cause I'll die for my woman *any* day. What about you, *D-Walk*?"

Blaque and Walker glared at each other. They stood so close that their lips almost touched.

Finally breaking the long, silent staredown, Walker replied, "You should already know I'll die *and* kill for mine."

"We're more alike than you think," Blaque stated with a sly grin. "Now, get to the reason why you're here."

Walker grabbed a large manila folder from the bar top and politely handed it to me with a smile.

"Pearle, everything you need is in this envelope."

"Hell no, Walker!" Blaque yelled with a rage I had never heard from him. "This is between you and me!"

Puzzled and curious, I pulled out the first 8x10, which was a picture of my father.

"Why is my father's picture in here?"

Walker smiled. "Hopefully, he is your motivation. Based on the disappearance of the Escobars choreographed by your husband, I've been reassigned to a special task force to take down Rafelina Torres, the head of a Mexican cartel operating in Texas."

"Hell no!" Blaque shouted.

"Christian, I told you, you two are one. Pearle, your father's picture is in there because he will come home to your mother as soon as we bring Rafelina down. That reduces his sentence by almost ten years. I know how much you would love to do that for your family."

Tears ran freely down my face. Blaque kissed my cheek.

He whispered, "Don't do this, baby."

"Pearle, this is perfect for you," Walker interrupted. "You're a good actress and speak fluent Spanish. There is a team already set up, and they're close to bringing them down. You and I will swoop in and finish this so we can get home to our families. Agent Rosa Flores will pick you up from Hobby Airport in Houston tomorrow evening."

"*Tomorrow?*" Blaque and I responded in unison.

Walker pulled out a pen. "Just sign these papers stating you'll be a confidential informant, and I'll be out of your way."

Blaque clenched his jaws tightly. "Damn you, Walker. You are not using my wife as your pawn."

I touched Blaque's hand to calm him and asked Walker, "Can I start next week? We are going on our honeymoon."

Walker grabbed his box of cigars. "Nah, your honeymoon is over."

Blaque shook his head no, but I signed on the line anyway— Pearle Monalise Savage. The first time I signed something using my new name. Defeated, I placed the paper in Walker's winning upper hand.

"We'll see you tomorrow in Houston, Mrs. Savage. Take care, Jack. I mean, Christian."

On my wedding day, DEA Special Agent David Walker and his task force brought me out of retirement to play Sol Milian, the woman who would bring down the Torres Cartel and free my father.

CHAPTER 22
DADDY LESSONS

SOL MILIAN
HOUSTON 2000

GOING FROM FLIGHTS on a private jet with only two passengers to being seated in the last row, middle seat on a packed Air Tran 737 was like eating a juicy filet mignon at Mr. Chow's for lunch to a ground beef chuck burger at Mickey D's for dinner. I was wedged between an overweight couple who had bought the aisle and window seats. The couple let up their armrests, leaving only room for half of a person to sit comfortably. For seven hours, my arms and thighs were covered on each side by their extra flesh, and because we were in the last row, I couldn't recline at all during the flight.

I complained to the flight attendant but was told it was the only available seat on the overbooked flight. So, I had no choice but to endure the hot mess. With my daddy's freedom within my reach, their sweaty skin was the least of my concerns.

Agent Flores—or Rosa, her undercover name—picked me up in a dingy white van with tinted windows. She was a beautiful Mexican woman with long, wavy black hair, brown eyes, and pink lips. She was extremely petite, especially behind the driver's seat of the large van, but had a loud, commanding voice.

"Pearle, your name is Sol Milian, and you and I met on MySpace. I recruited you to join Scarlet Entertainment as a model, which is actually an illegal sexual exploitation business."

"*What*?" I screamed. "Why in the hell would you guys use me to do this? I'm married. Hell no. This is ridiculous. I thought we were bringing down drug dealers."

Agent Flores was an FBI special agent. The special task force that Walker had referred to after my wedding yesterday was comprised of the DEA and FBI. They had come together to bring down the Torres Mexican Cartel, which ran one of the largest human trafficking operations between Mexico and the U.S. The cartel also transported marijuana and cocaine into America.

Agent Flores posed as an outside contractor who recruited and drove female victims for the Torres Cartel. Houston, Texas, was the largest major city in the horrific scheme. I had no idea of the boiling pot of gumbo I'd been thrown into, and I knew Blaque would not go for it once he found out.

"Pearle, this is terrible, I know," Agent Flores said. "This is why we want to shut down the Torres operation and ones like it for good. We want you to get close to Honey and Isabel, two young recruiters, to get information. I'm only a driver, and once I drop the girls off, I don't know where they go. You will be safe, though. We will have eyes on you the entire time. After three days, we will pull you out. You can go home to your husband, and we will free your father."

I rolled my eyes. "I want my father released on day three."

Flores touched my hand. "Pearle, you have my word. I'm sorry Walker didn't explain it to you but think about the lives of the young women you will save."

My heart immediately sank. I thought of a girl from my neighborhood in Compton who had been kidnapped. The word on the street was that she had been swept into a similar illegal operation. Unsuspecting young girls and women were lured and deceived for exploitation by internet predators and robbed of their innocence and dignity. This sickened my soul.

For the first time, I felt horrible for all the things I had done to the many men I'd deceived and robbed. I knew I wanted and needed to help, not only for other women and girls but also for my redemption.

From Houston Hobby Airport, we dove into deep potholes like those in Kingston and Compton. We cruised past several abandoned row homes, dingy motels, and small palm trees. The Check-to-Cash establishments, liquor stores, and dirty streets were hood indicators. My mind drifted, and I heard DJ Quik in my mind—Houston…"*is just like Compton.*"

We jumped onto Highway 45, and Agent Flores drove us to an area called Third Ward near Houston's downtown. We exited Macgregor off SH 288 and passed several impressive homes and mansions Flores stated were occupied mainly by wealthy black families. On the same block, condemned and abandoned mansions appeared haunted by spirits.

We crossed a bridge, turned on a couple of long streets, and passed a few corner boys selling drugs. Parked in front of several homes were Skittle-colored old-school cars with chrome rims. We sped past the projects and turned onto a quiet street tucked tidily in Riverside Terrace, a nice neighborhood in Third Ward.

Agent Flores and I went through my instructions several times.

"Pearle, these girls will be nice and attempt to charm you. Play along with your model career aspirations and squeeze them for information. We will pull you out in three days. Keep this cell phone on you at all times. This is how we will track you."

Awaiting my arrival were Honey and Isabel. Honey was a pretty, brown-skinned woman in her twenties with an hourglass-shaped figure and honey-blonde highlights. Isabel was a sexy Latina with curly hair, perfect hips, and green eyes. They both looked like overly glammed dolls. They flashed a deceiving smile and asked me to follow them into a two-story light blue and grey brick house.

Inside, the home looked ordinary and basic, except for one room downstairs that had been converted into an elaborate photo studio. I sighed with disgust at the fake "model" photo studio I knew was used to exploit and abuse unsuspecting victims.

One of the heifers looked at me and said, "Sol, this is where all the magic happens. You will launch your exciting modeling career if you pass the three-day interview process."

I used the strength of every muscle in my body to crack a smile. "Can't wait."

Upstairs, there were three bedrooms. One room was for Honey and Isabel. The other two rooms rotated girls who would either pass or fail their interview. I shared a room with Eliza, a pretty, nineteen-year-old Creole girl from New Orleans. She had creamy tanned skin, thick straight hair, high cheekbones, and beautiful brown eyes. The other room was occupied by a beautiful Houston native named Pamela, who was a sexy, thick-in-all-the-right-places chocolate belle, and Angelina, a quiet Puerto Rican beauty from Chicago.

Once we got settled, Honey and Isabel led Eliza and me downstairs to a glam squad, who administered makeovers and gave us new wardrobes. We each received different hairstyles, lashes, and makeup. My makeover included a bleached blonde hair color. Our new clothes were the smallest, most revealing articles on the market. My outfit consisted of a red vest with no bra and matching coochie cutters with half my ass out. After we were dolled up, we took pictures in the photo studio and left out.

We slid into Honey's candy apple red Cadillac Escalade and

headed to the Third Ward, where the club scene was jumping. At Faces, the first club, we danced to Tru's "No Limit Soldiers." Honey and Isabel surveyed our moves. While acting out my part, I couldn't stop thinking about how Blaque and I were supposed to be sailing the Caribbean Sea on our honeymoon. Still, I would give my greatest performance to free my daddy.

At the exit door of Faces, we were greeted by the fresh aroma of barbecue ribs from a food cart. We sat outside the club and finished our ribs sponsored by a friendly, heavyset southern gentleman with a gold chain and matching grill in his mouth.

Like thunder before the storm, loud bass boomed and rattled, and UGK's "Pocket Full of Stones" filled the streets. Everyone on the block looked to see a kiwi-colored 1985 Cadillac Seville cruising around the corner.

All eyes were glued on the candy green slab with black tinted windows and bright white-wall tires. My crew turned and dropped their mouths as the Caddy pulled up next to us and hit the switches. The car bounced up and down like a basketball and tilted to the left and right. The music blaring from the speakers started a mini block party. Females twerked and danced in the streets, vying for the driver's attention. Irritated by the extra foolery, I rolled my eyes and shook my head. The side window cracked enough to allow spliff smoke to escape, and the music lowered.

"Hey, Shawty Red," the driver called out in his country grammar.

The light-skinned girls in our crew looked around with thirst in their eyes. I, on the other hand, didn't bother to look up or glance his way.

"I want the sexy blonde in the red shorts."

Everyone looked at me. I stared at the tinted window in disbelief.

"Yeah, you, sexy," the smooth baritone said. "Come here, baby."

My heart jumped out of my chest, and I thought I was dreaming.

Honey hit my arm. "Sol, if you don't get your ass over there, I will. See if he'll sponsor us for the rest of the night."

I sprinted to the driver's side. Through the crack, I saw an orange and navy Houston Astros fitted cap, which sat low over his face. In his ears were two diamond studs, and a thick platinum and diamond chain hung around his neck. He sported a crisp white t-shirt and a Rolex.

Blaque looked up and licked his lips. "What it do, baby?"

My heart melted; I could barely contain my excitement. "Whatever you want it to."

He laughed. "What's your name, Red?"

"Sol Milian."

"That's a pretty name. I like you, Sol Milian. Get your sexy ass in the car."

"My girls are trying to have a good time tonight. Are you sponsoring?"

Blaque slid five crisp one-hundred-dollar bills through the window. "Yeah, but you're the only one I want."

I passed one C-note to each girl. "Don't wait up. I won't be home tonight."

The girls smiled, although I could tell they were secretly jealous.

I jumped in the passenger seat. Blaque rolled up his window, and we dipped off.

Once we were down the street, I screamed and kissed all over his face.

"Blaque, baby, I love you so much. You are crazy, man."

His hand touched my face. "You know I can't go a day without you, Mrs. Savage. So, I'm bringing our honeymoon to where my wife is—Houston."

I unbuttoned his pants and devoured every inch of manhood

I could get into my mouth. He moaned loudly, and after his third swerve on Almeda Road, he pulled over and parked under a group of trees in Hermann Park. Blaque quenched my thirst when his salted caramel melted down my throat.

After quickly removing my red shorts, he guided me to his lap. He reclined his seat, and I unzipped my vest. With my back against the steering wheel, he controlled my movements like the switches on his old-school Caddy until we climaxed.

The windows were fogged from our heated breath and Houston's nighttime humidity. My face was stuck to Blaque's shoulder. He rubbed my new blonde tresses as I looked into his hazel eyes. He stroked my face and kissed me passionately. Suddenly, my phone rang, interrupting my bliss.

"Hello, Sol. Are you okay?" asked Agent Rosa.

"Yes, I'm fine. I'll be back at the house tomorrow," I told her, then hung up and wrapped my arms around Blaque's neck. "Mr. Savage, are you following me?"

"Yes, Mrs. Savage. I'm having you followed by a private investigator so I can always have eyes on you. I don't trust Walker's ass," he told me, then looked at his watch and whispered in my ear, "Are you down to go on an adventure with me, Trinity?"

I nodded, and he kissed my lips.

Chopped and screwed, we rolled slowly through Third Ward jamming to DJ Screw's "Leanin'". I exhaled smoke through the crack in my window while watching girls dance and dudes nod with approval as we passed by. I looked at Blaque, who was leaned back in his seat and bobbing his head to the beat. He was so fine. When he winked, butterflies fluttered through my body.

With no fear of any danger, my body rolled slowly in the front seat while he rubbed my thigh. He hit 610, and we drove for an hour before pulling into a large cattle ranch.

When Blaque opened my door, I jumped into his arms.

Once I released him, he pulled two suitcases from the trunk. We walked through the front door and were greeted by a tall, coffee-complexioned man dressed like a modern-day cowboy in leather cowboy boots and a tan Stetson. He smiled and grabbed our luggage.

"Howdy, Mr. and Mrs. Savage." Our host had a strong southern accent with a heavy drawl. "I'm Harry Rosemont. Welcome to Rosemont Estate. Follow me."

The ranch-style home was one level and spacious. The living room's centerpiece was a Texas longhorn statue that stretched eight feet from tip to tip. The floors were wooden throughout, and the décor was rustic and homey. We followed Harry to the master bedroom, where I was ready for Blaque and me to strip out our clothes.

Harry tipped his hat. "See you guys in the living room in five minutes."

When Harry left the room, Blaque spun me around and smacked the flesh hanging out from underneath the bottom of my shorts.

"Mrs. Savage, your hair is cute, but you're going to have to explain this costume."

The thought made me sick. "Blaque, baby, it's too much to talk about, and I'm not in the mood. I promise I'll fill you in tomorrow. Right now, let's enjoy our honeymoon."

He pulled me close and kissed my lips. "Okay, baby."

Blaque grabbed my hand and led me to the living room, where Harry awaited us with two cowboy hats. Blaque took off his Astros cap and replaced it with a black Stetson. My hat was a cream-colored cowgirl hat with a black leather braid.

Holding hands, we went to the side door. Rosemont Estate sat on hundreds of acres of grassy fields that appeared endless, like a green sea. As we approached a stable, I immediately got excited and jumped into Blaque's arms, wrapping my arms around his neck.

"Blaque, baby, I've always wanted to go horseback riding."

"I know."

In the stable were over a dozen horses. Harry instructed us to pick out a horse for our nighttime excursion.

"What does it matter?" Blaque asked. "Isn't a horse a horse?"

Harry laughed out loud. "'Of course, of course. You two are probably too young to know the song from the TV show *Mr. Ed.* It was a sitcom about a talking horse."

We stared blankly in silence, and he smiled.

"I guess it was before your time. Anyway, there should be a connection between you and your horse. You'll know the right one."

Harry and Blaque watched me patiently as I walked along the stable with my eyes closed, stroking each horse's head until I received a response from my touch. Peanut was my choice until he startled me with a sudden movement. The last horse was Snowflake, a beautiful, all-white thoroughbred. Her brown eyes called me to her. I stroked her head and pulled her reins. After I rubbed her side, she wagged her tail. I slid onto the brown leather saddle and felt at home. Blaque struggled to mount a black stallion he had chosen because it matched his hat.

Harry gave us lessons on how to guide and ride our horses.

"Will the horses have trouble on the trail at night?" I asked him.

"No, ma'am. These horses can ride these trails with their eyes closed."

Led by Harry, Blaque and I trotted along the trail lit by the brilliant midnight moon and stars. With my inner thighs and legs, I learned Snowflake's rhythm and understood how she moved. We communicated with each other. I trusted her guidance, and she moved under my command. The horse and I moved gracefully in sync.

Houston was very flat, and I found beauty in the trees and open night sky. The night had become my favorite part of the day. The quiet stillness calmed my mind, and the moonbeams gave me clarity to see my path.

Blaque struggled behind us. His horse, 8-Ball, stopped on the trail to eat, then ran to catch up as Harry and I waited. Blaque bounced up and down on the saddle and was nearly knocked off when the stallion came to an abrupt halt.

"Man, how do you do this every day?" Blaque asked, looking miserably at Harry. "I'm ready to get off this damn thing right now."

The horse must have felt his dismay. She bucked forward, and he almost fell off again.

We rode on, and when I looked back at Blaque, he was sitting lopsided on 8-Ball and being tossed around like a small red ball attached to a paddle. After forty-five minutes, we headed back to the stable.

Blaque stared at me as I hugged Snowflake. "No fair. 8-Ball was a thug."

I laughed. "Next time, be choosier with your horse like you are with your woman."

He laughed, too. "Hell no. There won't be a next time for me."

"Blaque, but I want a horse of my own," I whined, poking out my bottom lip.

Harry looked at Blaque. "Mrs. Savage does ride naturally, like a pro. You can always buy a horse from us, and we'll keep it here so she can ride whenever she wants."

Blaque limped slowly and placed his hands between his legs. "I won't be riding ever again, but I'll get you one in L.A."

With that, I smiled. If I didn't know it before, which I did, I knew then that there wasn't anything my husband wouldn't do for me.

Upon returning to the room, we jumped in the shower to cleanse ourselves of the horse smells and night air. Afterwards, Blaque sat on the side of the comfortable king-sized bed and massaged his inner thighs from his painful horse ride.

I crawled between his legs. "Aww, do you need me to kiss it for you?"

He nodded. *"Si, por favor."*

I caressed and licked everywhere below his waist.

"My turn, *Mamacita*," he said, laying back. "Let's go, cowgirl."

I put on my cowgirl hat, climbed on top of him, and started rocking and swaying like a professional bull rider.

"Damn, that cowgirl hat is driving me crazy, Mrs. Savage."

With one hand holding my hat and my other hand on his chest, I continued riding him until he released all his love inside of me.

The next morning, there was a knock at the bedroom door. Dorothy Rosemont, Harry's beautifully thin, cocoa-brown wife, brought us sausage, eggs, biscuits, fresh fruit, and orange juice.

"Good morning, honey," she greeted with a smile as bright as the sun. "Here is some breakfast. I know you guys were out late, so you can enjoy breakfast in bed. Everything on your plate, down to the sage in the sausage, comes directly from our land."

I smiled graciously. "Wow! Rosemont is black owned?"

"It's been in Henry's family for over a century. He's very proud to carry forth his family's legacy."

"That's amazing, and the food smells wonderful. I can't wait to taste everything. Thank you."

I sat next to Blaque and placed the food tray between us. "Blaque, we need to talk."

Having his full attention, I explained the nature of my assignment and told him what I had learned about the girls. After giving him my initial observation of the operation, he snapped.

"There's no way in *hell* I'm taking you back there. What if you get pulled too deep into that shit and come up missing? I wouldn't be able to live with myself. The thought of all the awful things they'd do to you—makes me sick to think of it. Give me that cell phone. I'm telling Walker's shady ass and Flores that you're out."

I gently touched his hand. "Blaque, I have to do this, baby. I can help save other girls and women. The very thoughts making you sick are actually happening to someone else's loved one. It will only be two more days, and then I'll be back with you in L.A."

Blaque looked at me like I had lost my mind.

"Pearle, that's a *hell no*." He bit into his sausage. "Damn, this sausage is good."

I folded my arms. "Blaque, you can't say hell no. Not only will I be helping young girls, but it will get my daddy out of prison ten years early. Please?"

I tried to seduce him with my kisses, but he leaned back away from me and shook his head in protest.

"Pearle, I'll do anything for you but this. You are my wife, and I'm putting my foot down. I know you want your dad out, but there's no way he would agree to you getting caught up in a human trafficking operation."

Tears rolled from my eyes. "You're right that he wouldn't want me to do this for him, but my daddy taught me not to turn my back when people are in trouble. These girls and women need my help. I'm also doing this for myself since I've done some terrible things in the past. I guess you can say it's my way of trying to right some of my past wrongs. Blaque, this is bigger than us. For the first time, I hear a voice in my spirit telling me this is my purpose."

"Pearle, yes, we're criminals and have done horrible shit, but human trafficking is no game, baby. Anything—unspeakable things—could happen to you. As my wife, you are my sole responsibility. I'll go to jail—hell, I'll *die* first before I let you stay one night in that house."

He wouldn't budge.

"Can I have a few hours?" I asked, sliding across his lap.

"No. We're going back to Los Angeles tonight."

"*Papi*, at least give me four hours to collect information. We're going to the rodeo at the Astrodome later. I'll leave early, and you and I can catch a red-eye back to L.A. tonight. You've hired a private investigator. Plus, the FBI *and* DEA are also watching me. I promise to be extra careful. We'll meet at ten o'clock outside the stadium. I'll book our flights now, babe."

I pulled out his cell phone and credit card to book our flights.

Blaque shook his head. "I've got a bad feeling about this."

After I booked our midnight flights to LAX and a round of morning lovemaking, Blaque's mood lightened. By the time he drove me back to Third Ward, it was late afternoon. He called the private investigator when we hit the last pothole going into Riverside Terrace.

Blaque parked and held my hand while he talked. "I need you to make sure you're watching Pearle. If there is any suspicious activity in the neighborhood, pull her out by any means necessary."

He hung up and squeezed my hand, his eyes filled with worry.

"Pearle, I love you so much, baby. This feels wrong, and my gut never fails me."

I grabbed his face. "Mr. Savage, it's just a few more hours. Don't worry. Your Gangsta Boo got this."

"What's the name of the fake-ass operation again?"

"Scarlet Entertainment."

He pulled my head against his chest.

"Be careful," he whispered, then kissed me with so much love that I lost my breath. He put three fingers in my face. "Mrs. Savage, I want you to meet me at *nine o'clock* instead of ten. That's in *tres horas.* Call me if anything looks or feels strange. My PI and I will be watching you."

"Yes, my Lion King. Everything will be fine," I reassured him.

"I love you. See you at nine."

He caressed my hand and looked at me with his hazel puppy dog eyes.

"Don't go."

He was hard to resist, but my mind was made up. He finally released my hand with one last kiss.

Before I could exit the car, he handed me a stack and a 9mm to keep in my purse.

"I'll be fine. Three hours," I told him, giving him a final kiss. Then I slid out of the car and ran to the house.

The girls were excited to hear about my nighttime escapade, which I downplayed as a late-night Chacho's takeout run and rendezvous in Crowne Plaza nearby.

As Honey and Isabel smiled with approval, I thought to myself, *I got this.*

Black Heritage Day was a one-day celebration during the twenty-day-long Houston Rodeo. It was a day to recognize and commemorate black farmers, black cowboys, and black businesses in Houston and the state of Texas. The girls and I got ready to attend a New Orleans-style Zydeco pre-party for VIPs. My roommate Eliza was excited because it reminded her of home in Louisiana.

A black artist always performed in concert, and this year, the artist was H-Town. The atmosphere in the Astrodome was electric. The energy was unfamiliar and shocked me. I never imagined I would see tens of thousands of black people in western wear all under one roof.

The women wore various colored cowgirl hats, boots, and belts adorned with rhinestones and bling. The western accessories were styled with club dresses, fitted denim and bra tops, short shorts, skirts, and one-piece catsuits. The men rocked cowboy hats, boots, and fresh sneakers with sagging Wranglers, Sean John, and sports jerseys. I was drawn to all the style and flavor and wanted to come back with Blaque so we could experience the vibe uninterrupted.

The girls and I made it inside the VIP room. We were given tickets sponsored by a local group of ballers to watch the concert from the skybox. While we waited for H-Town to rock da' boots, Zydeco blasted, and immediately, we were surrounded by sharks of men and handed drinks. Everyone congregated and was dancing. I played along while waiting for the right moment to make my exit.

I was anxiously waiting to speak to Agent Flores. Before the girls and I left the house in Third Ward, I was getting ready in the bathroom and overheard Isabel and a man named José Luis quietly whispering in Spanish under the buzzing sound of the outdoor AC unit. They discussed how we were getting placed in trap-house "modeling gigs" around the country. The cities mentioned were Houston, L.A., Atlanta, and Miami. Isabel had given José suggestions of where she thought we would fit in best. Laredo, Texas, was where he and a man named Larazo would house us until we were officially placed.

My heart raced in anticipation as I thought of how my intel would help the FBI bust the operation and rescue the girls in the house before they were taken. Even better, my father's freedom was only two days away.

The lights dimmed, and right before H-Town hit the stage, I told Honey that I had to run to the restroom. From there, I called Agent Flores. She answered, but there were too many people around for me to speak freely, and inside the stall, the music echoed too loudly for us to hear each other. I hung up and looked at the time—*8:45 p.m.* I left quickly from the restroom to find a quieter place to talk. After running to the elevator and departing the skybox level, I called Blaque. He answered on the first ring.

"What's up, handsome?" I said while shuffling through the crowds of attendees.

I could hear his smile through the phone. "Hey, sexy. I saw you in the pink cowgirl hat earlier. We are using that tonight when we get back to L.A. I'm already outside waiting for you. Bring your fine ass to me right now, Mrs. Savage."

I smiled. "Yes, *papi*. I'm on my way."

When we hung up, I moved quickly out the stadium doors. I sighed a deep breath of relief once the night air hit my face. Shoulder-to-shoulder with swanky cowboys and cowgirls, I descended five escalators and walked down what felt like never-ending slopes of ramps. When I finally arrived at the ground level, there were more flocks of people. We were packed together like herds of cattle outside the Astrodome. Gripping my purse and cell phone, I pushed forward. My phone rang. It was Agent Flores. I scrambled to answer.

"Where are you?" she asked.

"I'll call you as soon as I get to Blaque's car."

As soon as I hung up, Blaque called.

"Hey, baby, I see you. Do you see me parked across Fannin Street?"

I laughed. "I saw that neon green Caddy from the top level of the stadium."

Loud, screwed music from Scarface bumped from a distance. Car traffic was stopped. Trotting our way was a line of horses attached to candy-colored stagecoaches. The wheels of the tricked-out carriages were shiny and gold. The drivers were dressed in suits and cowboy hats.

"I wish I had a camera," I told Blaque and swayed to the beat. "This is the coolest thing I've ever seen."

"We'll come back next year, baby. Stay on the phone with me until you make it across the street."

The stagecoaches stopped in front of me and unloaded hundreds of people. As more boarded, I was pushed and pulled through the crowd. I'd lost view of Blaque and the street.

"Where are you, Pearle?" he asked.

Before I could respond, I felt a sharp pinch on my neck, which startled me, and I dropped my phone. When I bent down to grab it, everything went silent, and my vision faded to black.

CHAPTER 23
DEBO

CHRISTIAN "BLAQUE" LAURENT SAVAGE

"PEARLE, BABY? HELLO? Pearle? Where are you?"

While listening to Pearle make her way through the crowd, I heard what sounded like her phone hitting the ground. The only thing I could hear was people talking and feet shuffling. Immediately, I began to panic, especially since she wasn't in my eyesight.

I turned off the car and sprinted like Michael Duane Johnson across the street. My PI ran from the opposite direction. My heart raced and sweat dripped from my forehead and down my face as we frantically searched the crowd for any sign of Pearle.

I pressed the phone to my ear and yelled her name. "*Pearle!*"

"Who is this?" a male voice finally said from the other end.

"This is her husband, motherfucker," I responded, ready to kill. "Who the fuck is this, and where is my wife?"

At that moment, my foot crushed Pearle's pink cowgirl hat into the sidewalk. Looking down, I saw her Chanel bag lying next to it.

"It's Walker, Christian."

His tone said it all. I went numb, and my body hit the pavement. Pearle had disappeared less than fifty yards from me, the FBI, DEA, and my private investigator. After grabbing her purse and hat, I was helped to a black van parked a few feet from where Pearle was last seen.

Inside the government van were Walker and an attractive Latina, Agent Rosa Flores. They informed me that the streets had been blocked, and other field agents were searching the premises.

Agent Flores, Walker, and I reviewed video footage of two Hispanic men snatching Pearle. They had gotten off at Sam's Club parking lot, only one stop from the stadium. I watched as the men flung Pearle around like a rag doll, and my heart shattered. An indescribable pain surged throughout every inch of my being. With Pearle gone, I felt lifeless.

My fist launched my pain directly into Walker's face. He staggered backward. I hated him. Before my fist struck again, Agent Flores stepped in the middle.

"Whoa, Mr. Savage. We will lock your ass up for that."

"I don't give a fuck about jail!" I yelled. "Walker had a personal issue with me and brought my wife into a human trafficking operation on our wedding day. I'm supposed to be on my fucking honeymoon."

Walker landed a hard punch on the right side of my jaw.

"No, you continuously fuck up well-designed operations by going rogue. This is on your crooked ass, Christian."

We got in each other's faces, and I glared at him.

"Be a man and admit you used my wife to get back at me. You took your eyes off Pearle just like you took eyes off the Escobars. You're the real fuck-up who can't do his job."

Agent Flores interrupted. "Gentlemen, sit down. We have an innocent woman to save. The next forty-eight hours will be crucial to locating her. We need to work together."

My stomach churned from the reality. Walker was right. I had fucked up, and my wife was paying the price for the path I had chosen.

My PI had nothing. Pearle had vanished. After forty-eight hours in the tightly packed van and no leads on Pearle, Walker drove me to my car on Fannin Street. It was gone.

"Fuck!" I shouted.

Walker pulled out his phone and found my car at a tow yard nearby.

"We'll find her," he told me when he dropped me off.

I gave him the middle finger, and he sped off. I started making phone calls. Explaining Pearle's disappearance to Goldie was one of the most heart-wrenching things I had ever done.

"Blaque, how in the fuck did she get kidnapped on your honeymoon on a fucking yacht?" he yelled, damn near busting my eardrum.

"Goldie, I'll explain everything to you and your mother when I get to L.A. tomorrow."

He hollered until his voice broke.

"I promise, Goldie, I won't sleep until I find her."

He struggled with his words. "No, if *you* tell my mother, it will kill her."

Before I could say anything else, he hung up. Painfully exhausted in my spirit, I called Blue.

Since I'd set up the family as the main cocaine supplier for the cities we operated, he had taken over Los Angeles as planned. We had returned the Escobar brothers to Columbia, and they were strategically hidden. They were now our allies. As gratitude for preventing their DEA capture, they provided us direct access to Columbian supply at wholesale prices. But like The Notorious B.I.G. song, we had "Mo' Money, Mo' Problems." The alliance was a choice that I wished I could undo. Because I double-crossed the DEA, my wife was now in human captivity.

"What up with business, Blue?" I asked, although I really didn't care at the moment.

"Business is moving, but the block is hot. Yesterday, we lost the Pasadena driver, and this morning, the Compton driver got sideswiped and ran off the road. And just an hour ago, I got the news Arion got locked up in Michigan. Shit is crazy. How are things with you and Pearle?"

I sighed. "Damn, they were our best drivers. I can't believe Arion is doing a bid. I love that dude. He looked out when I first moved to L.A. It's too much shit going on. As for Pearle, I'll fill you in when I get back home tonight."

Upon arriving at LAX, I walked through the airport like a zombie. Once outside, I was comforted by seeing Blue waiting for me in the Bentley. We embraced, and it was the longest hug I'd ever received. Then a thought hit me like a ton of bricks.

"Blue, what was the name of the agency Jules said she got her models from?"

"Scarlet Entertainment."

"*Fuucckk.*" The air was sucked out of my stomach, and tears filled my eyes. "Take me to Jules, *now.*"

He touched my shoulder. "I can't do that, man."

"What? Why?"

"She and all her Jewels are missing."

I searched for God in the sky. *Where are you?*

"Jules was a no-show for the last drop, which was one million dollars' worth of product *she* requested," Blue continued. "I tried to call her, but all lines were disconnected. I went to her crib, and it was completely empty. While I was there, my phone rang from a private number. It was Jules. She said, 'There are eyes on the sparrow,' then hung up. Man, I ran out of there so fast. I thought her crib was going to blow up. I have everybody looking for her ass. Koran knows people who find people, and they are looking all over the city. I heard she was in Cuba, South Africa, and Dubai, but no one has seen her. I figure she'll pop up, but right now, Jules and those damn Jewels are ghosts."

After I told Blue everything, he embraced me like a brother.

"Call Walker and tell him he has another man on the team. I've got your back till the end."

Emotionally overwhelmed, I spoke in a dry whisper. "Man, you don't know how much that means to me."

"What are we going to do about Pearle?"

Gazing out the window, I replied, "I don't know yet, but I won't rest until I find her."

We parked in front of BLACK. Since we were in a street war, we planned a truce meeting with Watts, Hollywood, and Englewood. Blue exited the car, put out his cigar on the street, and opened my door.

Before I could get out, my phone rang, and I looked at the screen. "Blue, this is Walker."

He gave me dap. "We'll only go up from here, bro. Love you."

"I love you more, bro. I'll meet you inside."

Blue flashed a comforting smile and closed the door. I watched him jog across Sunset Boulevard and stop traffic like we'd always done.

As Walker started to speak, I could hear defeat in his voice.

"Christian, I wanted to touch base—"

Suddenly, screeching tires could be heard as an all-black Chevy Impala came to an abrupt stop in front of the club. My phone fell out of my hand upon the sound of rapid gunfire. Screams of fear filled the air, and I felt the chill of death's presence. I jumped out of the car with my Glock, but it was too late. The car sped off, and people scattered like ants through the streets and sidewalks.

I sprinted to Blue and fell to my knees.

"Why, God?" I screamed.

His body floated on a red sea on the concrete. My pain stabbed deeper into the open wound of my spirit.

My brother, Blue, faded and died in my arms.

CHAPTER 24
ADRENALINE RUSH

MAURICE "GOLDIE" BROWN
LOS ANGELES 2000

Karma was a predatorial curse, and I had been its prey ever since I was a boy. When cancer killed my mother, I was too young to have wronged the universe. Years later, the law murdered my brother and incarcerated my father in the same week. I had struggled with God, asking Him, *Why me? What transgression did I commit to deserve karma's wrath?* The trauma sent my mind to dark places. To escape the pain, I would fire up blunts and drink until I was numb. But Pearle was the only real cure that brought me to light. Sure, I had robbed and lied for money. However, I never expected karma to come back around and hurt Pearle to get back at me. My greed started this mess, but Blaque's neglect fucked it into a deadly debacle.

It was almost lunchtime, and I was in the bushes, stroking Pussy's neck. Since Matias's capture, Pussy had become my Pussy.

Driving slowly towards us in his Maserati was Blaque. He was alone.

Pussy purred, and I smiled. "I see his ass, girl."

It had been a long night. Blaque's flight was scheduled to land at ten o'clock the night before, and I wanted to be the first face he saw when he made it to Bel Air. Pussy and I waited for hours in the bushes, and he had finally arrived.

Stopping at the gate, he rolled down his window and then sat there like he was waiting for someone. I sprinted from behind the bushes and pressed the barrel of my .45 caliber against his temple.

"Where's my sister, motherfucker?"

He didn't move, nor did he appear surprised.

"Put your gun away, Goldie."

"Where's your security?"

"They've been here, watching you. I told them not to bother you."

I tossed Pussy in his face. She scratched at him like a cheetah before landing at my feet. His guards had me surrounded at gunpoint, but I didn't care.

"Fuck you and your whack-ass security. Where were you motherfuckers when my sister went missing?"

"Put your guns away and go," Blaque commanded his soldiers. He touched his neck and licked the blood from his fingertips. When they didn't move, he yelled, *"Go!"*

They lowered their weapons, turned around, and vanished behind the tall bushes.

"Goldie, get in. I promise to tell you everything."

"Hell no. Tell me now."

"Please, I only want to tell this story one more time, and there's someone else who deserves to hear it from me."

"I told you, telling my mother is off limits to you."

"I'm not talking about your mother."

He reached over and pushed the passenger door open. I had an idea of who he was speaking of, and I hesitantly walked over. Positioned like a person in the passenger seat was Pearle's pink Baby Phat jogging suit. Blaque carefully slid the pant legs across the console and onto his lap, then wrapped the jacket's sleeves around his neck like they were arms. After picking up Pussy, I got inside.

I wanted to hate Blaque's guts. He had lost one of the most important people in my life, but when I saw the agony written all over his face, I felt no one could hate him more than he hated himself.

We arrived at Woodlawn Memorial and parked in front of Nike's grave. Blaque opened his glove compartment. Two pre-rolled blunts were awaiting us. We each took one and headed for Nike's grave. We sat on the lawn, fired up, and Blaque started his and Pearle's story from the beginning.

After he finished, I was speechless. There was so much to process. My mind rewound to the Escobar contract and moved forward to the present. I painfully relived how I had convinced Pearle to agree to the job when she was against it. I got sick to my stomach when I replayed Pearle whispering in my ear, "What if Blaque's a fed?" I hadn't trusted her gut.

"*Fuck!*" I cried out.

"Goldie, I'm sorry," Blaque said.

"She *knew* your ass was a cop, but I didn't listen."

"I'm not a cop."

"You're worse. You're a fed snitch, and my sister loved you so much that she let you turn her into one."

"I love Pearle more than anyone or anything in this world. I promise I will find her and bring her back."

I got up and started pacing. The next image took my breath away and sent me back to the ground. I reached over and grabbed Blaque's collar. He motioned for his security to stay back. Tears streamed down my face.

"Please, tell me how in the hell, if you have any ounce of love for my sister, did you allow her to become a sex slave? You have to be the worst husband in the world to agree to that."

Huge drops fell from his eyes, and he broke down like a baby. I loosened my grip, letting him go. He moved his lips, but no words came out.

"I need an answer. And do not insult me by saying it was for my father, because he would trade in the rest of his ten-year bid for a life sentence before he would ever agree to let my sister place one toe in an enslavement trap house."

Blaque's face was covered with painful tears as he responded, "I swear before all the angels in this cemetery that what I allowed to happen to my wife does not represent the godly love and respect I have for her. Pearle looked me in my eyes and said her spirit told her that she would save those girls, and my spirit told me I would save Pearle. I trusted my spirit more than my heart, and I've been questioning my religion ever since. Pearle is my heart and soul, and I won't leave this earth without her safely returned in my arms."

The more he cried, the more my hate for him broke down.

I sighed. "Something in my spirit believes in you, nigga, so now is not the time to lose your religion. Pearle needs Blaque Savage, the one possessed by Freddy Krueger and ready to slice any motherfucker in the way of finding her. And you need to find her quickly, or I swear on my brother's grave, I will kill you."

Blaque got on his knees. "Let us pray."

We bowed our heads.

"Please, Father, bring Pearle back to me safely, and I promise I'll do whatever it takes to get back in Your graces. But, right now, I need Your forgiveness in advance because I'm going to kill every motherfucker involved in my wife's disappearance. Amen."

I saw the fire return to his eyes, and I smiled. "Amen, gotdamnit."

Blaque's phone rang as we stood up, and he answered after looking at the caller ID.

"I'm on the way," he told the caller.

We pulled into Tam's parking lot, and Koran ran to Blaque's window.

"What's up, y'all? You look like shit."

"What info do you have about Jules?" Blaque asked.

"My homeboy works valet at Beverly Wilshire and said a brown-skinned Sade look-a-like with sexy lips and a beauty mark checked into room 112 as Brenda Manderson. All she had in her hands was a purse and a big-ass painting."

Blaque tossed Koran a wad of money.

"Thanks, and remember to keep any business conversations short and discreet over the phone."

"I know the drill. Oh, and sorry I couldn't make the wedding, but congrats to you and Pearle. Peace, Goldie."

Blaque and I gave Koran the peace sign, and Blaque drove off.

Before heading to the Wilshire in Beverly Hills, I had lowered the passenger side mirror and was grossed out by my reflection. When I looked over at Blaque, he looked worse. Koran was right—we both looked like shit. I knew we wouldn't make it past security looking like bums, so I suggested we swing by Bloomingdale's. Since it wasn't a leisure shopping spree, I ran in to purchase us some fresh clothes and shoes, while Blaque waited for me in the car. I even grabbed a diaper bag for Pussy. I was in and out in under thirty minutes. By the time we got to the Wilshire Hotel, it was dark outside, and Rodeo Drive was brightly lit like Christmas. The streets and hotel were flooded with people.

As we sat in the car, I asked Blaque, "Isn't Jules your ex-girlfriend?"

"She's an ex-employee."

"Do you think she has information about my sister's kidnapping?"

"Yes."

We got out of the car and walked through the revolving hotel door. Blaque's shoes clacked against the marble floor, and he was walking like he had a wedgy. Clearly, he was uncomfortable with his selection of clothing. We caught the eye of a police officer, who began looking at us suspiciously and following us while we walked across the lobby. As a distraction, I pulled Pussy out of the diaper bag. She purred, and I smiled at the officer.

"Thank you for your service to our great country, sir."

He relaxed his posture and blew Pussy kisses.

I smiled. "She likes you. Would you like to pet her?"

He smiled back and rubbed her head. Then he tipped his hat.

"Cute kitty. You gentlemen have a great day."

When he walked away, I whispered to Blaque, "Shut your shoes up and stop walking like you have something up your ass. You almost got us busted, nigga."

He pointed to his ashy ankles and too-small shoes.

"Really, Goldie? You knew this shit was too small when you bought it."

I chuckled slightly and replied, "Suck it up, dude, and come on."

We walked down the hall and made it to room 112. Blaque knocked on the door, but no one answered. I removed my wallet from my pocket and retrieved the universal magnetic strip cards I had kept for moments like this. The first two cards didn't work. I slid another one through the lock, but the door still didn't budge.

"What are you doing?" Blaque whispered.

"I'm a thief, remember? It's Inspector Gadget shit."

After trying three more cards, the door finally unlocked. We walked cautiously inside, and the room was empty. So, we sat on the couch facing the door and kept checking our watches. Thirty minutes later, Jules walked through the door. She looked surprised but maintained a cool demeanor. In her hand, she was clenching a painting of herself floating in water. At first, she stared at Blaque.

Then she looked at me studying her portrait. She frowned, rolled her eyes, and sat it down facing the wall.

She poured two glasses of bourbon and placed them on the coffee table in front of Blaque and me. She sat in a chair across from us and crossed her legs.

"I knew I would see you again, boss. Your wedding band, brother-in-law's presence, and ridiculous attire tell me you aren't here to invite me to a *ménage à trois*. So why are you here?"

"How are you, *Brenda Manderson*?" Blaque asked.

"Better than you, *Merman*. What can I do for you?"

"I need your contact at Scarlet Entertainment."

She directed her eyes and attention to me. "I don't talk in front of strangers."

I extended my hand. "We haven't formally met. My name is Maurice Brown, and I'm from Compton. Everyone calls me Goldie."

She shook it slowly. "I'm Jules from the hood."

"Which hood?"

"The one in the ghetto." She cut her eyes to Pussy. "Why are you walking around Beverly Hills with a cat in a diaper bag like a weirdo?"

"What's weird is how you're flirting and chasing after my sister's husband."

"You just broke into my room, and your sister's *husband* chased after *me*."

Blaque snapped his finger. "I'm a married man who didn't chase after anyone. Jules, you disrespected me when you left Blue hanging with one million dollars' worth of product."

"I'm sorry, boss. I'll get you the money."

"I don't care about the money. I need what I just asked you for—your contact at Scarlet Entertainment."

"I'm sorry, but giving you my direct contact will get me killed."

"What about Halle and the Jewels? Where are they?" he asked.

"Hidden in different places, living in plain sight." She paused.

"Trust me, you do not want to get in bed with anyone at Scarlet Entertainment. They will burn you in more ways than one."

"Jules, I need your help. They have Pearle," Blaque told her.

"How in the hell did that happen?"

"I fucked up." They held eye contact, and he said, "You know how much I love Pearle, so I need a name."

"Are you asking me to die for her?"

"Of course not," Blaque replied, "but I know you can give me something."

"I don't fuck for free."

"How much do you want?" he asked.

She smiled seductively in response while reaching inside her purse.

I cringed from their mysterious, flirtatious vibe. Unable to take it anymore, I snapped.

"What in the fuck is going on between *you* two? My sister is missing, and I'm done watching you eye fuck each other."

Blaque and Jules broke their gaze, and he shot me a chilling look that told me to shut the fuck up. I sank my teeth into my lips to restrain myself from saying anything more.

Jules immediately closed her purse and crossed her legs.

"Blaque, come back without your brother-in-law. He obviously has a problem with me."

"Fuck him," he said. "All I care about is my wife."

She looked me up and down again, then asked, "Are *we* fucking good, Goldie?"

I gave her a thumbs-up. "*All* fucking good."

She reached back inside her purse and grabbed a pen and paper, handing it to Blaque.

"I don't need your money, Blaque. I need a good criminal attorney."

He wrote something down and returned the pen and paper to

her. "This is the number for my cousin, Judge. He lives in Atlanta. Tell him I sent you."

She wrote something down and gave it to him. "Go to this address tomorrow night."

"What is this place?" he asked.

"It's a club. If a tall, Dwayne "The Roc" Johnson look-a-like is standing at the door, the person you need is inside. Dress like you're rich, be charming, and spend frivolously. Catch the attention of a girl in a red dress, and you're in."

I shook my head. "Excuse me, but we don't have time for riddles."

"Blaque, it's the only way."

"Fine, count me in," I said. "I'm charming as hell."

"And I'm rich as hell," Jules snickered, "but I'll never be Oprah Winfrey."

"Blaque, *ella es siempre así?*" I asked.

"English," she commanded.

I huffed. "Are you always like this?"

"Are you always a weirdo?"

Blaque snapped his fingers again. "Jules, do you have any idea where my wife could be?"

"I really don't know." Just then, her phone rang. "I'm sorry, but I have to take this call."

We all walked to the door, and on Blaque's way out, he stopped.

"Why did you stiff Blue all of a sudden, and what did you mean when you told him 'eyes are on the sparrow?'"

"The feds are watching us, and I'm on the run. I was trying to warn him," Jules replied.

"Have you ever told anyone about me or Blue or how you got your product?"

"Not a soul, but you already knew that."

"Take care of yourself," Blaque told her. "And thank you."

She grabbed her painting and placed the phone up to her ear. "You, too, and I do hope you find Pearle."

When we got to the car, I snatched Blaque's keys. "I think we should go back. You need to press Jules harder for more information. I think she's hiding something."

He got in the passenger seat and placed Pearle's cowboy hat that he had been keeping in the car over his face. "No, she gave us enough."

"You're putting a lot of trust in your *ex*-employee. Did you fuck her?" I asked as he reclined his seat.

"No."

"Would you tell me if you did?"

"No."

"That's why my sister had to beat your ass in my club."

"Your sister had convicted an innocent man."

"Whatever, *Merman*."

"Whatever, *Weirdo*." He sat up and took the hat off his face. "Pearle is the only woman I've ever loved, and I love her more than anything. She is my life, and I will do whatever it takes to get her back. You told me to slice motherfuckers in my path, and your big mouth almost got in my way. So, I advise you to shut the hell up," he warned, then placed Pearle's hat back over his face.

I started the car. "Whatever."

Before I pulled off, Jules quickly walked out the Wilshire's front door, followed by a tall, beautiful woman holding Jules' painting and purse.

I pushed Blaque's arm. "Hey! Who is that with Jules?"

He sat up and squinted his eyes. "Halle, her assistant. Drive a little closer."

The valet opened the doors of a white Lincoln Navigator, but before Jules could get inside, a dark-skinned brother dressed in a black suit and Air Jordans walked coolly toward her.

Blaque mumbled through his teeth. *"Walker."*

"Who is Walker? The feds?" I asked. "He's the dirty DEA agent who lost Pearle."

"Motherfucker."

Walker was followed by a group of men and women dressed in black business suits. They surrounded Jules' car, and she and Halle surrendered.

"They got Jules," I said.

"I'm not worried about her."

Blaque reclined his seat, covered himself with Pearle's hoodie, and put her hat back over his face. Pussy hopped on his lap, and before we left the parking lot, they were snoring.

Pearle's disappearance did more than strike a deep pain inside me. Losing her made me realize that my choices had the power to impact more than me. I'd almost gotten Pearle, Blaque, and me killed. I had nearly lost my mother's house and everything I'd worked for, and I had hurt and humiliated my boo, Tina, for years. Since we were teenagers, all she'd ever done was love me. I'd witnessed Blaque have a mental breakdown from regretful choices he had made, and I didn't want to bear that type of weight anymore. I told Pearle that when bad no longer felt good, it was time to change, and my time had come.

After Blaque and I parted ways that night, I went home defeated, and like always, Tina was waiting for me. She held me while I cried and confessed everything Blaque had told me. I was the most vulnerable I had been in my life.

The next morning, it sounded like karma banging on my front door, and the bangs only got louder the longer I lay there. Knowing I couldn't delay the inevitable forever, I kissed Tina passionately, like it was going to be our last kiss. Then I fired up a blunt, exhaled the smoke, put it out, and rolled out of bed.

Tina sat up. "Goldie, what's wrong? What's going on?"

I quickly got dressed and reached inside the closet to grab my bulletproof vest, which I wrapped around my chest. Then I slathered Vaseline on my face.

"Get dressed, boo," I told her.

Tina quickly slid into her dress and grabbed a Tech-9 from under the bed.

"Let's go," she said, ready for battle.

I smiled and handed her a video camera. "Put down the gun, boo. Five-o is here for me."

Hesitantly, she placed the gun under the mattress. "How do you know?" she asked.

"I know that knock, but I need you to record in case they try to Rodney King a nigga."

Following my instructions, Tina pressed record. "They better not try anything."

I picked up Pussy and smiled for what I thought would be the last time for many years. Then Tina and I sauntered down the hallway, moving slowly as if we were walking the green mile. Once I reached the door, I swung it open. Unable to believe what I saw on the other side, I slammed it shut and turned to stare into the camera.

Tina, who was still filming, started crying. "Open the door, Goldie."

I caught my breath and wiped the tears from my face. The doorbell rang. When I opened the door again, my father rushed inside. We threw our arms around each other and embraced like we would never let go. Mama walked in behind him, and she and Tina joined our hug. It was one of the happiest moments of my life. The DEA agent, Walker, threw up the deuces and shut my front door. I hated him for losing Pearle, but I had my father, mama, and Tina in my arms. Now all I needed was for Blaque to bring my sister back to me to make my life complete.

CHAPTER 25
HOLY GRAIL

CHRISTIAN "BLAQUE" LAURENT SAVAGE
LOS ANGELES 2000

I HAD KNOWN EVERY inch of my property, but without Pearle living in it, it was foreign territory. I'd kept everything in the house exactly how she left it. I tattooed her face on my chest, spritzed her perfume on my skin, and slept with something she had worn while lying next to me. I did these things as a constant reminder that I would see, smell, and feel her again.

I was standing in front of the mirror inside my spacious walk-in closet, fumbling with my tie, when I caught Uncle Henry watching me. He walked behind me and turned me around.

"Let me help you, nephew." He began tying my tie and stopped. "Why did you dismiss your security?"

"They are a useless distraction."

"And you missed Blue's funeral. Christian, everyone is worried about you."

"I know."

"You've never shut us out, and with Pearle missing, you need both families now more than ever."

"Not this time, Uncle. I've got to do this alone."

He sighed. "But you are not working alone. You're working with the U.S. government."

"I am, but I'm not."

"You *are* working with them, and Agent Walker is downstairs waiting for you. I don't trust him at all."

"Neither do I."

He tightened my tie with the perfect knot. "Then why in the hell are you working with him instead of family?"

"Uncle Henry, I need you and everyone else to back off so I can focus on finding Pearle," I snapped. "If I need your help, I will let you all know."

He frowned with disapproval while helping me put on my suit jacket. Then he brushed my shoulders and followed me downstairs. Agent Walker was standing in the foyer, scanning the room. When I saw him, I felt a strong sickness in my stomach. He had released Pearle's father as promised, and I gave him credit for that. However, the family reunion was bitter because Pearle wasn't there.

Uncle Henry stood beside me with his hands folded in front of him.

"Leave us alone, Uncle."

He glared at Agent Walker and then went back up the stairs.

"Walker, unless you have information about Pearle, I need you to go," I told him. "Tonight is not the night, and I'm in a hurry."

"I told you, Christian, to stay out of my way. I know you went to see Juliette Remington at the Wilshire."

"Yeah, so?"

"I need to know what she told you."

"She didn't tell me anything."

"Christian, help me, and in return, I'll help you. I am privy to information that can help you find Pearle."

I despised his fake sincerity.

"You don't give a damn about Pearle," I spat. "All you care about is your promotion."

"You've assumed it's just about a promotion. I care about protecting my family by cleaning up our community. My father died of an overdose because cartels like the Escobars and Torres brought drugs here and poisoned our neighborhoods. So, catching big fish criminals is personal for me. I have a wife and family that I must provide for and protect, and like you, I live and die for mine. So, let me help you, and we can get what we both want. Also, I will need any information you have about the Escobars' whereabouts."

I didn't care about him or the Escobars.

Sighing, I replied, "Fine, but I don't want to ever see you again after this, and I mean it this time."

He extended his hand. "Trust me, after this case is closed, you won't."

Hesitantly, I shook his hand. "Jules gave me an address to a possible lead, and I'm on my way. I'll let you know what I find out in the morning."

I rushed past him and onto the porch outside. He followed.

"I'm going with you," he said.

I shook my head. "No. I'm doing this solo."

He walked to his car and opened the back door like a chauffeur. "Get in. I'll be your driver."

"There's no way I'm riding in a hooptie with anyone dressed in a Sears suit, especially a cop."

"First, this is a new, freshly detailed Honda Accord, and my suit was bought from Nordstrom's and is tailored, spoiled brat."

"My bad for the diss, but you do look like a fed. You'll get us killed."

"I was D-Walk before I was Agent Walker, *Blaque*."

I didn't trust a word out of Walker's mouth, but I trusted his intel. If it weren't for Walker, I wouldn't have known the Escobars had hired Pearle and Goldie to rob me. And if I were going to find Pearle, his confidential secrets would get me to her quicker.

Walker stood there, sporting a decent suit with fresh Air Jordans. I'd always thought if he wasn't a cop I despised, I could

see myself shooting hoops with him. He had enough swag and
street smarts to blend into a hood environment. We were the same
frame and build, and I believed, with a mini-makeover, we could
pull Walker off as my driver.

Within ten minutes, Walker had transformed into D-Walk. I
replaced his Kenneth Cole suit with Armani, zirconia studs with
diamonds, and his Accord with a Bentley. The only thing he
wouldn't change was his shoes. He was fresh, and I had to admit,
bad looked good on him.

We drove to the address Jules had given me. Thinking we
were lost the first time we saw the place, we circled back around.
We were in a random neighborhood, and Walker was driving
slowly down an empty street.

I looked at the address again and said, "Stop. This is the place."

Walker stopped in front of a vintage-styled store with an
illuminated "CLOSED" sign hanging in the window. The words
"Glass House" were painted on the door. Inside, I could see tables
with various glass sculptures on top of each one.

Walker parked and turned to me. "Jules played you."

"She wouldn't do that. Just chill."

Minutes later, a man dressed in a white welder's uniform
walked out of the Glass House door and into the middle of the
street. Walker and I sat silently observing.

The Dwayne Johnson look-a-like peered through the glass
door. He and I exchanged glances, but he didn't leave the store.

"Do you know him?" I asked Walker.

"His name is Rocco Greene."

"Who does he work for?"

"A ghost the FBI has been trying to capture."

A few minutes passed, and a silver garage door next to the store opened. Walker slowly drove inside. There was a Ferrari ahead of us. Valet workers were dressed in welder suits. The worker in front of us took the driver's keys and parked the car less than twenty feet away.

Walker pulled out his wallet and snatched a twenty-dollar bill from inside. He grunted.

"There's no way in hell this man deserves a tip."

I tossed two stacks over Walker's shoulder. "When spending money while with me, whatever your brain says to pay, multiply it by five."

"You want me to give that man one hundred dollars to move the car ten feet?"

"Yes. You are a baller, D-Walk. Summon your inner thug."

The valet opened our doors. I inhaled Pearle's floral scent on my wrist before stepping out of the car and onto the red carpet. I was officially Blaque Savage, possessed by Freddy Kreuger, and ready to slice a motherfucker up. Next to me was D-Walk from College Park in Georgia, and I could see he had left all traces of Agent Walker inside the car.

Rocco Greene removed the red velvet rope blocking the entrance and opened a glass door. Walker and I stepped inside and walked down a long, graffiti-painted hallway. We stopped at a dead-end in front of a black and pearl-colored glass sculpture that caught my eye. On both sides of the hallway were two closet doors facing each other, each marked "Art Supplies."

The handle on the left closet door jiggled, and the door opened. After Walker and I entered, we were surrounded by girls wrapped in fitted black dresses and jeweled-colored pumps—the same attire I'd seen when I met Jules. In their hands were bottles of champagne and sprinklers. House music was blasting loudly through the speakers. Glass Door was actually a swanky speakeasy. As we followed the ladies through the crowd, I observed a larger male ratio than women.

An exotic-looking woman in green stilettos wrapped her fingers around my hand.

"Hey, handsome. I'm Emerald. What's your name?"

"Whatever you want it to be," I replied while following her to a large booth, where she poured me a glass of champagne and sat on my lap.

She placed her hand on my face and whispered in my ear, "I'm yours all night. If you need anything, let me know."

I slipped five one-hundred-dollar bills between her breasts. "Can you bring my partner and me a cigar and two shots of bourbon?"

She left and returned with two Cuban cigars and our drinks.

Walker was drinking with a lady in blue, and he and I exchanged glances. Wanting to scope the place, I handed Emerald my cigar.

"Can you hold this for me? I'll be back."

She smiled. "I'll be waiting."

I ran to the restroom, doused my face with water, and locked myself in the stall. A minute later, the restroom door slammed and locked. Then there was a light knock on the stall's door. When I looked down, I saw a pair of green pumps peeking from under it.

What am I doing? I asked myself.

I slowly opened the door, and Emerald threw her arms around my neck. She removed a clear vial from between her breasts and unscrewed the top.

"Do you want to party?" she asked.

I placed my hands around hers. "Hi, beautiful. May I see that?"

She handed the vial to me. The bottle was similar to my product, Pearl, but a bootlegged version. I took a taste of the cocaine with my finger. It was trash.

"Are you ready?" she asked.

"Do you know how I can get more?"

"It's a secret," she whispered.

I reached inside my pocket and counted out ten one-hundred-dollar bills.

"I promise it will stay between us."

She took the money. Her lips trembled and opened like she was going to speak, but the sudden banging on the restroom door startled her into silence.

She placed the money back in my hand.

"I'm sorry. I have to go," she said, then stumbled out of the stall and rushed out of the restroom.

Damn! Emerald had slipped through my fingers, and it made me sick. Despite the bathroom having gotten busy, I locked myself back inside the stall. I deeply inhaled my wrist again and closed my eyes. Pearle's face flashed before me in my mind. Desperation filled my veins at my deep desire to see her in the flesh again.

CHAPTER 26
DREAMS

SOL MILIAN
LAREDO 2000

As I REGAINED consciousness, I was nearly deafened by ringing in my ears. I was lying on a cold stone floor and could faintly hear Spanish music playing. I didn't know if it was daytime or night. I was unaware of how long I'd been incoherent, but I estimated I'd been out for days from the weakness and sickness I felt in my bones. I rubbed my legs together for warmth, and my skin felt covered with dirt. The smell of urine and funk infiltrated my nostrils, causing me to gag and dry heave. My body was heavy like bricks. I opened my eyes. Although the room was completely dark, rainbow-colored lights flickered on the right side of my brain. The flashers blinded me. I attempted to move, but excruciating pain kept me bound.

A soft hand touched my back, and I jumped.

"Shhh," she whispered. "Just act sleep."

In a state of shock, I stayed stiff as a board. I was too dehydrated to shed a tear, so I whimpered quietly. The gentle touch on my back comforted me. Regret and agony filled my spirit as I grasped my reality. I was captured.

A bright light filled the room and triggered my nausea. The sickness intensified the throbbing pain and dizziness. I closed my eyes but found no relief. My throat was parched, and I coughed.

Two men walked down the stairs, followed by a thin, petite

Latina who was striking and appeared no older than thirty years old. She covered her nose with a handkerchief to lessen her exposure to the foul stench.

"Who is that coughing?" she asked. Her voice was loud and more mature than her appearance. When no one spoke, she yelled, "If I ask again, everyone will be punished."

I tried to lift my head. *"Señora."*

"What's your name?" she barked.

"Mi nombre es Sol Milian."

She motioned for me to come to her. When I attempted to stand, vertigo knocked me down.

She smacked one of the men in the head. "Help Sol stand and bring her to me."

The short, stubby man held a .45 caliber in his hand. He shuffled bodies with the soles of his shoe like dirt, creating a path. When he got to me, he grabbed my hand and yanked me to my feet. I stumbled past several black and brown females, all appearing no older than twenty.

The woman grabbed my face. "Did I talk to you in Spanish, Sol?"

Terrified, I held my hand over my mouth to prevent myself from vomiting in her face.

"No, ma'am."

She pulled my hair, and I threw up in my mouth.

"Don't do shit without my permission again. Do you understand me?"

Weakened, I hit the ground.

"What's wrong with you?"

I swallowed. "Migraine, ma'am."

She looked at the stubby man and slapped his face. "José Luis, you are responsible for taking care of the girls. How can we demand high prices if we starve them to death? We have a potential big buyer and need to clean them up. Take Sol upstairs and give her water and food."

I sat on the cool kitchen floor with a glass of water and a piece of white sandwich bread. The woman handed me two Excedrin migraine caplets and another glass of water. She then helped me up and guided me to a small bedroom with a twin-sized bed, nightstand, and lamp.

"Sol, lie down and get some rest."

After I lay down, she stared at me for several seconds before leaving and closing the door.

I woke up migraine-free, but surprisingly, I was still nauseated. The woman sat across from me in a chair next to my bed. I didn't move. On the nightstand next to the lamp were a Subway sandwich, jalapeno chips, and a paper cup. My mouth watered from the scent of the freshly baked bread. We locked eyes.

"Eat."

As usual, I scarfed down my food.

"Thank you," I said.

"Sol, tell me about yourself."

I gave her Sol's life story. As a young girl, I'd moved between foster homes and dreamt of becoming a model. I met a woman named Rosa on MySpace, who told me about Scarlet Entertainment, where I could be a promotional model.

She held my face with cold, skinny fingers. "I examined your body while you were asleep. Besides your tattoo, you don't have any scars or marks and no drug tracks. You speak Spanish and look perfect. I'm making you my pet." She smiled with evil eyes. "You will do whatever I ask. Your main responsibility will be taking care of the girls and me. I have a potential order for about thirty girls of color. The buyer would need them cleaned up. My guys drug the girls to keep them quiet, but you can make sure they are fed, cleaned, and healthy for buyers. How does that sound?"

I nodded and stuttered. "What do I call you?"

She got up and walked to the door. "Rafel…but call me, ma'am."

She slammed the door behind her, and I was left feeling even more terrified. The woman was who I had suspected—Rafelina Torres.

When Rafelina left the room, I cried myself to sleep. The loud sound of a busted car alarm honked directly into my eardrum. The door swung open, and clothes smacked my face.

José Luis stood in the doorway, fully dressed in an ill-fitted black suit.

"*Vamanos, puta.*"

I followed him down a dark hallway with wooden floors wet and smelling of Pine Sol. We stood outside a white door adorned with a large golden crucifix. José Luis slowly opened it.

Rafelina was on her knees, swaying and chanting a prayer that began with "Hail Mary full of grace." She held a cross and beaded necklace in her right hand.

José and I froze like ice sculptures. A praying woman should not be frightening, but José Luis, the closest person to her, was just as terrified as me. From that moment forth, I nicknamed her Devilina.

After a few additional mumbled prayers, she rose and came to us. Her lips were weird, between a smile and a frown.

"From now on, your name is Pet. If you tell anyone your real name, I'll kill you and them. If you think about leaving, I'll kill you. Understand?"

I nodded obediently. "Yes, ma'am."

"Good, Pet. You look like shit. Clean yourself up. Pull your hair back into a tight bun."

"Yes, ma'am."

She smiled. "And hurry the fuck up."

I bolted to the bathroom and threw up. I didn't know how many days had passed since my capture, but when I looked in the mirror, I'd aged several years. My face was covered with dust, and my lips were dried and cracked. My bleached blonde hair was knotted and clumped all over my head. The worst part of my face was my eyes. They were dark and looked sunken in the sockets. My pupils were dilated, and the whites were bright pink. I sobbed with silent tears.

After taking a lukewarm shower, washing my hair, and applying lotion to my body, I still looked like shit. As instructed, I slicked down my hair with gel from a large clear tub and slipped into a ridiculous all-black *I Dream of Jeanie* outfit and gold choker.

There were two heavy pounds on the door. *"Vamanos, Puta."*

I stared into the mirror. In my reflection was karma, revenge from Maxwell and the others I had deceived—payback for lives I'd destroyed. I looked at my vanished smile and deflated ass. *Poison.*

CHAPTER 27
KING OF DIAMONDS

CHRISTIAN "BLAQUE" LAURENT SAVAGE
LOS ANGELES 2000

WALKER AND I had been at Glass House for a couple of hours. As Jules had instructed, I had worn my most expensive clothes and jewelry, spent my money frivolously, and charmed my way into the hearts of all the women I had come in contact with. My eyes had scanned the club all night, but no woman in a red dress was in sight. I was emotionally and physically drained and sickened from defeat. The crowd was slowly thinning, and my aura was fading.

Walker leaned over. "We should go. You are starting to look bored. We can try again next week."

I knew he was right, but leaving before the club closed felt like giving up on Pearle, and I refused to do that.

"I just need some fresh air. I'll be back."

"I'll come with you," he said.

"Hell no. I need alone time and a brief change of scenery."

Before he could respond, I left and walked briskly through the club. I needed to escape the flickering strobe lights, loud music, and clingy girls. I needed time to breathe and clear my mind.

I wandered out of the door we had entered, and it locked behind me. I started to knock but changed my mind. The sudden silence and dimmed lights in the hallway were exactly what I needed. I strolled down the hallway towards the Glass Door entrance to feel the night air, but the graffiti art on the walls pulled me in. There was texture and details I hadn't noticed the first time, and I followed the artist's path that ended at the black and white glass sculpture I had admired when I first arrived. Captivated, I got lost in emotion, feeling the love and pain of the artist who created it.

"Hello," a man said.

I turned to face an impeccably dressed Hispanic man with a long ponytail. I had no idea who he was, but anyone rocking over fifty thousand dollars' worth of clothing and jewelry was someone I felt like I needed to know.

"Hello," I replied.

"I've never seen anyone take the time to look at anything in this hallway."

"I'm an admirer of the work."

"What do you like about it?" he asked.

"The contrast. I gravitate towards art that makes me feel conflicted. And the graffiti on the wall reminds me of home."

"How so?"

"There are different aspects of the struggle between love and war throughout."

He looked impressed. "Where are you from?"

"Jamaica. What about you?"

"Mexico. You don't sound Jamaican."

"And you don't sound Mexican."

We both laughed, and he said, "You keep eyeing the sculpture. Why?"

"I have something similar in my art gallery, except it fuses white glass with black metal."

"That sounds beautiful. Where did you get it?"

"I sculpted it at an art school in Kingston."

"So, you're a Jamaican artist?"

"I would love to create all day, but I'm too busy running shit."
He laughed, and I continued, "Why are you asking me so many
questions? Do you know the artist?"

"Yes, this is my work."

I extended my hand. "I'm a big fan, *señor. Como se llama?*"

He smiled. *"Hablas espanol?"*

"Si."

"Me llamo, Larazo, *y tu?"*

"Blaque. *Mucho gusto*, Larazo."

"Nice to meet you, too, *Señor* Blaque. What type of 'shit' do
you run that prevents you from pursuing your passion?"

"I run a family business that exports sugar to America."

"Why type of sugar?"

"All kinds—brown, white, and powdered."

"Is Jamaican sugar better than other countries?" Larazo asked.

"It's the sweetest and much purer than what I just had in the
restroom."

"Do you think I'm interested in that type of sugar?"

"I think a man who wears a twenty-thousand-dollar pair of
Testoni shoes and five-carat VVS cuff links may be interested in
sugar," I replied. "But if you are not that man, I think you and I
could agree on a price that will connect me to a man who is."

"Who's your favorite artist, Blaque?"

"Jean Michel Basquiat. What about you?"

"Andy Warhol. What Basquiat piece do you wish you could
get your hands on?"

"It's already hanging on my gallery wall," I replied. "What
about yours?"

"It's in my office. Would you like to see it?"

"It would be my pleasure."

My heart had stopped for a moment while Larazo and I were talking. I didn't know exactly who Larazo was, but meeting him created the most anxiety I had ever felt. I knew in my gut that the unexpected way our paths had intersected would somehow lead me directly to Pearle. I also knew meeting a man like Larazo the way I had was a once-in-a-lifetime opportunity. I had one mission, and that was not to fuck it up.

There was a keypad on the art supplies door located on the right side of the wall. Larazo entered a code, unlocking the door. We stepped inside, and the atmosphere was the opposite of the club on the left. There was dead energy in the room. The crowd was meek, the music was somber classical, and the women working were like beautiful zombies.

I followed Larazo to a wall of small glass figurines. There was an opening on the right, and we walked through it. We stopped in front of a black metal door. He entered a code on the keypad. It opened without him touching it. We walked inside. The room was very eclectic, with colorful art and sculptures scattered throughout. He had two Andy Warhol paintings on the wall, and we discussed art as two eager enthusiasts. We finally sat down, and he looked ready to discuss business.

"Blaque, no one has ever seen this room. It is very sacred, but you are the only person I have met with the same art interests as me. Tell me why you chose to come to Glass House. The club scene does not fit you."

"It is not my scene. I came here for business reasons, honestly. I heard Glass House provides the most impeccable service in L.A., and I wanted to experience it myself. In addition to my export operation in Jamaica, I own several clubs around the U.S."

Larazo's demeanor was emotionless.

"I am attracting clientele who have very deep pockets," I continued. "I know I can provide them with the highest quality of product, but as it stands, my clubs do not offer my clientele the highest level of service they deserve."

"Again, what makes you think I am the man who can help you with this?"

By his disposition shift, I felt him slipping away, so to reconnect, I said, "Larazo, you have shared your art inspiration, along with your sacred place with me. No man, other than family, has given me this level of respect. Business aside, I would like to invite you to my art gallery inside my home, which is very sacred to me."

My heart raced as I waited for him to answer.

He stood up and stuck out his hand. "That is very generous, Blaque, but I do not visit the homes of people I do not know. I'm sure you understand."

My heart crashed to the floor. "I do."

He walked me outside of his office. "This side of the club is an exclusive level higher than VIP. You and the man you came with can enjoy the service and amenities—on the house, of course."

I extended my hand. "*Gracious,* but I have other business to attend to. Again, I love your work, and it was a pleasure, Larazo."

After Larazo went back behind the wall, I stood there with my feelings flat on the ground. I felt like I had missed the basketball free throw that would have won my team the NBA championship. I took a few deep breaths and searched for the door to return to Walker, but I found him seated alone at the bar.

I walked over to him. "How did you get over here?" I asked.

"Rocco came and got me. Where were you?"

"It's not important."

"Are you hiding something from me?"

"No. Let's go," I replied, trying to hide my frustration.

We tried to exit the door we had entered but were unsuccessful. The lady in the red dress finally came over.

"Are you looking for something, gentlemen?" she asked.

I managed to crack a smile. "The exit, please."

She smiled back, and we followed her to a side glass door. The Bentley was parked and waiting, and Walker and I stepped outside. The valet driver opened our doors. I plopped down in my seat, feeling depleted and defeated. Goldie had told me that it wasn't the time for me to lose my religion, but my faith had shrunken to the size of a mustard seed.

I shut my eyes, and Walker started driving. In an attempt to get comfortable in the seat, I rolled over to the left. While doing so, I opened my eyes. That's when I noticed a white box on the floor. A card was attached to the top with my name on it. My heart jumpstarted as I picked up the box like it was the holy grail. Opening the card, I started to read it:

I hope to see your Basquiat and this inside your art gallery very soon.
Larazo

"Walker, have you heard of a man named Larazo? He's wealthy and wears a long ponytail."

"I know of a Larazo Torres, Rafelina's younger brother," he replied. "But as far as I know, she keeps him distanced from her business. Why?"

Having been on an emotional rollercoaster all night, the only thing I could do was laugh. I laughed so hard that tears fell down my face.

Walker took his eyes off the road long enough to turn around and ask, "What's so funny?"

I wiped my face. "God."

With the box on my lap, I lifted its lid. Wrapped inside was Larazo's black and white glass sculpture. Next to it was a cell phone.

I inhaled my wrist; Pearle's fragrance was still there.

Closing my eyes, I whispered, "I will never lose my faith again."

CHAPTER 28
HAUNTED

SOL MILIAN
LAREDO 2000

I FOLLOWED DEVILINA DOWN the cold steps into the dungeon and was introduced to everyone as Pet. Each girl was stripped of their name and given a number for their identification. They wore black spandex that fit so tight it looked like a second layer of skin. We wore our hair snatched into tight buns. Devilina did not want to see a strand of hair out of place, and she meticulously inspected each girl every morning to make sure our appearance was to her liking. She'd get vicious whenever a girl didn't meet her expectation of "perfection."

Every day, we rose at five a.m. and used one sink. Each girl was given five minutes to wash her body and brush her teeth. We used our washcloths as toothbrushes. Seven-thirty a.m. was inspection time. At eight a.m., we cleaned the entire dungeon. Breakfast was at nine a.m. and consisted of water, fruit, and sunflower seeds. At ten a.m., we exercised, and at eleven a.m., I read Bible scriptures to the girls. We ate lettuce, carrots, and sunflower seeds at noon and drank water. At one o'clock, we had free time to read more of the Bible or draw. At four p.m., we were served dinner—lunch meat, cold broccoli, white bread, and water. Before bed, each girl was again given five minutes to wash up and clean her teeth. Lights were out at eight p.m. That's when I would go upstairs to eat my six-inch Subway sandwich, chips, and drink, then shower before going to sleep.

This was the schedule Devilina expected me to execute flawlessly. There was no time for illnesses that required real medical attention. The only medicine she administered was Pepto Bismol or Excedrin. Those girls who experienced ailments that stemmed from drug and alcohol withdrawals received no care.

Devilina had zero tolerance for fighting, but how could she expect order in a hostile environment? I tried to keep things quiet, but sometimes the girls wanted to fight me, feeling I had special treatment. Didn't they know I was also being held captive and only doing as instructed?

If anyone, including myself, were deemed out of line, she would administer one public lash of her animal whip. One thrash didn't damage our skin enough to affect her profits, but it scarred us emotionally.

Week three had the strongest-willed group of girls. They organized a hunger strike. I wanted to join, but my mind was on the brink of insanity. Plus, my body had cravings that couldn't defy nourishment. Devilina randomly picked Twenty and whipped her in front of everyone until she was bloodied and delirious, making her authority clear to avoid further organized defiance.

Seventeen, from week three, was very special to me. She was naturally pretty but hardened, especially around the eyes, from too much time spent in darkness. She reminded me so much of myself. She loved acting. Like me, she used her acting skills to escape her surroundings. She even attended a performing arts school in her hometown of Gary, Indiana. The only thing I knew about her city was it was the hometown of the famous Jackson family.

Seventeen surprised me when she told me that Gary had been named the nation's murder capital. She described her neighborhood and how she grew up exposed to drugs and violence.

Seventeen had given me hope; she was the first to talk about escaping. She was an expert at picking locks and hotwiring cars. She spoke so strongly that I risked my life and gave her my real name. I told her everything.

We planned our escape—the seventh day of the week at 2:17 a.m. was our time to run. The day before, we moved with more energy and giggled with excitement. Oddly, I wasn't scared, anxious, or uneasy. Everything was right. That night, I confidently set my alarm clock for 1:30 a.m. and placed it under my pillow.

There was a soft knock on my door. I looked at the clock—1:07 a.m. I tiptoed to the door and prayed Seventeen wanted to leave early. Through the crack, I saw one hazel eye. I gasped, and tears poured down my face.

"Shhh, Pearle," Blaque whispered. "It's me."

He walked in and slowly closed the door. I jumped into his arms— my safety.

"Blaque, I missed you so much. We have to get Seventeen and go."

He kissed me with so much power I lost my breath.

"Pearle, I missed you, too, baby. Why didn't you listen to me? Why didn't you let me protect you, baby?"

"I'm so sorry, Blaque. I just wanted to do something right. Goldie said God would reveal my time to make a life change, and I felt it. The feeling was so strong I couldn't fight it. But, please, let's go. I fucking hate it here."

He grabbed my face and kissed my tears.

I held onto him, but he wouldn't move. "Blaque, por favor. Please, let's go. Vamanos."

Each kiss from his lips felt softer and softer until I felt nothing.

I woke up with my pillow soaked in tears. Salty tears stung my eyes. I pulled out my alarm clock. It was 1:05 a.m. My dream had been so real that I peeked out the door to see if Blaque was in the hallway, but there was only darkness.

I sat on my bed and smiled. The great escape was happening in an hour. Hype, I started Crip-walking around the room.

Moments later, a chorus of high-pitched screams echoed through the house. Sickness filled the pit of my stomach. My heart raced as I ran out my door. José Luis pulled out his .45 and pointed it at my face. I froze.

Devilina walked cautiously out of her room.

"José Luis, did you unlock my door and the basement?"

He showed her his keys and explained they had been on him the entire time. They looked at me, and I shrugged.

The shrills from the basement grew louder. If anyone lived nearby, they heard it.

Devilina and José Luis were scared white. They believed ghosts had unlocked the doors and left them open.

"Can I check on the girls?" I asked.

"Yes, Pet," Devilina barked. "Get your ass down there. Make them shut the fuck up."

I walked carefully down the stairs. When I saw the horrified look on Twenty-One's face, I knew something terrible had happened.

I trembled, afraid to ask. "What's wrong?"

"P...P...P...Pet, it's Seventeen," Eighteen stuttered.

Everyone pointed at the staircase. I looked around but didn't see anything.

"What's wrong with Seventeen?" I asked.

I clicked on the light, and everyone screamed again. A few ran and hid in the bathroom. As I moved further down the stairs, I felt something brush against my face and looked up. I closed and slowly re-opened my eyes, not wanting to believe what I saw.

Seventeen had hung herself with Devilina's whip. "Our Only Escape" was written on a piece of paper secured to her shirt with the bobby pins she must have used to pick the locks.

My knees slammed against the cold floor as I collapsed. "Why, God?" I screamed.

Just like that, my dreams of freedom were dashed, and my nightmarish captivity continued.

After Seventeen's suicide, a piece of me vanished. My saddened spirit lifted from me, and I watched the shell of my body merely exist.

We were in hell without the flames, and our torturer was Devilina. We were women and teenagers snatched, tricked, and condemned to slavery that began in a hellish dungeon. My only escape was mental fantasies. I would get lost in my thoughts, which kept me breathing. I repeated my daddy's words of wisdom about keeping my mind free even if my body was imprisoned.

My dreams kept me alive. Whenever I could, I dreamt of Blaque's face, touch, and smile. Our memories were planted in my mind, and our love deeply rooted in my heart.

In my fantasies, my family's existence was fresh. I envisioned my daddy's reunion with Mommy and Goldie. The wooden stage I once loved and performed on entered my thoughts.

Who would I be if I'd chosen to pursue my passion?

After Seventeen died, I began to pray daily. I learned to pray alone. I prayed for our release from captivity. I prayed relentlessly for a brighter fate for the ladies who moved in and out of the dungeon. I prayed for my sins. I prayed for my salvation.

Even though Seventeen had committed suicide, Devilina was convinced the house was haunted and that ghosts had killed Seventeen. She frequently called me into her bedroom at night to sleep on her floor to soothe her fears. As I lay there, I often thought about suffocating her. Occasionally, I worked up a sliver of courage to execute, but something inside me wouldn't release me to follow through. She was a tormented woman who used me as her therapist, forcing me to listen to her transgressions that she should have been confessing to God.

Devilina hosted weekly parties. Afterward, she would entertain different men in her room. As her Pet, I was at her beck and call to do whatever she wanted done. After one party, she had no man to keep her company. So, she summoned me to wash her hair.

As I rubbed the warm water on her back, she confided in her drunken state, "Pet, I know you wonder why I do this—how can a woman sell other women? The truth is no one gave a damn about me when I was on the streets at the age of eight. Men paid pennies to touch me in alleys, and I used that money for my brother and me to eat. I had to do what I had to do to survive. What I do now is no different. I'm surviving. Do you understand?"

I wanted to drown her and myself, but I prayed instead.

"Yes, ma'am," I said.

Unexpectantly, she kissed my lips and hugged me.

"Good girl, Pet. I knew you understood me."

That night, I trembled while rocking myself to sleep.

Devilina was out of character the following day, moving around the house with extra pep. She had invited a man—her favorite buyer—over for a business meeting. He had purchased most of her girls, and she wanted to discuss forming a partnership with him. My presence with anyone other than Devilina, the girls, or José Luis was forbidden, and I was grateful for that. I feared anyone who dealt with Devilina.

"José, Larazo says this man has spent ten million dollars in weeks. Get the good champagne."

"*Si, señora.*"

"Pet!" she called out.

"Yes, ma'am?"

"Make sure everyone is clean, perfectly dressed, and hair is in a tight bun."

Immediately after receiving my orders, I dashed to the bathroom to vomit.

Following behind me, Devilina asked, "What's wrong with you? Get yourself together. Take some migraine medicine or Pepto. And I don't know how you're getting fat when all you do is throw up all the damn time." She handed me a sheer black face covering while I was still kneeling in front of the porcelain toilet bowl. "You look like shit. Today is not the day for you to be sick."

"Yes, ma'am."

I cleaned my face and then put on the ridiculous covering. As I snapped the gold choker around my neck, I gagged. There were two knocks on the bathroom door, and I straightened up.

"*Vamanos, puta.*" José Luis barked from the other side.

I opened the door and started heading for the dungeon, but he shoved the barrel of his gun in my back and pushed me in the opposite direction towards the sitting room. Devilina was *very* compulsive about consistency, so the sudden shift in her routine terrified me. I crept slower than usual.

"*Vamanos, puta,*" José barked again.

I exhaled and looked at the floor. Against the red couch, I saw a pair of Christian Louboutin shoes that were the color of peanut butter. My eyes traveled upward to a tan Armani suit, a baby blue and tan striped tie, and a Presidential Rolex. On his caramel-colored left ring finger, I saw a double-bezel diamond band. My heart stopped when I looked into Blaque's eyes. *Am I dreaming again?*

Devilina smiled. "Blaque, I want you to meet—"

Before she could finish her sentence, my vision blurred, and I collapsed on the wooden floor. I blinked and inhaled the sweet manly mix of Issey Miyake, coconut, and cocoa butter. I saw Blaque sprint toward me. With one hand, he swept me up and fired his Glock with the other. Snapping out of my daze, I gripped his hand, and we ran down the hall past the kitchen.

"Fuck that planning shit!" he yelled. "Meet us at the front door!"

Rapid shots were fired at us. Blaque pushed me against the wall and shot José Luis, then turned and shot another man behind us. We gripped each other's hands and ran to the empty foyer. As I hurried to unlock the door, Devilina stepped out of nowhere with a TEC-9 and aimed directly at me, firing the weapon like a mad woman. Blaque quickly pulled me by my waist and covered me with his body. We fell to the ground. The front door swung open, and Devilina fell dead with two chest wounds from Agent Walker.

I felt the warmth of Blaque's body. I pulled off my face covering and kissed his face.

"Thank you, God."

Joyous tears ran from our eyes, but my joy was instantly snatched from me when I touched Blaque's face and noticed my hand was wet and red. My body shook with fear. I was covered in Blaque's blood but didn't know where it was coming from.

I gently kissed his lips. "No, Blaque. Hold on, baby. You cannot leave me now."

He beamed the brightest smile and touched my face, then

went limp in my arms. I screamed in agony while holding onto him. The pain came from the depths of my soul.

Before Rafelina Torres' demise, she had fired enough shots to take me out, but her bullets penetrated Blaque instead. I couldn't stop screaming. Agent Walker grabbed me as the paramedics quickly put Blaque on a stretcher, placed an oxygen mask on his face, started an IV, and worked on him using a defibrillator.

As we sped off in the ambulance, I prayed for Blaque's life to be spared. However, it seemed my prayers would be denied yet another time, because Blaque stopped breathing on the way to the hospital.

CHAPTER 29
LIFE AFTER DEATH

CHRISTIAN "BLAQUE" LAURENT SAVAGE
JAMAICA 2000

ROSE PETALS SURROUNDED me, and Pearle's familiar rose scent kept me in a daze. I could hear the sound of her heartbeat as she pressed her warm chest against me and wrapped her arms around my neck.

"You can keep dreaming, but don't leave me," she whispered. "I know you hear me, don't you, Blaque? I love you."

Coltrane sent dreams of Pearle in white with red lipstick and high heels. Her body was so soft, and we made love on the dance floor. I couldn't escape the scent of roses, lavender, and sage.

"Blaque, do you remember our song, baby?"

I was in a state of terrific torment. I smelled, sensed, and heard Pearle but couldn't touch her. She was so close but distant. She lived as a fantasy in my dreams.

NIRVANA 2000

Dressed in all-white linen, I was seated on the white sand, gazing into the pink, orange, and purple sky. The turquoise waves were fresh and beautifully quiet. There was no sun in the sky.

I looked behind me. Blue was seated at a white table on the beach,

279

dressed cleanly in an all-white suit.

I ran to him. "Man, I miss you. I'm so sorry. I should have done something to save you."

He stood up and hugged me. "Brother, this is where I'm supposed to be, to watch your back like always."

I sat on a soft chair at the table, sinking into the cushion. "Man, I'm so tired."

Blue pulled me out of the seat. "Nah, bro. Not yet. You have to leave this place before sunrise."

I stood up and threw my arms around him. "Blue, I messed up our family legacy. It's all my fault."

He held my embrace. "It's time for a new legacy, brother, and you know what to do."

"But I want to stay here."

He grabbed my shoulders. "Not yet. Remember, I got you. Now, go to Zion before it's too late."

The sky was getting brighter.

"How do I get there?"

Blue sat back down at the table. "Go to your favorite place, bro."

I sprinted toward the sea. Pearle's reflection was floating over the waves. Right before the sun popped above the horizon, I dived into the ocean.

JAMAICA 2000

I blinked, but my eyes were tired and closed shut. A mixed fragrance of sweet roses and coconut hit my nostrils like fresh air. My body was heavy, and I couldn't move. Pearle was pressed against me with her hand resting on my cheek. She was asleep. I knew it was her because I had placed my hands and lips on every inch of her body. Therefore, I was familiar with her touch. I knew she was asleep because I was familiar with the rhythm of her breathing whenever she drifted into that unconscious state of rest. The sound of loud, beeping machines surrounded me.

I couldn't speak. The wetness of the tears flowing down my face must have awakened her because Pearle quickly sat up.

"Blaque?" she softly said, holding my face in her palms.

I blinked.

"Blink again if you hear my voice, baby."

I blinked once more.

She pressed her lips against mine, and the reality of her kiss and tears brought me life. I attempted to move my hand to grab her but couldn't. She lifted my hand and kissed it.

"Oh my, God. *Ay Dio Mios*! Thank you. With teary eyes, she placed my hand on her bare stomach. The softness of her skin felt heavenly.

"Blink if you can feel that."

I blinked, and she kept my hand against her stomach.

"Blaque, this is our baby, and we need you to keep fighting to stay alive. Do you understand me?"

I was overjoyed. All I wanted to do was hold her, but I couldn't move anything but my eyes. So, I slowly blinked to let her know I had heard and understood her, and she kissed me all over my face.

"You were shot and have been in a coma for weeks, but you're going to be okay. I promise." Then Pearle screamed, "Walker! Blaque's awake!"

My eyes were like weights, but I forced them open.

David Walker rushed in and approached me from the other side of the bed.

"What's up, Christian? Can you hear me?"

He looked sincerely concerned, but I got that sick feeling like I always did whenever I saw his face. I acknowledged him with a disappointed blink.

"Pearle, we need a doctor—quickly," he said.

She picked up a phone next to the bed and slammed it down.

"Nothing works on this secluded-ass island."

Walker pulled out a cell phone from his pocket. "*Damn*. I forgot I don't have a signal."

"No one does. Wait. There's a man on this island— The Healer. He's not far from here. Stay with Blaque while I run and get him."

"Sure. No problem," he told Pearle with a smile and a nod.

"And, Walker, thank you for taking the time away from your cases to come and check on him."

"No thanks needed. Christian and I have had our differences, but both of you have risked your lives and saved a lot of people. A check-in is the least I can do."

Pearle leaned over me and pressed her lips against mine.

"Keep your eyes open and keep breathing, baby. I will take care of the rest. I'll be right back." She kissed me again. "I love you so much."

She then turned and left the room with Walker following her.

The room went quiet, and I rested my eyes. Then, a door slammed from another place in the house. The sound of stomping feet charged closer. Suddenly, the room door slammed.

"Blink if you hear me, Christian."

It was Walker. He had returned to my side and brought his foul energy with him. I didn't trust him. So, I fought to keep my eyes open, not wanting to even blink.

He smirked. "I know you don't like me, and the feeling is mutual. I came to tell you two things. First, all your dirty-ass uncles and cousins in the U.S. are being indicted." He paused to look at his watch. "Right now."

That news was a pitchfork to my heart; I didn't see it coming.

I hated him so much. I struggled to tell him, "Fuck you," but my lips were locked.

"Second, like you always suspected, my beef with you is personal, Christian. Do you remember me telling you that my father died of an overdose? Well, it was your father who brought the drugs to my neighborhood. So, the way I see it, your father killed my father, and me sitting next to you on your deathbed is karma. I watched your father shower you with an extravagant lifestyle from the money he made from my father's blood, and I hate both of you for it. I made a promise at my father's grave that I would make your father pay for what he did to him. I made it my mission to kill your family legacy by any means necessary. This is why the Savages are going down like the Titanic, Jack Dawson."

The worst nightmares were the ones when the monster was coming for you, and you couldn't run away or scream. Those dreams were reoccurring for me, and nothing felt better than waking up right before being caught. This time, however, I wasn't waking up because I wasn't asleep. David Walker was attacking me, and I wanted to kill him. But the only weapon I had was a deadly glare.

"Christian, I do hate seeing you like this. So, I'm going to end our family vendetta by putting you out of your misery, and no one will suspect me since you're a few breaths from death." He snatched the pillow from under my head. "I know I do dirty shit to dirty fish like you. Ultimately, I'm reversing the generational curses plaguing our communities. So, *maybe* that makes me a dirty hero." He pressed the pillow over my face. "But you're just a dirty-ass fish."

While fighting for air, I heard a familiar clicking sound muffled through the pillow.

CHAPTER 30
TO ZION

PEARLE "MONALISE" SAVAGE
JAMAICA 2000

F UCK A HEALER. *I need a doctor.*

My heart and mind were racing miles per second. I ran out of the house like a frazzled wild woman. Rushing towards me were three Jamaican guards. The family and I had decided Kingston was the safest place for us to be, and our location should be kept secret. Agent Walker was the only person outside of the family who knew where we were because he helped us get Blaque transported to Jamaica from the U.S.

"Is everything okay, my lady?" one guard asked.

I stood there trembling, my words not coming out fast enough. "I need Blaque's sister and a medical team here *now*. He's awake."

While one guard relayed the message on his walkie-talkie, another turned towards the porch steps. "I'll watch over boss."

I paced to slow my thoughts. "It's okay. Walker is keeping him awake. Can you go ahead and find the healer?" I told him, and he ran off into the sand dunes.

My heart swirled with every emotion imaginable. His parents needed to know Blaque had awakened, and I wanted to be the one to tell them.

"Give me your walkie-talkie," I said to the guard.

"Did yours stop working?" he asked while extending the device to me.

I was so frantic that it had slipped my mind I had one. "No. I left it in the house."

Suddenly, an invisible blow to my stomach radiated through every extremity of my body.

I dropped his walkie-talkie and doubled over from the pain. *"Fuck."*

"What's wrong, my lady?" the other guard asked.

For a second, I thought it was the baby, but it was a heart-wrenching pain inside my gut.

Remembering what "The Seer" told me, I panicked. "Give me a gun."

The guard in front of me looked confused but quickly removed one of the weapons from his holster and placed it in my hand.

Before either of them could ask me why I wanted it, I sprinted up the porch stairs. I opened the front door and heard them chasing a few steps behind me as I ran down the hallway.

Before I reached the bedroom, I heard Walker say, "You're just a dirty-ass fish."

I pushed the door open and aimed at him.

Click. Click.

Walker was seated on the bed next to Blaque. He turned his head and raised his hands in the air. My eyes traveled quickly from his eyes to the pillow over Blaque's face. Walker had to die. I pulled the trigger. The guards fired at the same time, and Walker fell to the floor. As security scurried around me, I jumped to Blaque's side and snatched the pillow from his face. His eyes were still open, and he was still breathing.

My love rained tears on his face, and I smiled. "My man's a fucking shark."

He smiled back with his eyes, then with his lips. I thanked

God he was able to smile and placed my lips over his. We exhaled in a sweet kiss. Our souls embraced.

"*Blaque Pearle forever.*"

I never needed an Oscar. My life was a dramatic film filled with romance, comedy, horror, and crime. I'd spent years as a thespian exploiting techniques to escape a world outside my reality, never imagining I could love myself while completely out of character. Once I embraced my own reflection, I finally realized all I wanted was love. *All I need is love.*

EPILOGUE
LEGACY

"SMILE!"

Blaque extended his camera phone out with a five-foot-long selfie stick. We had flown to Atlanta, Georgia, from Kingston, Jamaica, for a celebration. Zion, our oldest son, was starting his freshman year at Morehouse College.

Zion was so much like Blaque that it was freakish at times. They looked alike from the color of their eyes, skin tone, and dreadlocked hair. They were the same height and build and moved alike. Their Jamaican and American mixed accents were spoken through the same baritone voices, and they even had the same temperament and fought like brothers.

Because of the risks associated with our family business, I wanted Zion to find a school in Jamaica where he would have more protection. However, ever since he visited Morehouse's campus while visiting his cousins, he didn't want to attend college elsewhere.

We stood at the campus entrance in the middle of traffic during dorm move-in day. Zion laughed as people dodged and maneuvered around Blaque's camera phone.

"Hurry, Pops, before you hurt someone with that thing."

"Let them go around. I'm tired of family "usies" with my head cut off."

We all laughed and posed for the camera. Blaque was snapping pics when a handsome young man walked by us. Zion jumped from between us and in front of the young man.

"*Yo!* Look at my man's sneakers. Are those the original 1996 Air Jordan 11's??"

He looked at Zion like he had two heads. "Yeah."

"Those are fresh. I need to know where you got those."

"*D-Walk!*" a woman called from afar.

Blaque and I searched around like Ghostbusters. Then, we caught each other looking crazily. We laughed to ourselves.

The woman came from behind us. "There you are."

Blaque and I turned around, and I was shocked.

"*Tanya?*" I said, my voice going up several octaves.

It was Tanya Walker, the barber who used to work in my salon in Compton. She hadn't aged a bit.

She smiled. "Pearle and Blaque! Wow, it's so great to see you!"

"It's great to see you," I said as we hugged. "How have you been?"

She told us that she had moved back to Atlanta, where she had opened her barber shop. She then shared with her son how I had taught her how to run a successful business.

I smiled at the compliment. "You had the skills and vision, I just coached you through it." I grabbed Zion's hand. "This is our son, Zion. He's the oldest of our four children, and this is his first year at Morehouse."

He shook her hand. "Nice to meet you ma'am."

"David Walker, Jr. is my freshman and the baby of my four boys. His other brothers are students here, also. They are around here, somewhere."

I stood there in shock. I looked over at Blaque, and he looked just as surprised as I was. There was a part of me that believed her son's name and physical resemblance to Agent Walker was a coincidence.

Zion thankfully broke the sudden silence. "D-Walk, where did you get your shoes?"

"They were my dad's."

"His father has a shrine of Air Jordans," Tanya said.

"Oh my, God. Do you think he'll let me buy a pair?"

D-Walk rolled his eyes. "They aren't for sale."

"My bad, bro. I'm just a sneakerhead who loves a nice pair of J's."

"Zion, forgive my son. Today is very emotional for our family because Morehouse is my husband's alma mater. Today is the anniversary of when we believed he died, and his Air Jordans are sacred to my boys."

That confirmed it. I flashed back to the day I pulled the trigger, and the anniversary of Agent Walker's death would've been the day before. My heart skipped and sweat pushed through my pores.

"I'm so sorry to hear that. I didn't know you were married."

Tanya looked teary-eyed. "Not many people knew. David was a DEA agent during the crack epidemic and drug busts. He was very protective over his family."

D-Walk got loud. "But they never found his body, so I believe he's still out there."

"We should go." Tanya cracked an uncomfortable smile. "He gets fired up like his father. He is his daddy's son. It was great seeing you, Blaque and Pearle. And you're going to love Morehouse, Zion."

Blaque and I waved.

"It was great seeing you, too," I said. "I'm sorry again about your husband."

She grabbed D-Walk's hand, and they walked off.

D-Walk suddenly stopped and spun around with a mysterious look on his face.

"I'll see you around, Zion."

"No, the hell you won't," Zion mumbled under his breath.

Blaque cleared his throat. "Well, that was intense."

"I didn't like D-Walk's vibe. I understand he lost his pops, but if he ever looks at me sideways again, I will clear the negative energy from his chakra with my foot up his ass."

All of us laughed. God knows I needed that.

"Zion, you sound like your father, baby."

"That's because I'm *my* daddy's son. Right, pops?"

"That's actual and factual."

As Zion and Blaque tussled around, my mind drifted. Images of Agent Walker's face kept flashing in front of me. I thought back to the last time I had laid eyes on him and wondered, *Where is David Walker's body?*

Zion placed his arm around my shoulders. "Mom, why do you look like you just saw a ghost?"

"Because I just did," I replied while staring off in the direction that Tanya and her son had walked.

FROM THE AUTHOR

I don't write Christian literature, but God speaks to me. One day while on my bathroom floor searching for my life's purpose, God told me, "Get up." When I did, he said, "Write a book."

Immediately, characters started speaking to me. I wanted to write but was conflicted. I had been given a divine assignment, but I am not sanctified. Plus, the characters begging me to tell their stories were not saints. But who I am is a woman of God who possesses a burning desire to inspire others.

It took another breakthrough while listening to Beyoncé's "Black Parade" for me to embrace God's instruction. So, on Juneteenth, the holiday we commemorate our freedom from enslavement, I also celebrate the day I freed myself from myself, and Juneteenth 2020 is the day I became a writer.

I grew up in Gary, Indiana, during the 1990s—the best decade ever. I experienced the hip-hop and R&B explosion—my emotional saviors from trauma—and emersed myself in the hairstyles, fashion, and culture of the time.

I was raised by my grandparents, who introduced me to the arts and instilled a disciplined work ethic that has led me to become the woman I am today. I watched my surroundings morph from a middle-class steel town to "America's Murder Capital."

During that era, swarms of us roamed the streets from the morning until the streetlights flickered. The freedom allowed hours of exploration and innocent play, which later transitioned into lurking in danger zones and predatorial crosshairs.

By age fourteen, I'd seen, done, and heard more than women double my age. I'd been violated physically, emotionally, and spiritually. Lessons learned too soon made me sharp, smart, and street savvy by the time I was sixteen.

I've been blessed to have been surrounded by loving and

supportive people all my life. I hold sacred the healthy, lasting, and loving relationships of the present and from my past. I have experienced some of the highest of high times in my life. I graduated from college, got married, prospered in a successful career, and had two beautiful children, only to end up on the bathroom floor. The beauty of the story is I got up. And when I did, I prayed, *"Please, God, tell me what to do, and I promise I will give You the glory. And not only will I never get back on the floor, but I will also help as many people as I can to get up and stay up."* That's when He spoke to me.

My life's mission is to intertwine my art with my life experiences in hopes that it will motivate you to get up and stay up. If my testimony helps at least one person get closer to their purpose, I can quote Tay Money and sing, *"I understood the assignment."*

ACKNOWLEDGEMENTS

Thank you, God. I started my journey as a little girl with dreams—one who ate government cheese and saltines. With you, I've danced, fought, laughed, struggled, succeeded, failed, loved, lost, cried, lived, and resurrected as an author. Thank You for all of it.

Thank you, Tarris Dolores, my grandma and heavenly angel, for implanting the writer's seed into my soul.

Thank you, Thomas William, my grandfather, for exposing me to the arts.

Thank you, Cynthia Rochelle, my mother, for my adventurous spirit.

Thank you, R&B and hip-hop, my refuge, for being my spiritual antidote.

Thank you, Gary, IN, my hometown, for all the memories and experiences that created me.

Thank you, Los Angeles, Atlanta, Houston, and Kingston for being dope cities and providing Blaque Pearle with flavorful settings.

Thank you, Geno, my husband, for giving me the treasured space to create. This sacrifice is priceless to me.

Thank you, Landon and Milan, my children—"my eyes" and "my vision"—for giving me purpose.

Thank you, Aunt Karen and Uncle Reggie, for your prayerful check-ins.

Thank you, my Queen Dream Team: Shavaun and Shaura for being my day ones, ride-or-die, 3-4 sister-cousins; Kristina for being my sister-cousin and first financial investor; Toiya Marie, my cousin, for being my daily lunchtime sunshine; Nicki for being my "Solid Gold" and always dropping priceless gems; Jasmine for plugging me into the spiritual universe; Dionne for being my heart connection; Ryan, my kindred spirit, for being my great "Xscape" to outer realms; Lorraine for our unbreakable 3-4 bond; Alaina Renae for your lyrical love guidance; Sharell, my cousin, for being the solar power to my light bulb; Tanisha for encouraging me to dance when I thought I'd lost my rhythm; Uanya for stepping in when I was stuck in la-la land; and Rhonda, my kid's year-round Santa Claus, for keeping them busy with art projects while I worked.

Thank you, Chris M. Murray, for being a constant encourager since the seventh grade.

Thank you, Connie, my therapist, for asking me if I was okay, because I wasn't.

Thank you, Roxanne Jones, my literary agent, for being one of the first people to believe in me. There are no words to express my gratitude.

Thank you Shontrell Wade and Carla M. Dean, my first-class editors, for your professionalism and keen third eye.

Thank you, Shawanda "N'Tyse" Williams, my publishing queen, for blazing literary and media trails for artists like me. You did everything you said you would and more. I couldn't be more grateful.

Thank you, Kreceda Tyler, and the entire Black Odyssey Media team for the wonderful voyage.

Thank you, Bruce McAllister—wise Yoda—for sensing my connection to the literary force. You are an amazing man.

Thank you to the countless people and family members who have supported me on this journey.

I love you all.

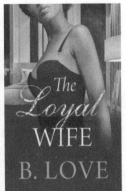

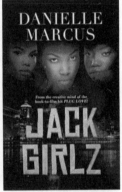